A FOREWORD FROM THE PAST...

In Spring of 1950, I auditioned for Rockhill Radio Productions, a New York City producer. They were casting the three leads of Tom Corbett Space Cadet, written from a Robert Heinlein book source as a live television and radio series for the Fall season. Though I was twenty-five years of age then, I looked about eighteen. I had a crew haircut and a genuine military background, having served four years during WW2 as a torpedoman in the US Navy. The producers were impressed; they first tried me as Cadet Tom, then had me read the role of Cadet Astro. Neither seemed right; I was given the lines of Senior Cadet Roger Manning and was promptly hired for the part. They asked if I'd read with other actors to help assemble the rest of the trio, and I agreed. During the weeks we interviewed many applicants, I returned to the Alvin Theater nightly where I was part of the cast of Mister Roberts, a long running Broadway hit. We found our Cadet Astro, a personable young actor named Al Markim, and not long afterwards Frankie Thomas entered the office. He was the curly-haired, engaging image of a handsome All-American Boy; there was no doubt in anyone's mind that he was our Tom Corbett. Our sci-fi series would be the first of the live television space series and the first to be seen on all the networks; it appeared in turn on CBS, NBC, ABC, and Dumont during the course of a memorable five-year run.

Willy Ley, one of the Founders of the German Rocket Society, was our technical advisor. Due to his insistence upon technical jargon, my role altered from its original conception. It happened during an episode in which Captain Strong floated helplessly in space far from the ship as Tom and Astro argued with me about how to get him back aboard safely. My reluctance was filled with the complicated scientific excuses supplied our scriptwriter by Mr. Ley. On air, conveyed live Coast to Coast via kinescope, Astro delivered his cue line anxiously, "Do you mean to say you'd leave Captain Strong out there to die?" I dried up, unable to remember a word, and retorted with a snarl, "Why not?" (Captain Strong was duly rescued after the cast and technical crew recovered.)

Bluewater has made a striking change from the original realistic comic strips rendered by Ray Bailey (Terry and the Pirates). Of course, those were done more than half a century ago, so these pages vividly present a bolder depiction of our daring adventures in a wilder colorful universe. I note wryly that my character has grown overly plump... a physical condition the Academy certainly wouldn't accept for its cadets... and Captain Strong now sports a fashionable beard. A new production team has provided us new uniforms, new rocketships, new antagonists, and a boundless frontier. Suit up and join us for all the perilous adventures to come.

's Luck!

—Jan Merlin

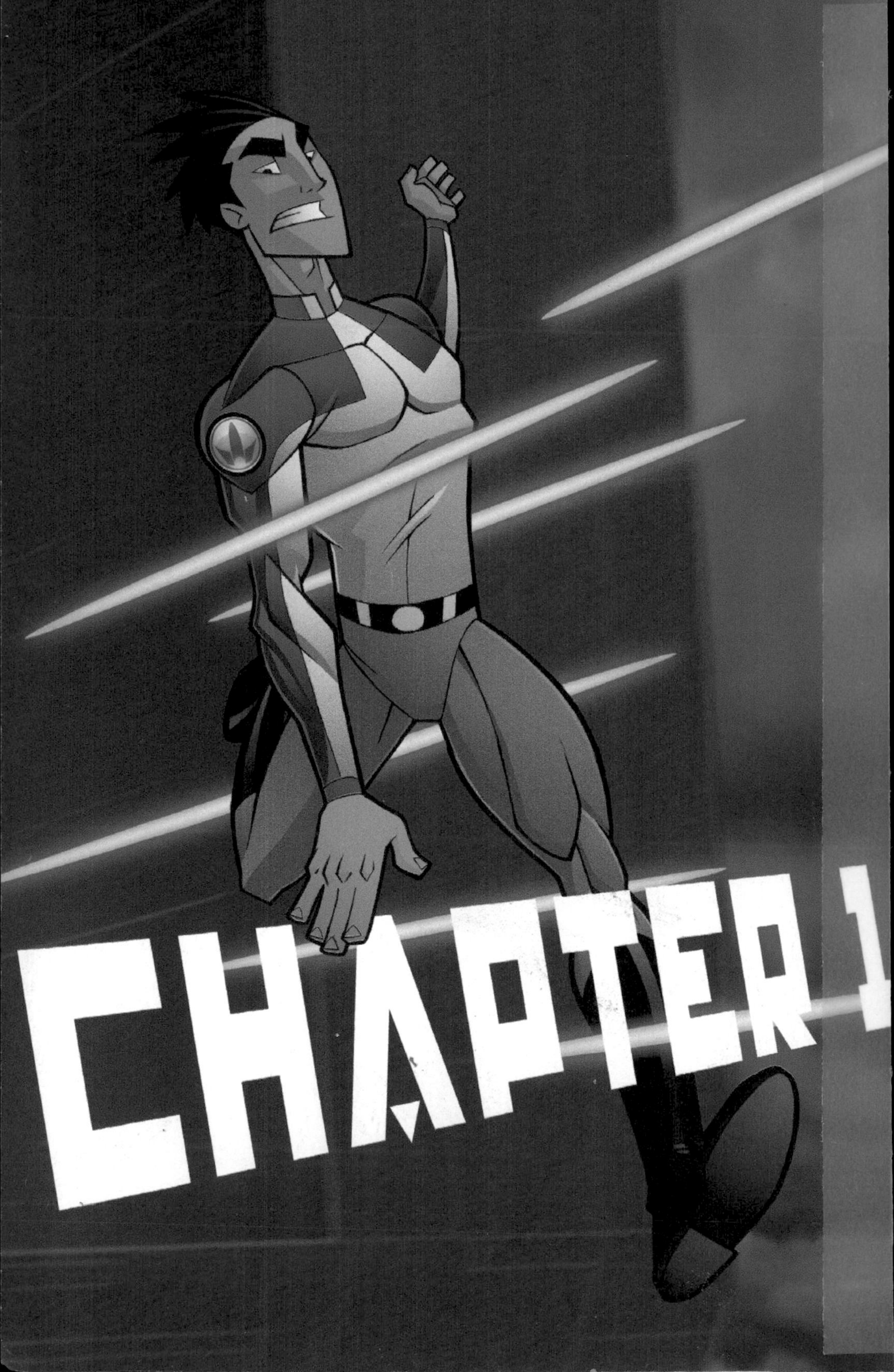
CHAPTER 1

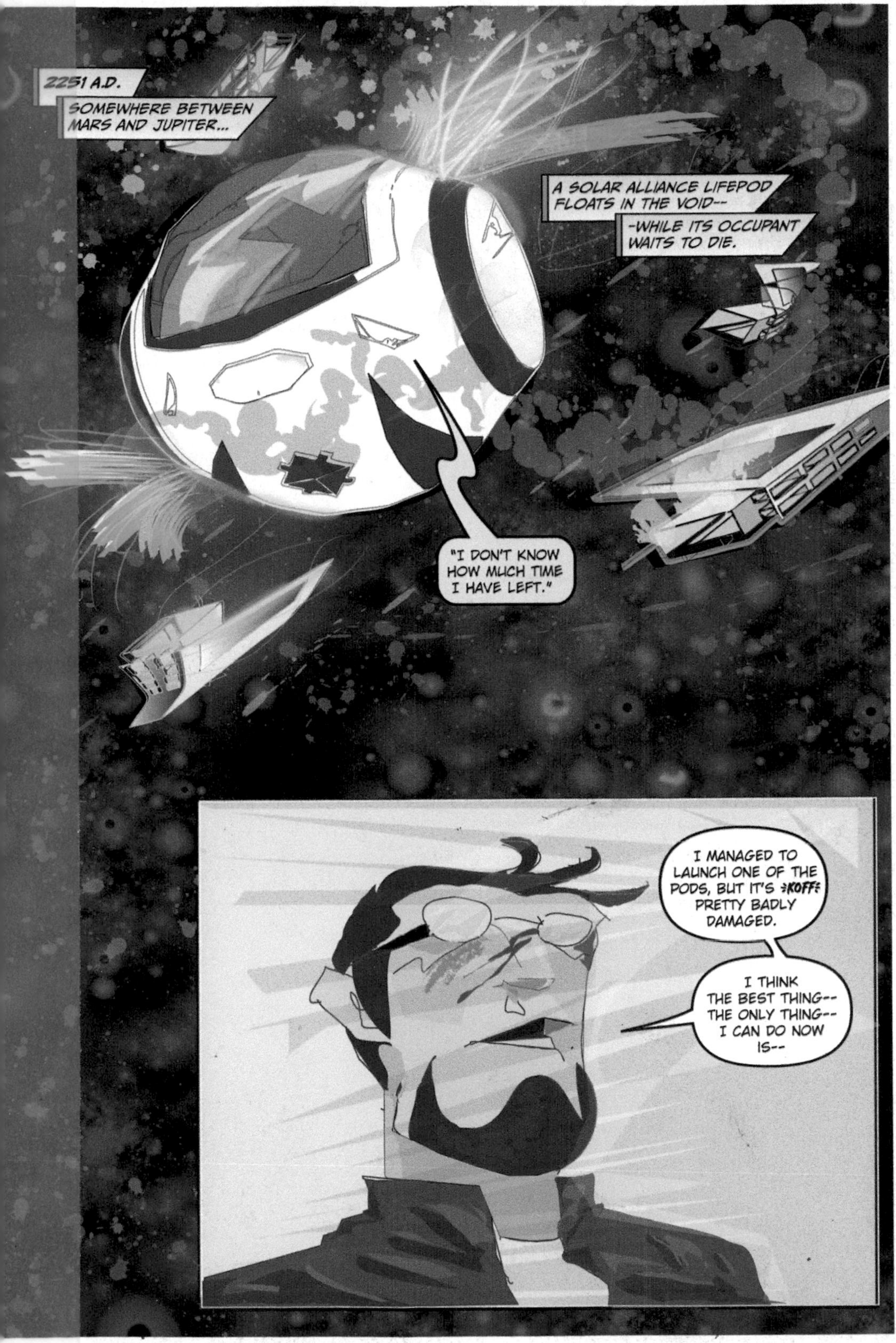
2251 A.D.
SOMEWHERE BETWEEN MARS AND JUPITER...
A SOLAR ALLIANCE LIFEPOD FLOATS IN THE VOID--
-WHILE ITS OCCUPANT WAITS TO DIE.
"I DON'T KNOW HOW MUCH TIME I HAVE LEFT."
I MANAGED TO LAUNCH ONE OF THE PODS, BUT IT'S *KOFF* PRETTY BADLY DAMAGED.
I THINK THE BEST THING-- THE ONLY THING-- I CAN DO NOW IS--

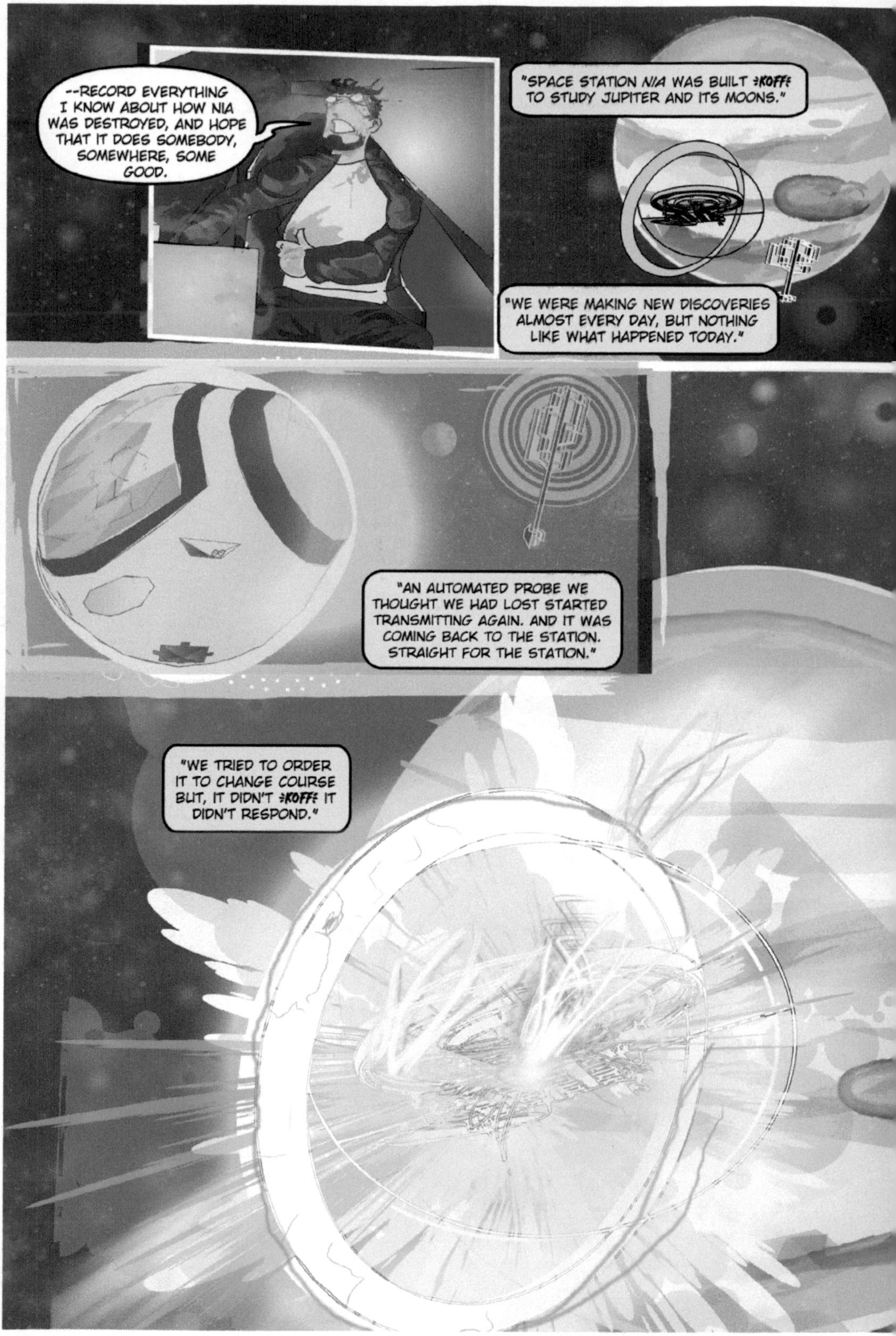
--RECORD EVERYTHING I KNOW ABOUT HOW NIA WAS DESTROYED, AND HOPE THAT IT DOES SOMEBODY, SOMEWHERE, SOME GOOD.
"SPACE STATION *NIA* WAS BUILT *KOFF* TO STUDY JUPITER AND ITS MOONS."
"WE WERE MAKING NEW DISCOVERIES ALMOST EVERY DAY, BUT NOTHING LIKE WHAT HAPPENED TODAY."
"AN AUTOMATED PROBE WE THOUGHT WE HAD LOST STARTED TRANSMITTING AGAIN. AND IT WAS COMING BACK TO THE STATION. STRAIGHT FOR THE STATION."
"WE TRIED TO ORDER IT TO CHANGE COURSE BUT, IT DIDN'T *KOFF* IT DIDN'T RESPOND."

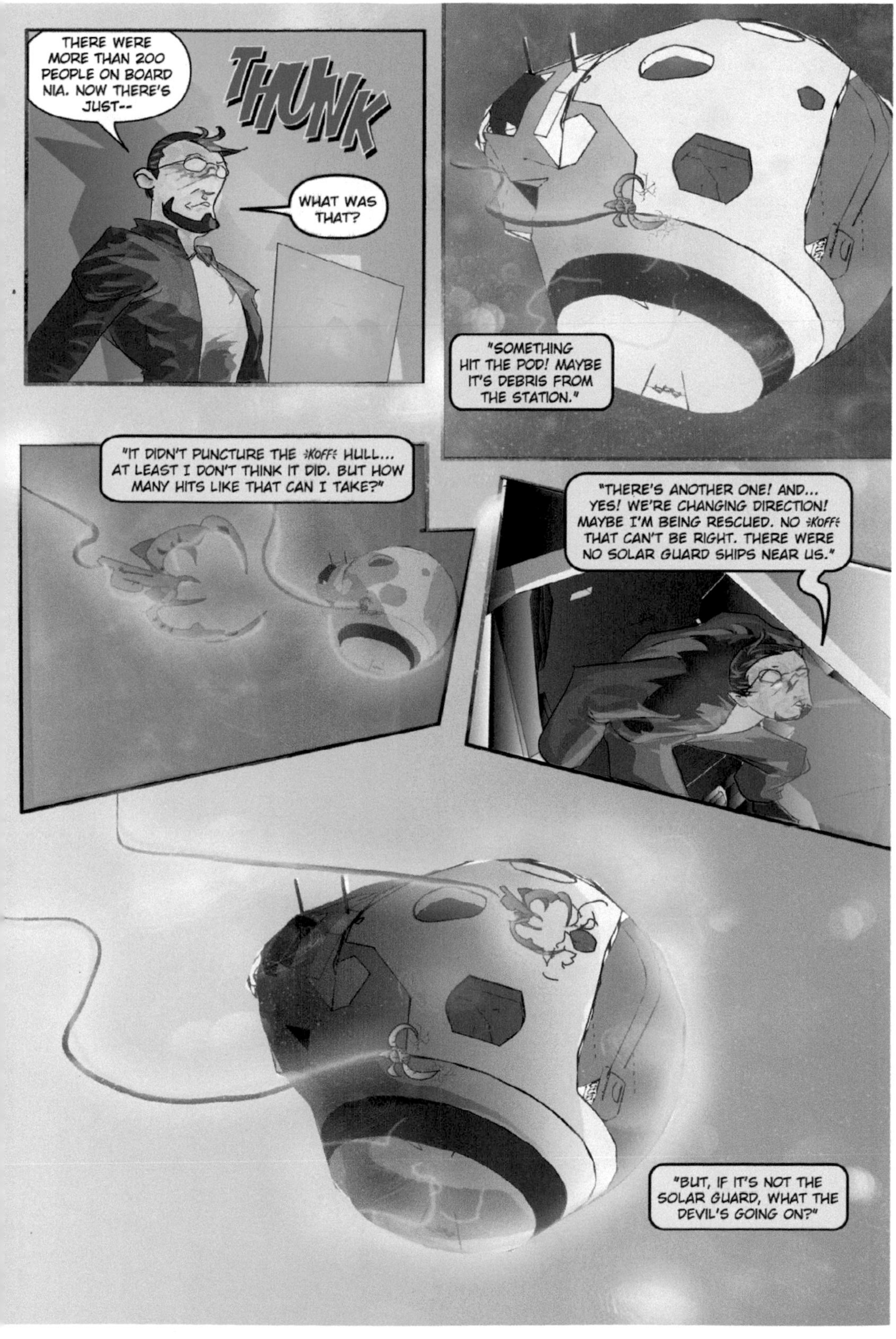
THERE WERE MORE THAN 200 PEOPLE ON BOARD NIA. NOW THERE'S JUST--
THUNK
WHAT WAS THAT?
"SOMETHING HIT THE POD! MAYBE IT'S DEBRIS FROM THE STATION."
"IT DIDN'T PUNCTURE THE *KOFF* HULL... AT LEAST I DON'T THINK IT DID. BUT HOW MANY HITS LIKE THAT CAN I TAKE?"
"THERE'S ANOTHER ONE! AND... YES! WE'RE CHANGING DIRECTION! MAYBE I'M BEING RESCUED. NO *KOFF* THAT CAN'T BE RIGHT. THERE WERE NO SOLAR GUARD SHIPS NEAR US."
"BUT, IF IT'S NOT THE SOLAR GUARD, WHAT THE DEVIL'S GOING ON?"

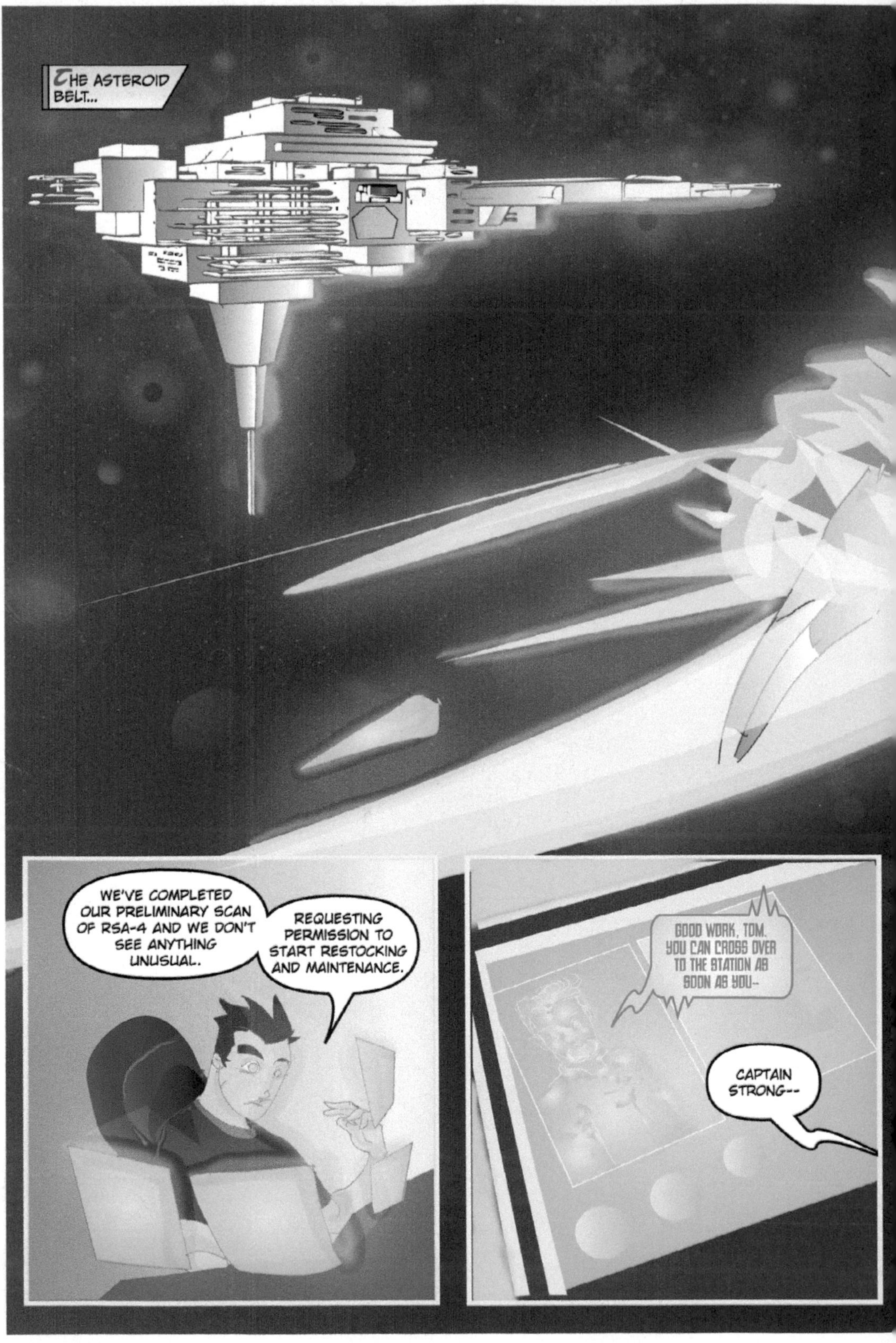
THE ASTEROID BELT...
WE'VE COMPLETED OUR PRELIMINARY SCAN OF RSA-4 AND WE DON'T SEE ANYTHING UNUSUAL.
REQUESTING PERMISSION TO START RESTOCKING AND MAINTENANCE.
GOOD WORK, TOM. YOU CAN CROSS OVER TO THE STATION AS SOON AS YOU--
CAPTAIN STRONG--

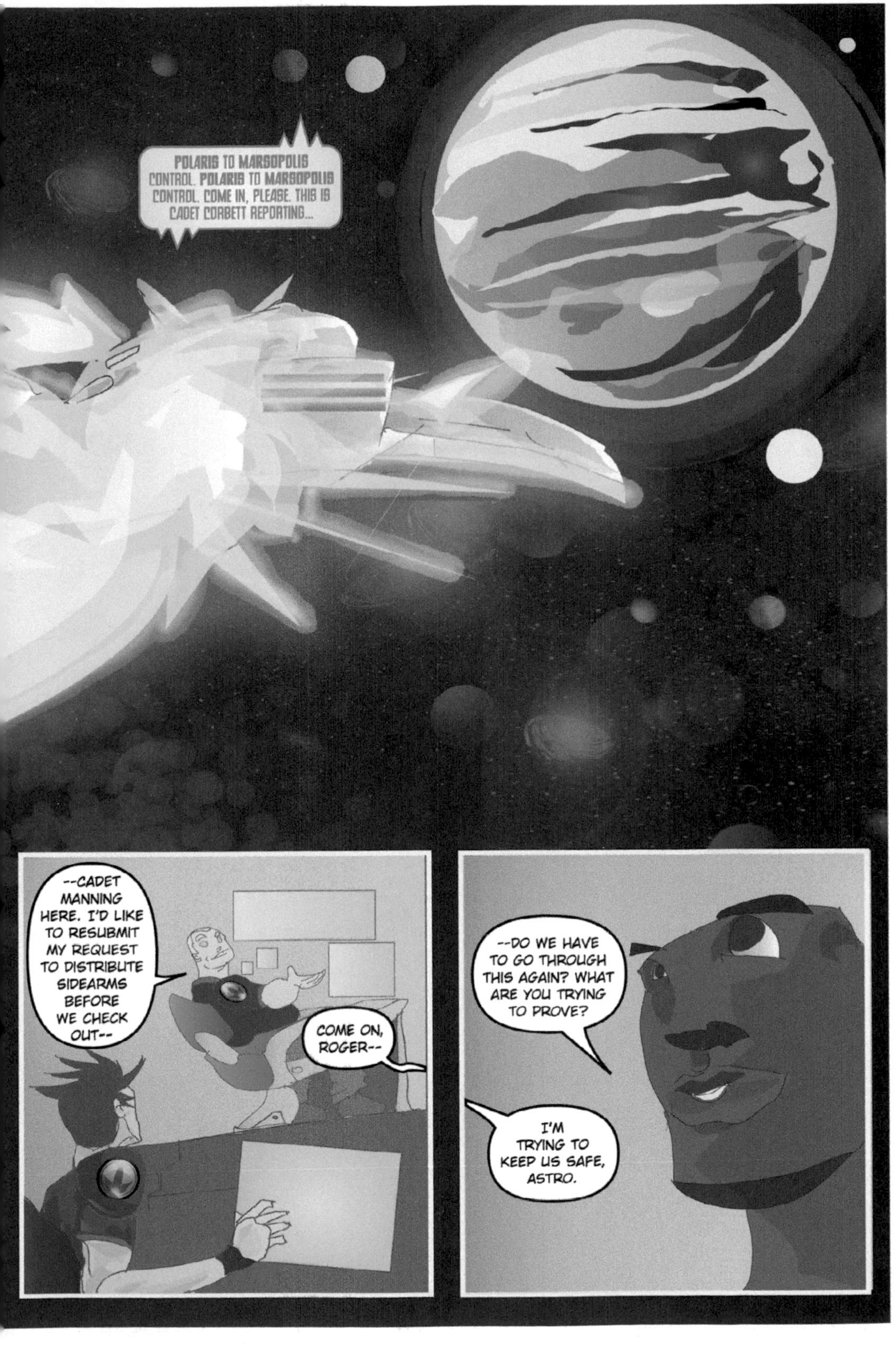
POLARIS TO MARSOPOLIS CONTROL. POLARIS TO MARSOPOLIS CONTROL. COME IN, PLEASE. THIS IS CADET CORBETT REPORTING...
--CADET MANNING HERE. I'D LIKE TO RESUBMIT MY REQUEST TO DISTRIBUTE SIDEARMS BEFORE WE CHECK OUT--
COME ON, ROGER--
--DO WE HAVE TO GO THROUGH THIS AGAIN? WHAT ARE YOU TRYING TO PROVE?
I'M TRYING TO KEEP US SAFE, ASTRO.

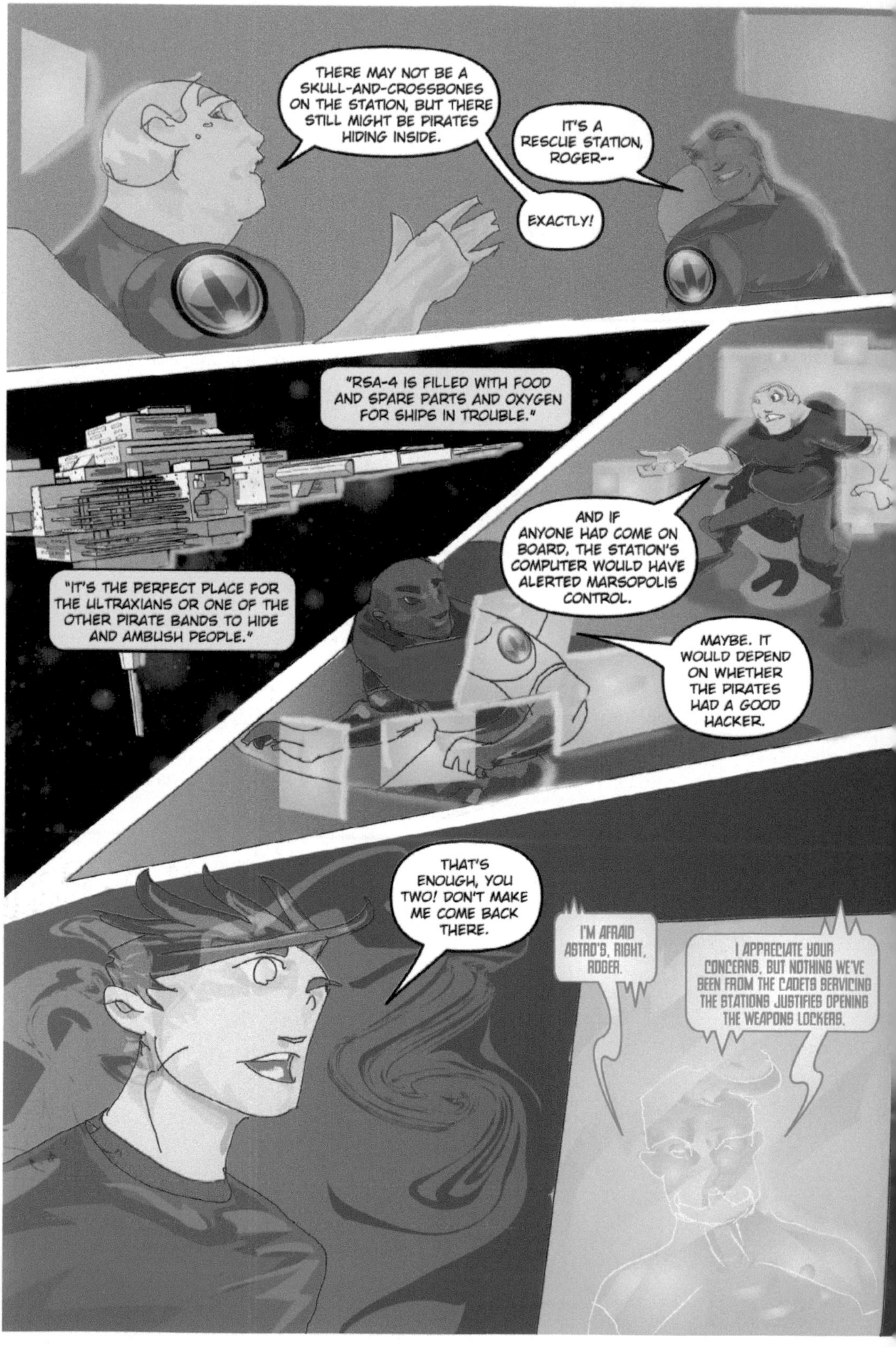
THERE MAY NOT BE A SKULL-AND-CROSSBONES ON THE STATION, BUT THERE STILL MIGHT BE PIRATES HIDING INSIDE.
IT'S A RESCUE STATION, ROGER--
EXACTLY!
"RSA-4 IS FILLED WITH FOOD AND SPARE PARTS AND OXYGEN FOR SHIPS IN TROUBLE."
"IT'S THE PERFECT PLACE FOR THE ULTRAXIANS OR ONE OF THE OTHER PIRATE BANDS TO HIDE AND AMBUSH PEOPLE."
AND IF ANYONE HAD COME ON BOARD, THE STATION'S COMPUTER WOULD HAVE ALERTED MARSOPOLIS CONTROL.
MAYBE. IT WOULD DEPEND ON WHETHER THE PIRATES HAD A GOOD HACKER.
THAT'S ENOUGH, YOU TWO! DON'T MAKE ME COME BACK THERE.
I'M AFRAID ASTRO'S RIGHT, ROGER.
I APPRECIATE YOUR CONCERNS, BUT NOTHING WE'VE SEEN FROM THE CADETS SERVICING THE STATIONS JUSTIFIES OPENING THE WEAPONS LOCKERS.

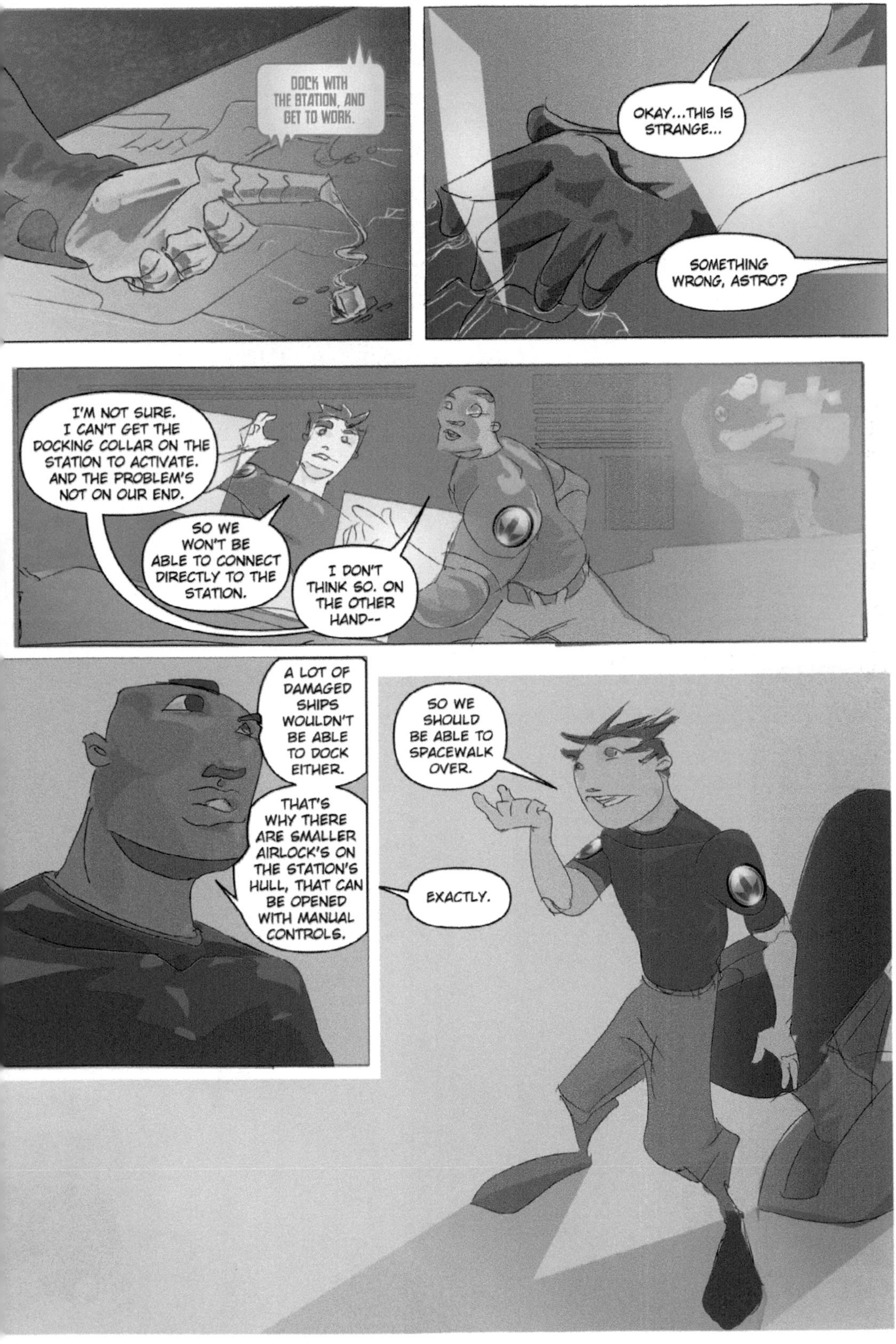
DOCK WITH THE STATION, AND GET TO WORK.
OKAY...THIS IS STRANGE...
SOMETHING WRONG, ASTRO?
I'M NOT SURE. I CAN'T GET THE DOCKING COLLAR ON THE STATION TO ACTIVATE. AND THE PROBLEM'S NOT ON OUR END.
SO WE WON'T BE ABLE TO CONNECT DIRECTLY TO THE STATION.
I DON'T THINK SO. ON THE OTHER HAND--
A LOT OF DAMAGED SHIPS WOULDN'T BE ABLE TO DOCK EITHER.
SO WE SHOULD BE ABLE TO SPACEWALK OVER.
THAT'S WHY THERE ARE SMALLER AIRLOCK'S ON THE STATION'S HULL, THAT CAN BE OPENED WITH MANUAL CONTROLS.
EXACTLY.

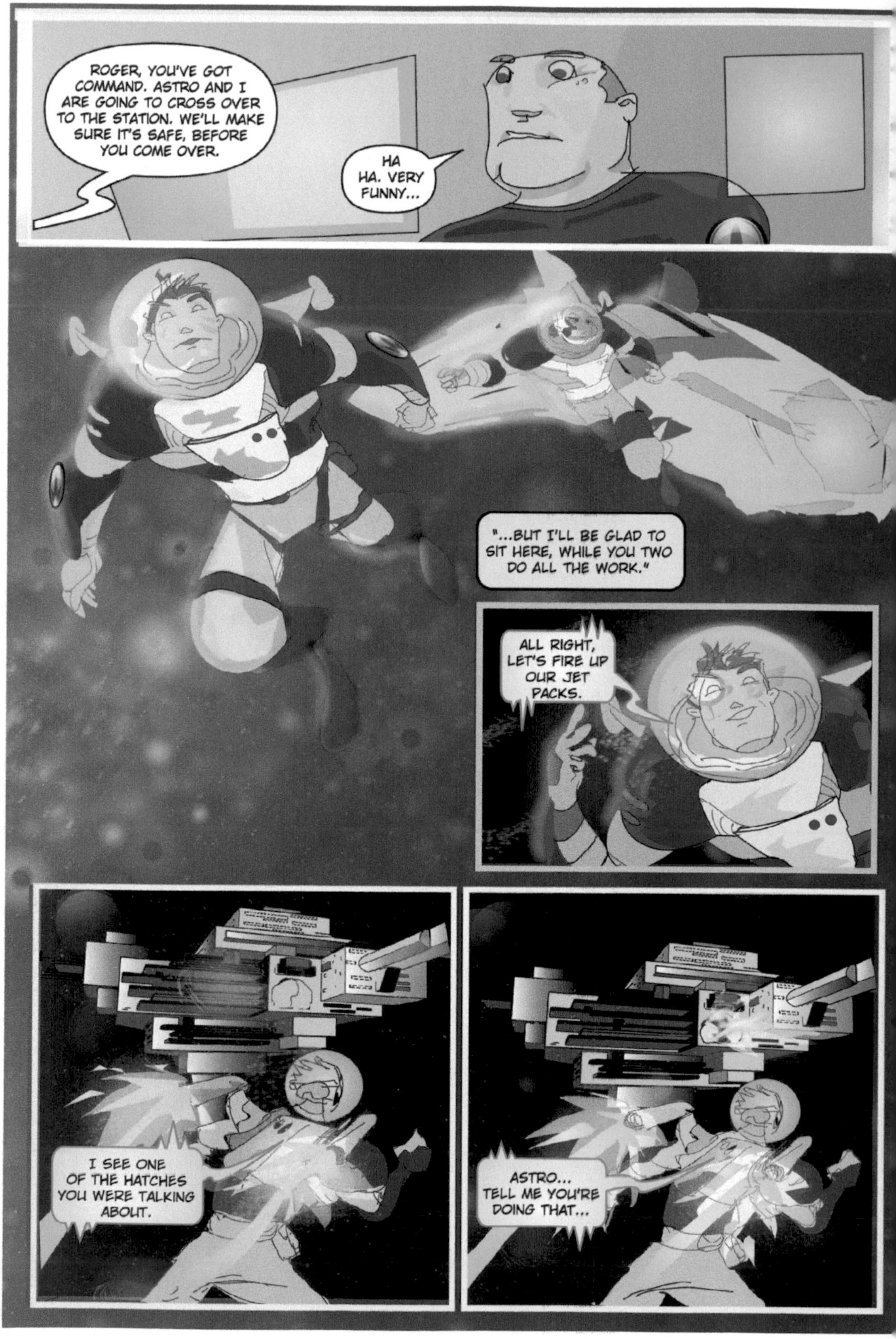
ROGER, YOU'VE GOT COMMAND. ASTRO AND I ARE GOING TO CROSS OVER TO THE STATION. WE'LL MAKE SURE IT'S SAFE, BEFORE YOU COME OVER.
HA HA. VERY FUNNY...
"...BUT I'LL BE GLAD TO SIT HERE, WHILE YOU TWO DO ALL THE WORK."
ALL RIGHT, LET'S FIRE UP OUR JET PACKS.
I SEE ONE OF THE HATCHES YOU WERE TALKING ABOUT.
ASTRO... TELL ME YOU'RE DOING THAT...

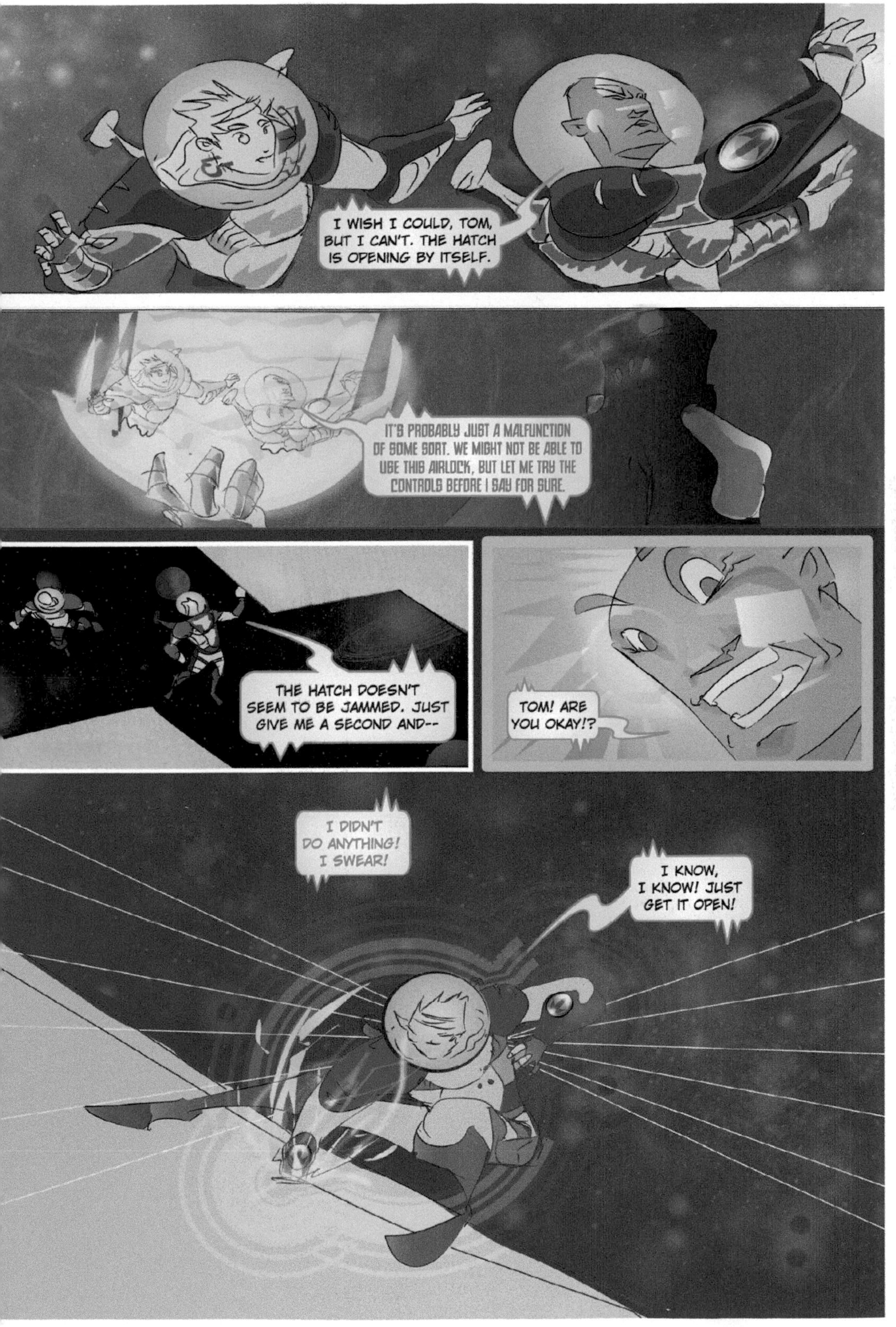
I WISH I COULD, TOM, BUT I CAN'T. THE HATCH IS OPENING BY ITSELF.
IT'S PROBABLY JUST A MALFUNCTION OF SOME SORT. WE MIGHT NOT BE ABLE TO USE THIS AIRLOCK, BUT LET ME TRY THE CONTROLS BEFORE I SAY FOR SURE.
THE HATCH DOESN'T SEEM TO BE JAMMED. JUST GIVE ME A SECOND AND--
TOM! ARE YOU OKAY!?
I DIDN'T DO ANYTHING! I SWEAR!
I KNOW, I KNOW! JUST GET IT OPEN!

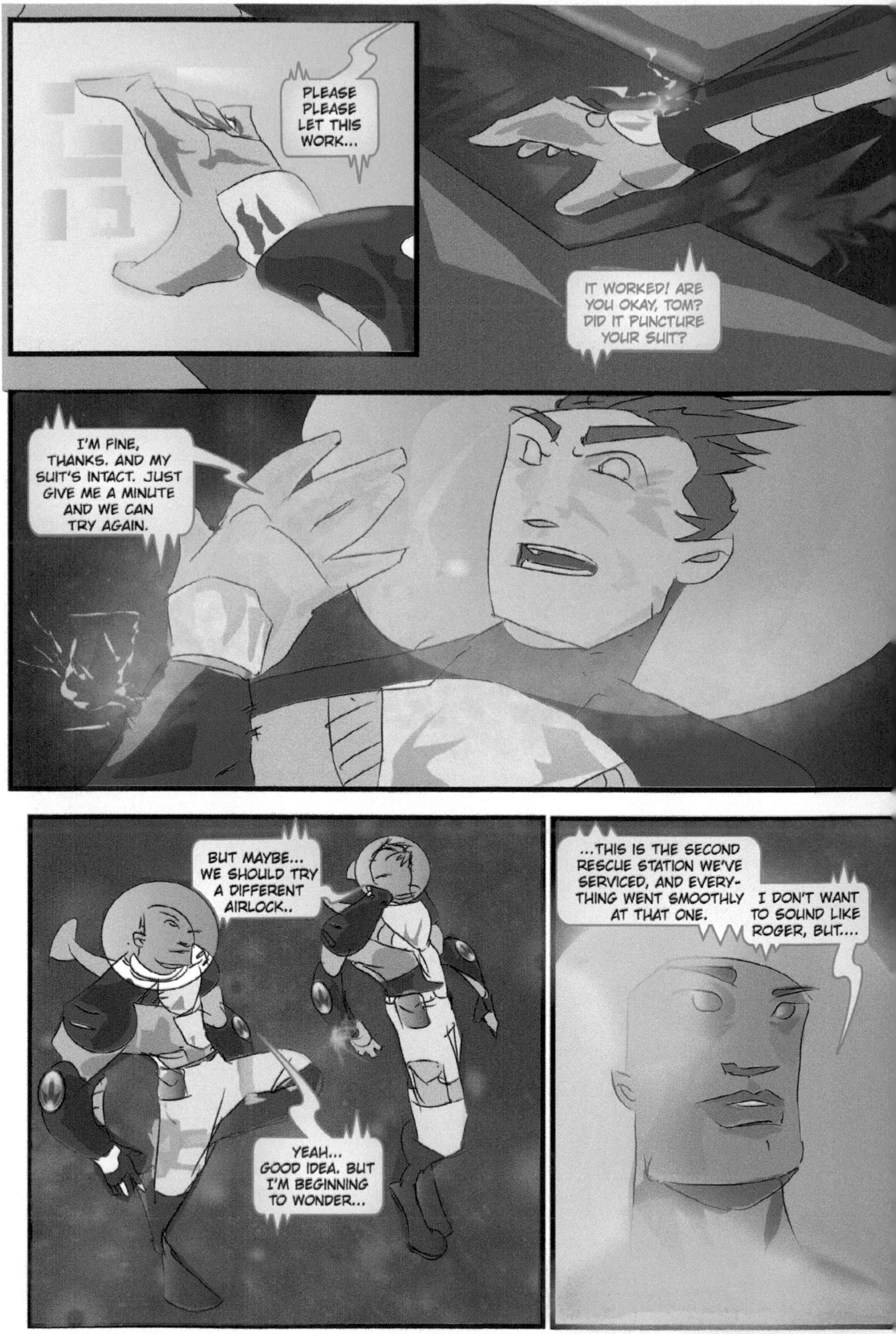
PLEASE PLEASE LET THIS WORK...
IT WORKED! ARE YOU OKAY, TOM? DID IT PUNCTURE YOUR SUIT?
I'M FINE, THANKS. AND MY SUIT'S INTACT. JUST GIVE ME A MINUTE AND WE CAN TRY AGAIN.
BUT MAYBE... WE SHOULD TRY A DIFFERENT AIRLOCK..
YEAH... GOOD IDEA. BUT I'M BEGINNING TO WONDER...
...THIS IS THE SECOND RESCUE STATION WE'VE SERVICED, AND EVERY-THING WENT SMOOTHLY AT THAT ONE.
I DON'T WANT TO SOUND LIKE ROGER, BUT....

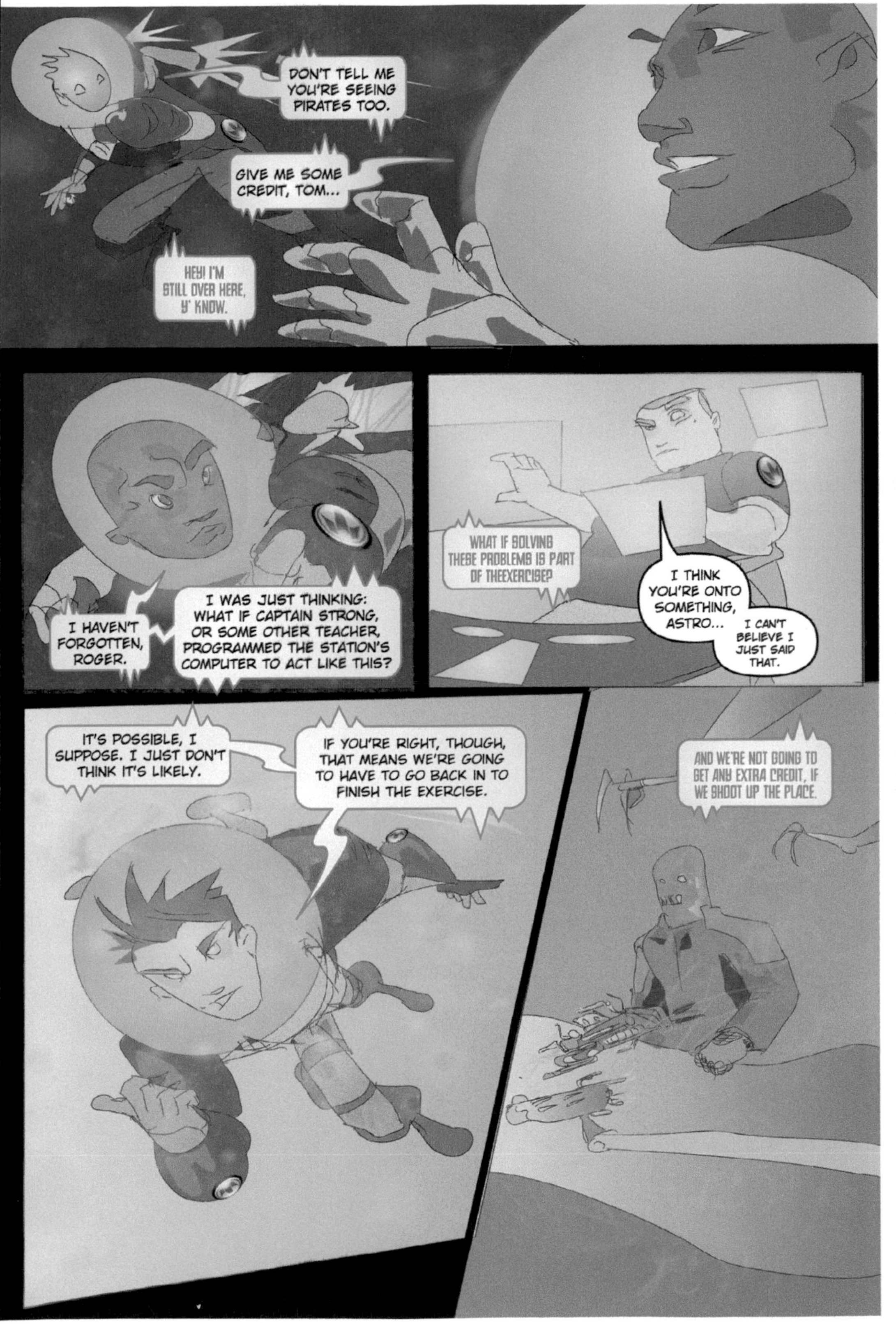
DON'T TELL ME YOU'RE SEEING PIRATES TOO.
GIVE ME SOME CREDIT, TOM...
HEY! I'M STILL OVER HERE, Y' KNOW.
I HAVEN'T FORGOTTEN, ROGER.
I WAS JUST THINKING: WHAT IF CAPTAIN STRONG, OR SOME OTHER TEACHER, PROGRAMMED THE STATION'S COMPUTER TO ACT LIKE THIS?
WHAT IF SOLVING THESE PROBLEMS IS PART OF THEEXERCISE?
I THINK YOU'RE ONTO SOMETHING, ASTRO...
I CAN'T BELIEVE I JUST SAID THAT.
IT'S POSSIBLE, I SUPPOSE. I JUST DON'T THINK IT'S LIKELY.
IF YOU'RE RIGHT, THOUGH, THAT MEANS WE'RE GOING TO HAVE TO GO BACK IN TO FINISH THE EXERCISE.
AND WE'RE NOT GOING TO GET ANY EXTRA CREDIT, IF WE SHOOT UP THE PLACE.

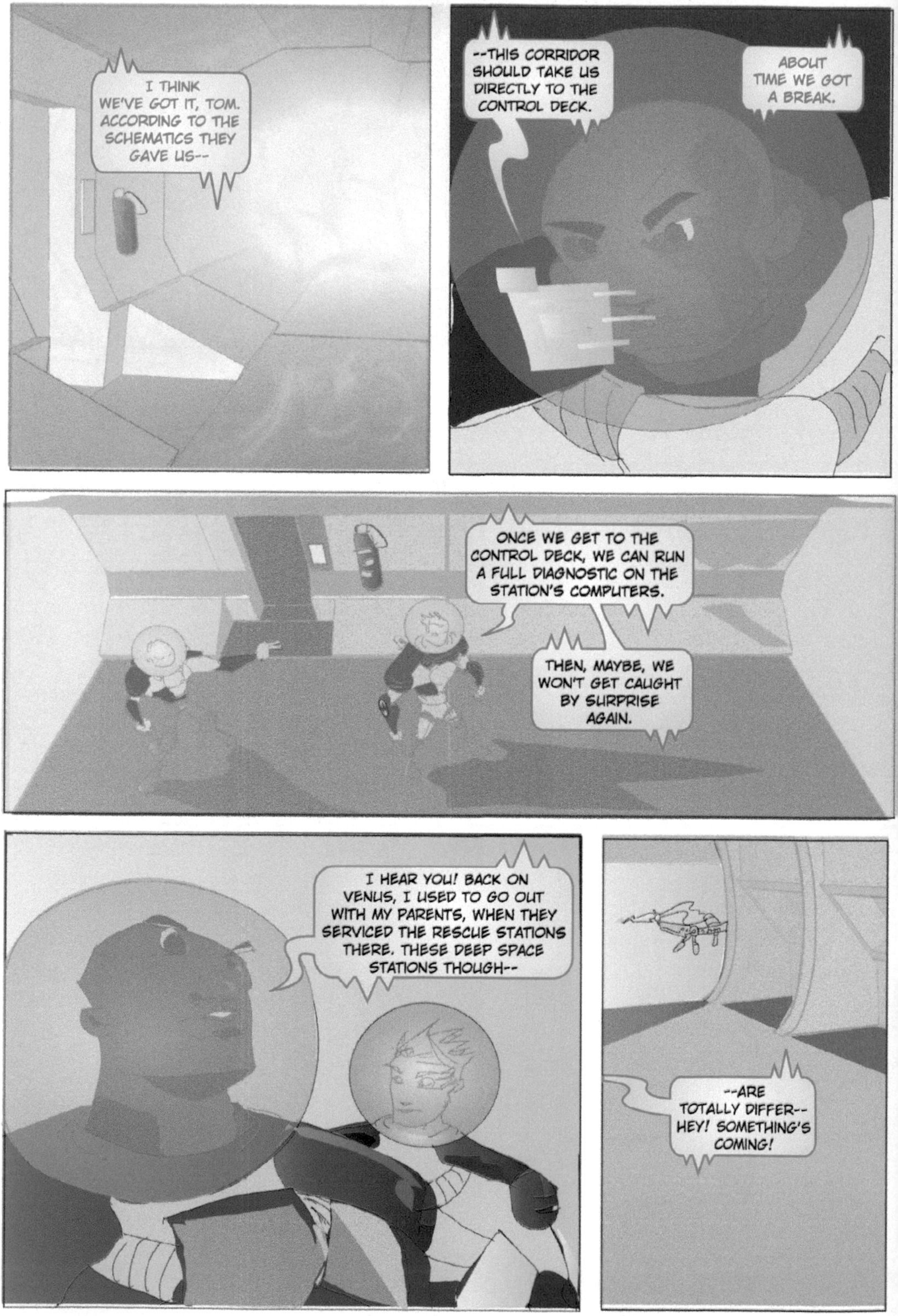
I THINK WE'VE GOT IT, TOM. ACCORDING TO THE SCHEMATICS THEY GAVE US--
--THIS CORRIDOR SHOULD TAKE US DIRECTLY TO THE CONTROL DECK.
ABOUT TIME WE GOT A BREAK.
ONCE WE GET TO THE CONTROL DECK, WE CAN RUN A FULL DIAGNOSTIC ON THE STATION'S COMPUTERS.
THEN, MAYBE, WE WON'T GET CAUGHT BY SURPRISE AGAIN.
I HEAR YOU! BACK ON VENUS, I USED TO GO OUT WITH MY PARENTS, WHEN THEY SERVICED THE RESCUE STATIONS THERE. THESE DEEP SPACE STATIONS THOUGH--
--ARE TOTALLY DIFFER-- HEY! SOMETHING'S COMING!

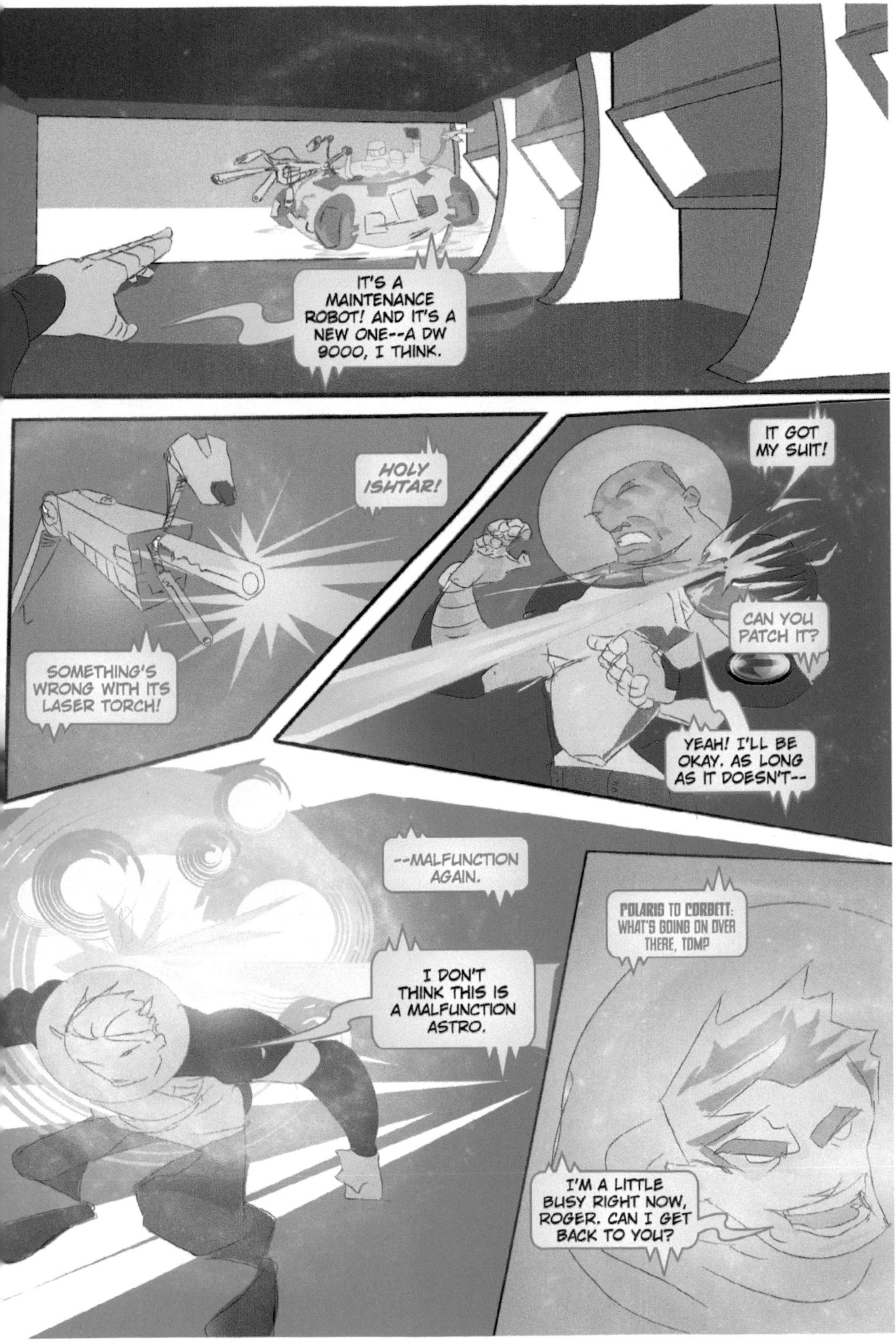
IT'S A MAINTENANCE ROBOT! AND IT'S A NEW ONE--A DW 9000, I THINK.
HOLY ISHTAR!
SOMETHING'S WRONG WITH ITS LASER TORCH!
IT GOT MY SUIT!
CAN YOU PATCH IT?
YEAH! I'LL BE OKAY. AS LONG AS IT DOESN'T--
--MALFUNCTION AGAIN.
I DON'T THINK THIS IS A MALFUNCTION ASTRO.
POLARIS TO CORBETT: WHAT'S GOING ON OVER THERE, TOM?
I'M A LITTLE BUSY RIGHT NOW, ROGER. CAN I GET BACK TO YOU?

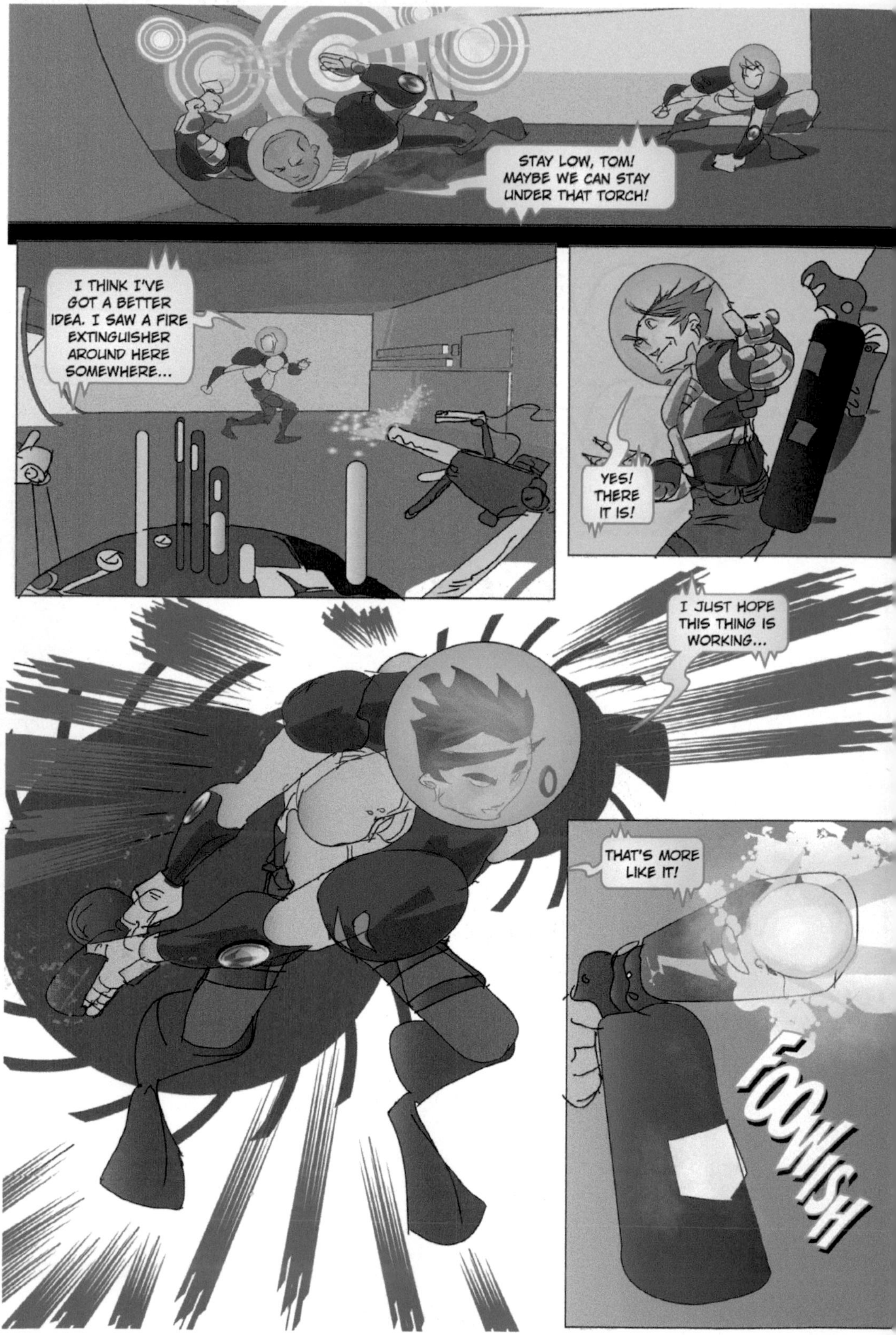
STAY LOW, TOM! MAYBE WE CAN STAY UNDER THAT TORCH!
I THINK I'VE GOT A BETTER IDEA. I SAW A FIRE EXTINGUISHER AROUND HERE SOMEWHERE...
YES! THERE IT IS!
I JUST HOPE THIS THING IS WORKING...
THAT'S MORE LIKE IT!
FOOWISH

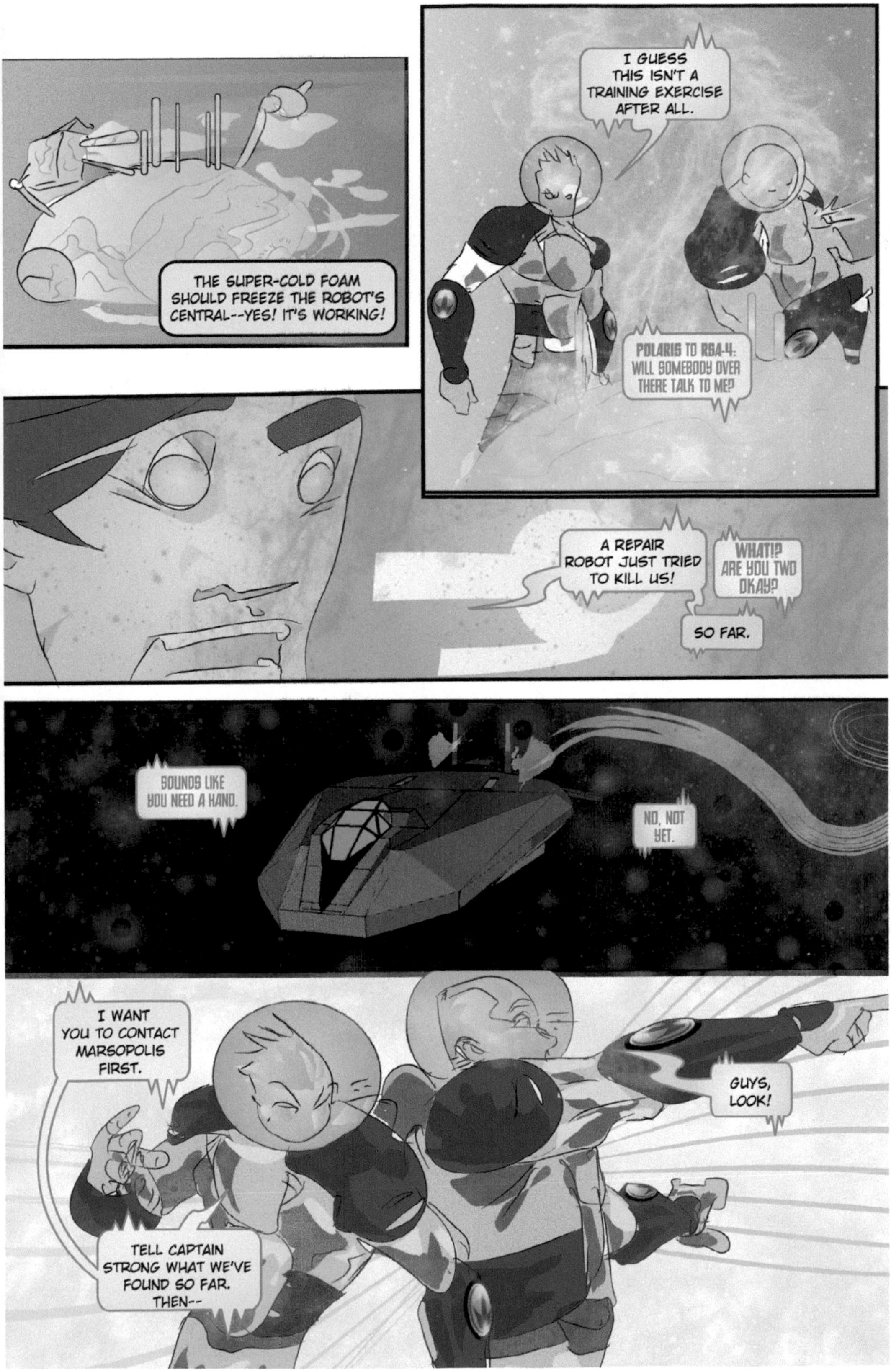
THE SUPER-COLD FOAM SHOULD FREEZE THE ROBOT'S CENTRAL--YES! IT'S WORKING!
I GUESS THIS ISN'T A TRAINING EXERCISE AFTER ALL.
POLARIS TO RSA-4: WILL SOMEBODY OVER THERE TALK TO ME?
A REPAIR ROBOT JUST TRIED TO KILL US!
WHAT!? ARE YOU TWO OKAY?
SO FAR.
SOUNDS LIKE YOU NEED A HAND.
NO, NOT YET.
I WANT YOU TO CONTACT MARSOPOLIS FIRST.
TELL CAPTAIN STRONG WHAT WE'VE FOUND SO FAR. THEN--
GUYS, LOOK!

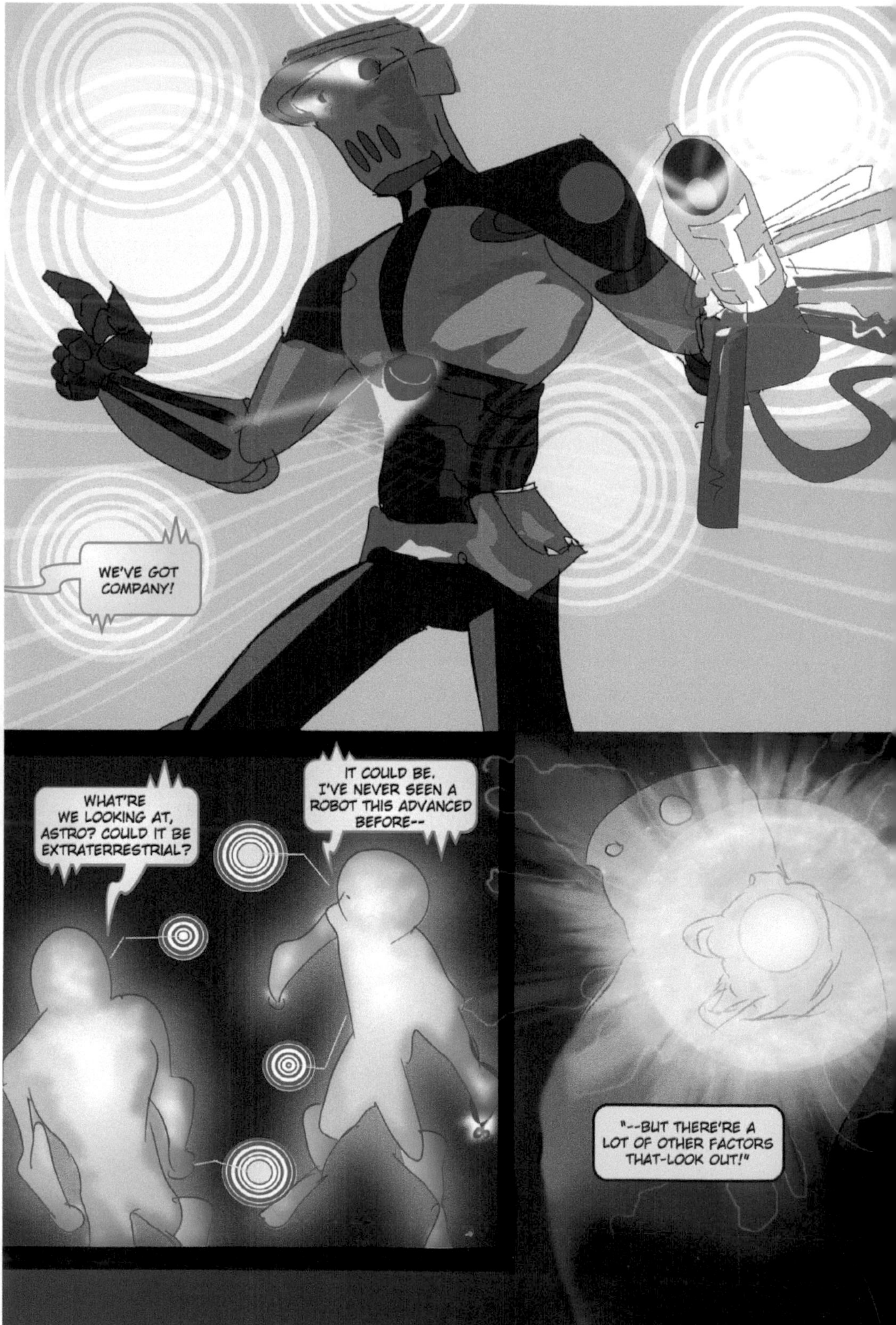
WE'VE GOT COMPANY!
WHAT'RE WE LOOKING AT, ASTRO? COULD IT BE EXTRATERRESTRIAL?
IT COULD BE. I'VE NEVER SEEN A ROBOT THIS ADVANCED BEFORE--
"--BUT THERE'RE A LOT OF OTHER FACTORS THAT-LOOK OUT!"

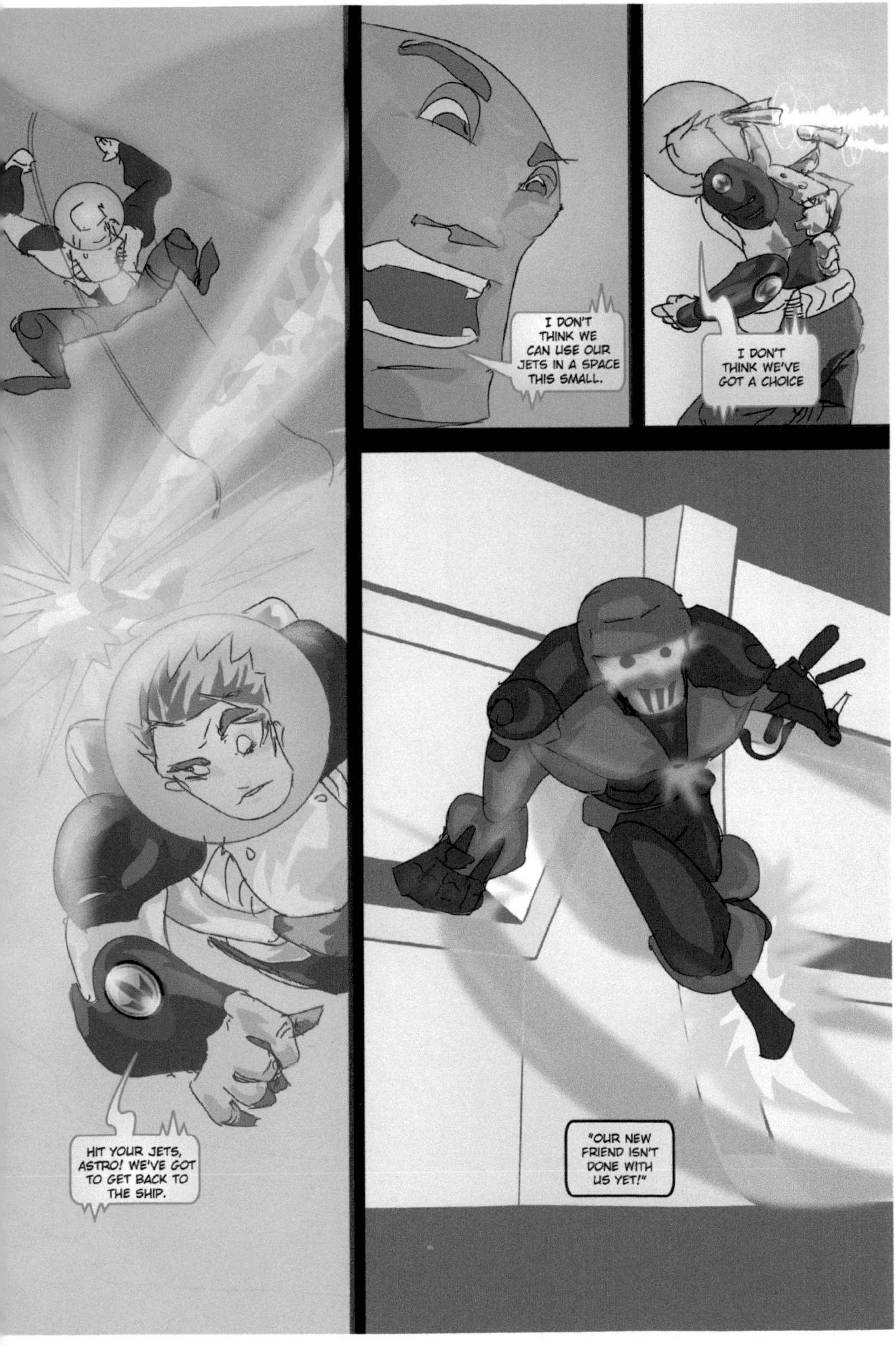
I DON'T THINK WE CAN USE OUR JETS IN A SPACE THIS SMALL.
I DON'T THINK WE'VE GOT A CHOICE
HIT YOUR JETS, ASTRO! WE'VE GOT TO GET BACK TO THE SHIP.
"OUR NEW FRIEND ISN'T DONE WITH US YET!"

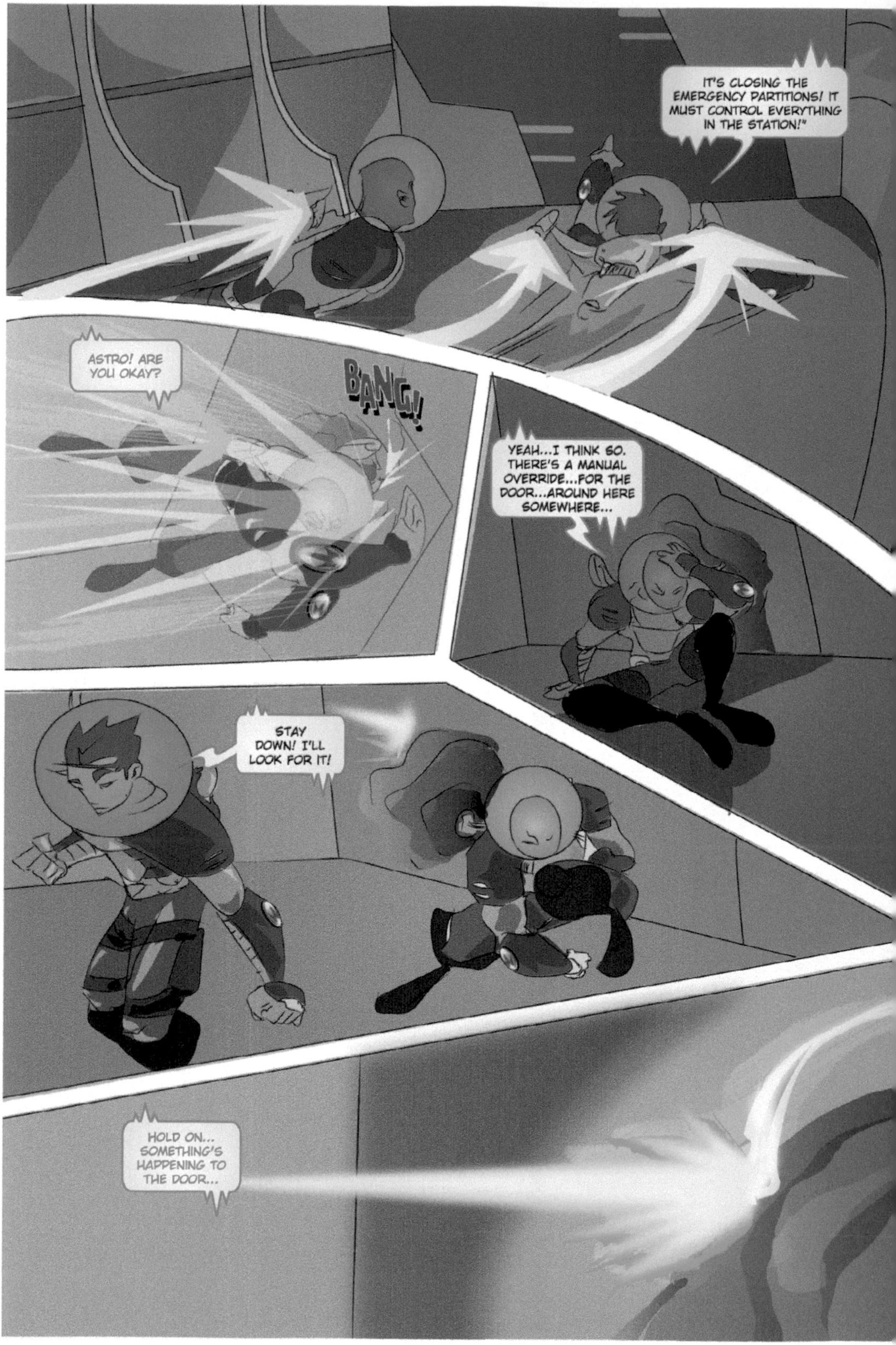
IT'S CLOSING THE EMERGENCY PARTITIONS! IT MUST CONTROL EVERYTHING IN THE STATION!"
ASTRO! ARE YOU OKAY?
BANG!!
YEAH...I THINK SO. THERE'S A MANUAL OVERRIDE...FOR THE DOOR...AROUND HERE SOMEWHERE...
STAY DOWN! I'LL LOOK FOR IT!
HOLD ON... SOMETHING'S HAPPENING TO THE DOOR...

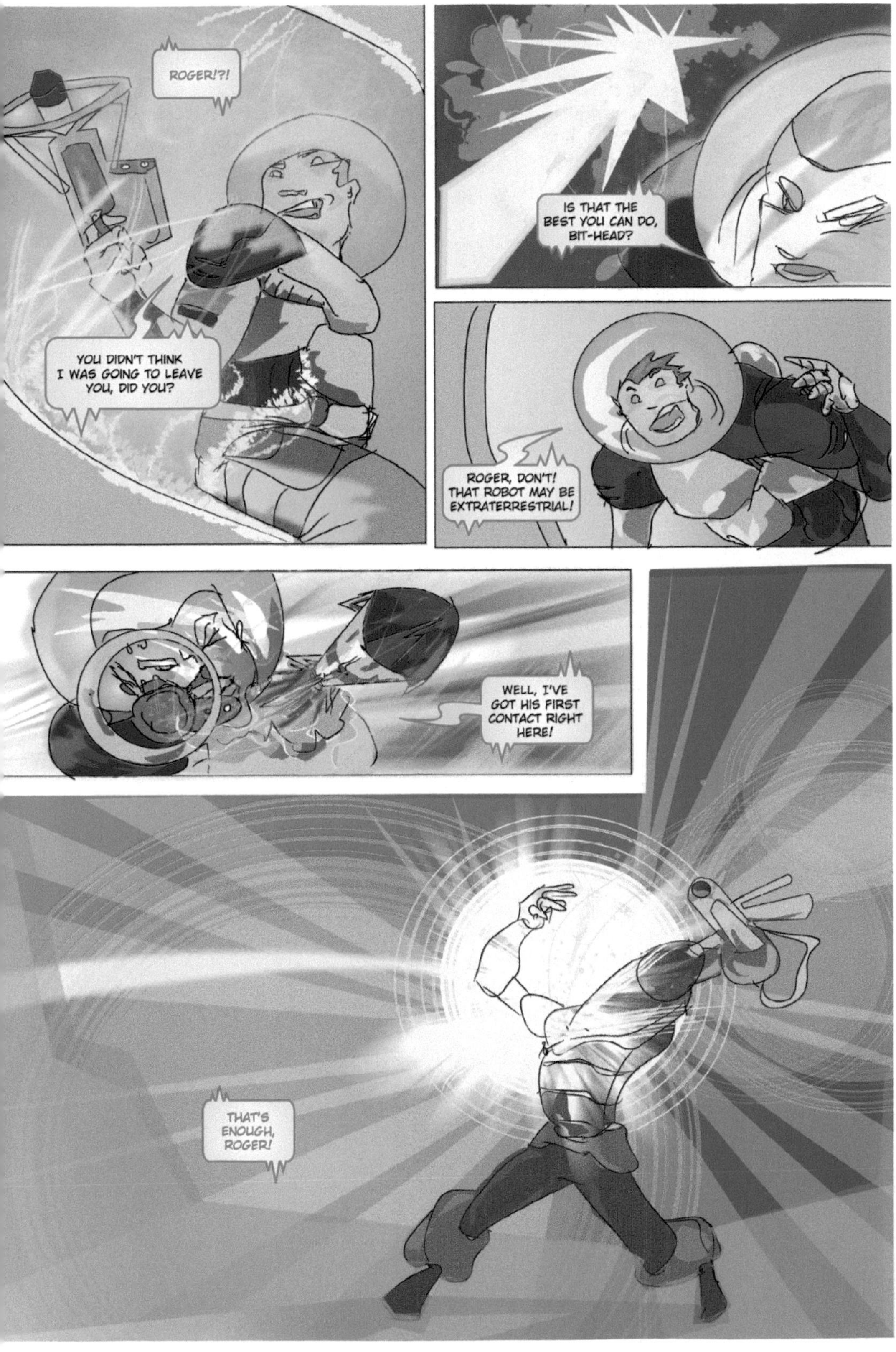
ROGER!?!
YOU DIDN'T THINK I WAS GOING TO LEAVE YOU, DID YOU?
IS THAT THE BEST YOU CAN DO, BIT-HEAD?
ROGER, DON'T! THAT ROBOT MAY BE EXTRATERRESTRIAL!
WELL, I'VE GOT HIS FIRST CONTACT RIGHT HERE!
THAT'S ENOUGH, ROGER!

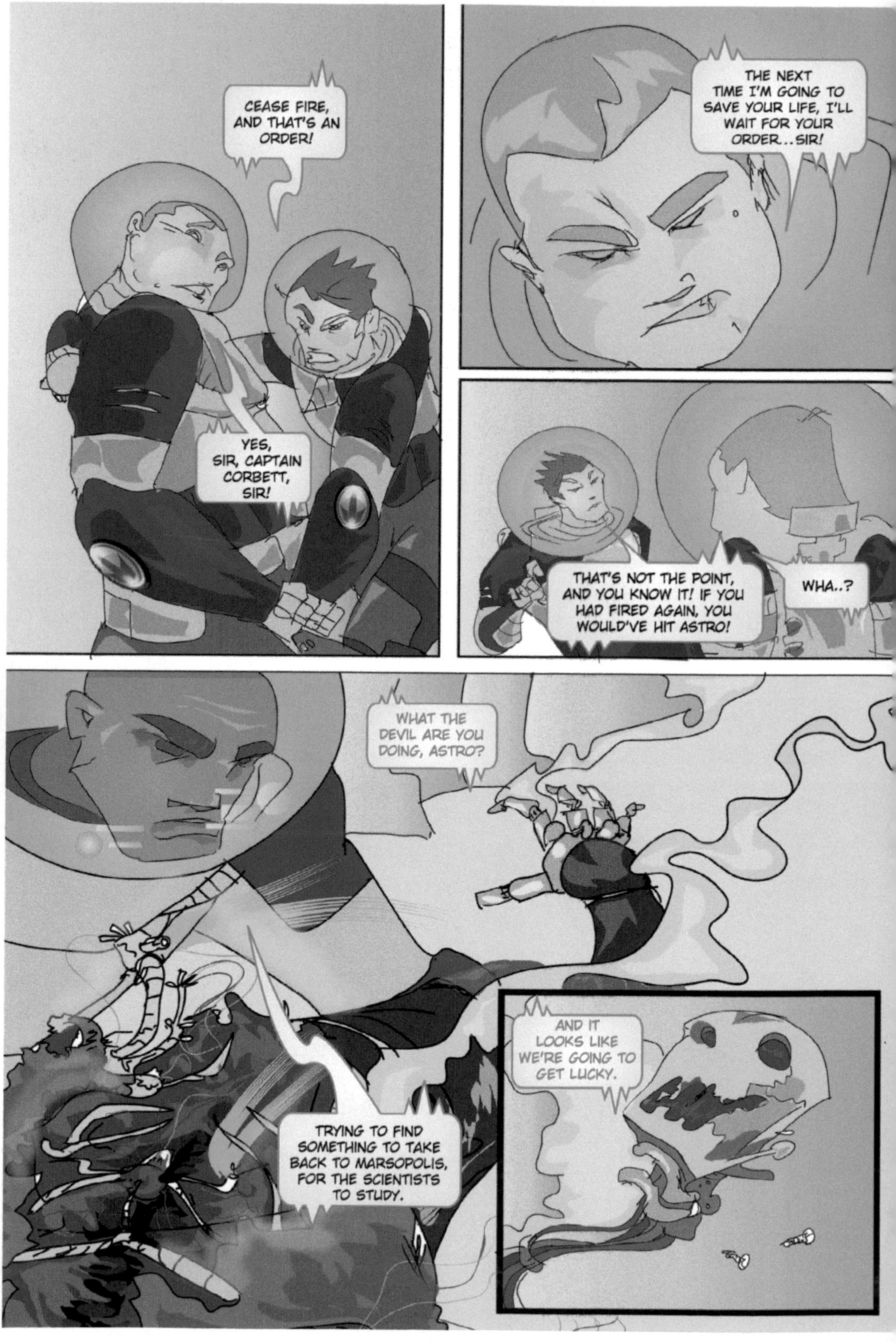
CEASE FIRE, AND THAT'S AN ORDER!
YES, SIR, CAPTAIN CORBETT, SIR!
THE NEXT TIME I'M GOING TO SAVE YOUR LIFE, I'LL WAIT FOR YOUR ORDER...SIR!
THAT'S NOT THE POINT, AND YOU KNOW IT! IF YOU HAD FIRED AGAIN, YOU WOULD'VE HIT ASTRO!
WHA..?
WHAT THE DEVIL ARE YOU DOING, ASTRO?
TRYING TO FIND SOMETHING TO TAKE BACK TO MARSOPOLIS, FOR THE SCIENTISTS TO STUDY.
AND IT LOOKS LIKE WE'RE GOING TO GET LUCKY.

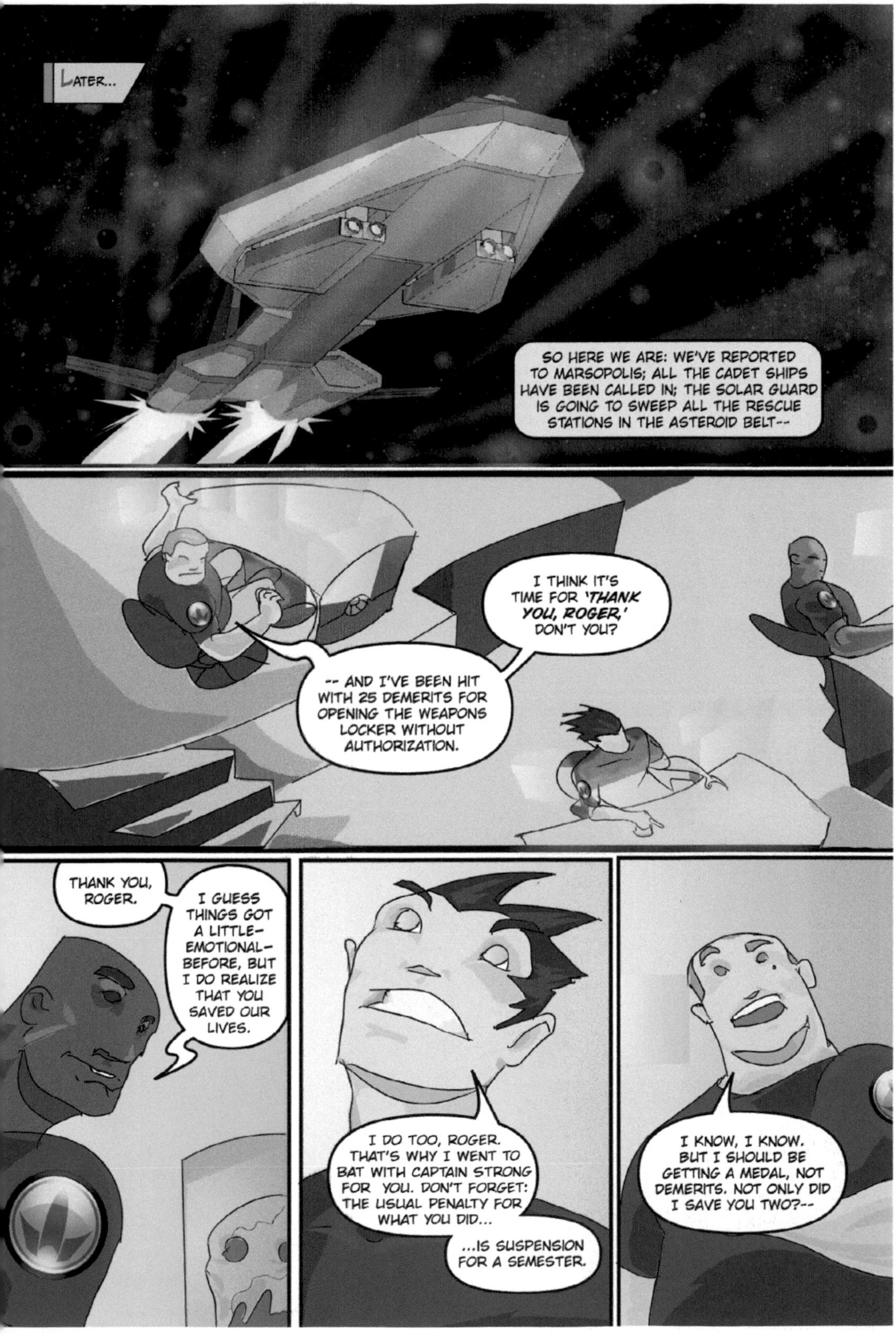
LATER...
SO HERE WE ARE: WE'VE REPORTED TO MARSOPOLIS; ALL THE CADET SHIPS HAVE BEEN CALLED IN; THE SOLAR GUARD IS GOING TO SWEEP ALL THE RESCUE STATIONS IN THE ASTEROID BELT--
-- AND I'VE BEEN HIT WITH 25 DEMERITS FOR OPENING THE WEAPONS LOCKER WITHOUT AUTHORIZATION.
I THINK IT'S TIME FOR 'THANK YOU, ROGER,' DON'T YOU?
THANK YOU, ROGER.
I GUESS THINGS GOT A LITTLE- EMOTIONAL- BEFORE, BUT I DO REALIZE THAT YOU SAVED OUR LIVES.
I DO TOO, ROGER. THAT'S WHY I WENT TO BAT WITH CAPTAIN STRONG FOR YOU. DON'T FORGET: THE USUAL PENALTY FOR WHAT YOU DID...
...IS SUSPENSION FOR A SEMESTER.
I KNOW, I KNOW. BUT I SHOULD BE GETTING A MEDAL, NOT DEMERITS. NOT ONLY DID I SAVE YOU TWO?--

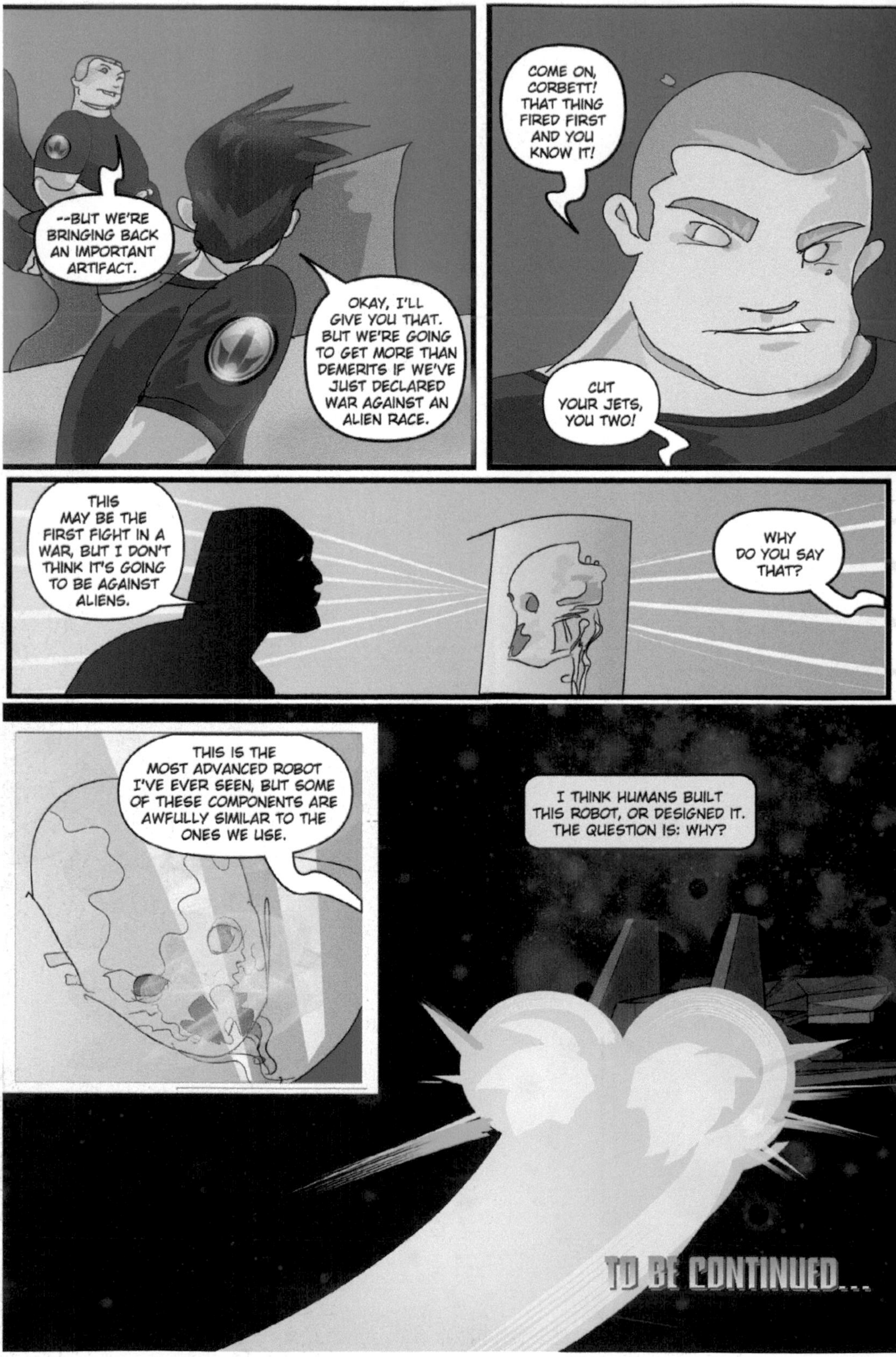
--BUT WE'RE BRINGING BACK AN IMPORTANT ARTIFACT.
OKAY, I'LL GIVE YOU THAT. BUT WE'RE GOING TO GET MORE THAN DEMERITS IF WE'VE JUST DECLARED WAR AGAINST AN ALIEN RACE.
COME ON, CORBETT! THAT THING FIRED FIRST AND YOU KNOW IT!
CUT YOUR JETS, YOU TWO!
THIS MAY BE THE FIRST FIGHT IN A WAR, BUT I DON'T THINK IT'S GOING TO BE AGAINST ALIENS.
WHY DO YOU SAY THAT?
THIS IS THE MOST ADVANCED ROBOT I'VE EVER SEEN, BUT SOME OF THESE COMPONENTS ARE AWFULLY SIMILAR TO THE ONES WE USE.
I THINK HUMANS BUILT THIS ROBOT, OR DESIGNED IT. THE QUESTION IS: WHY?
TO BE CONTINUED...

CHAPTER 2

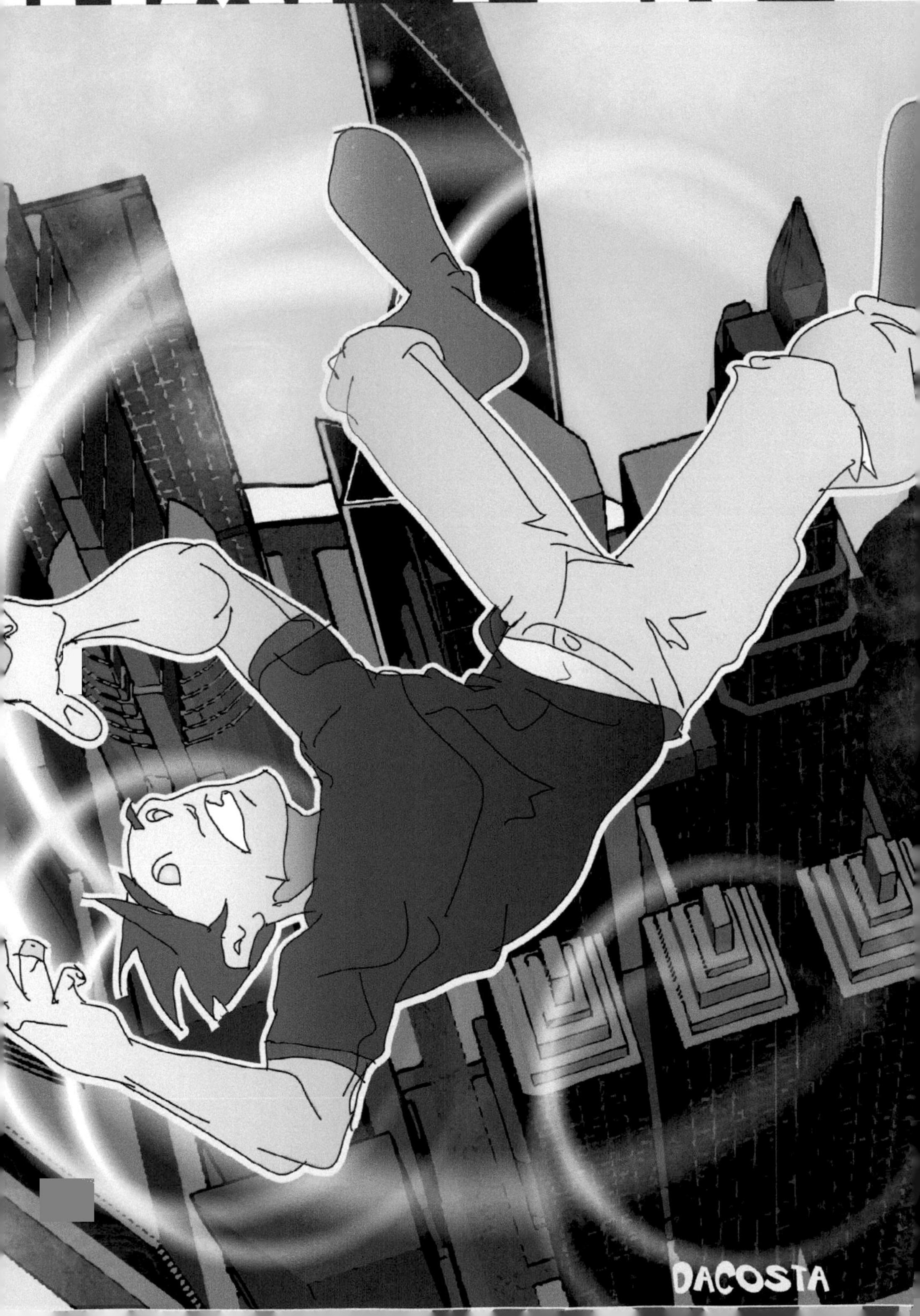
DACOSTA

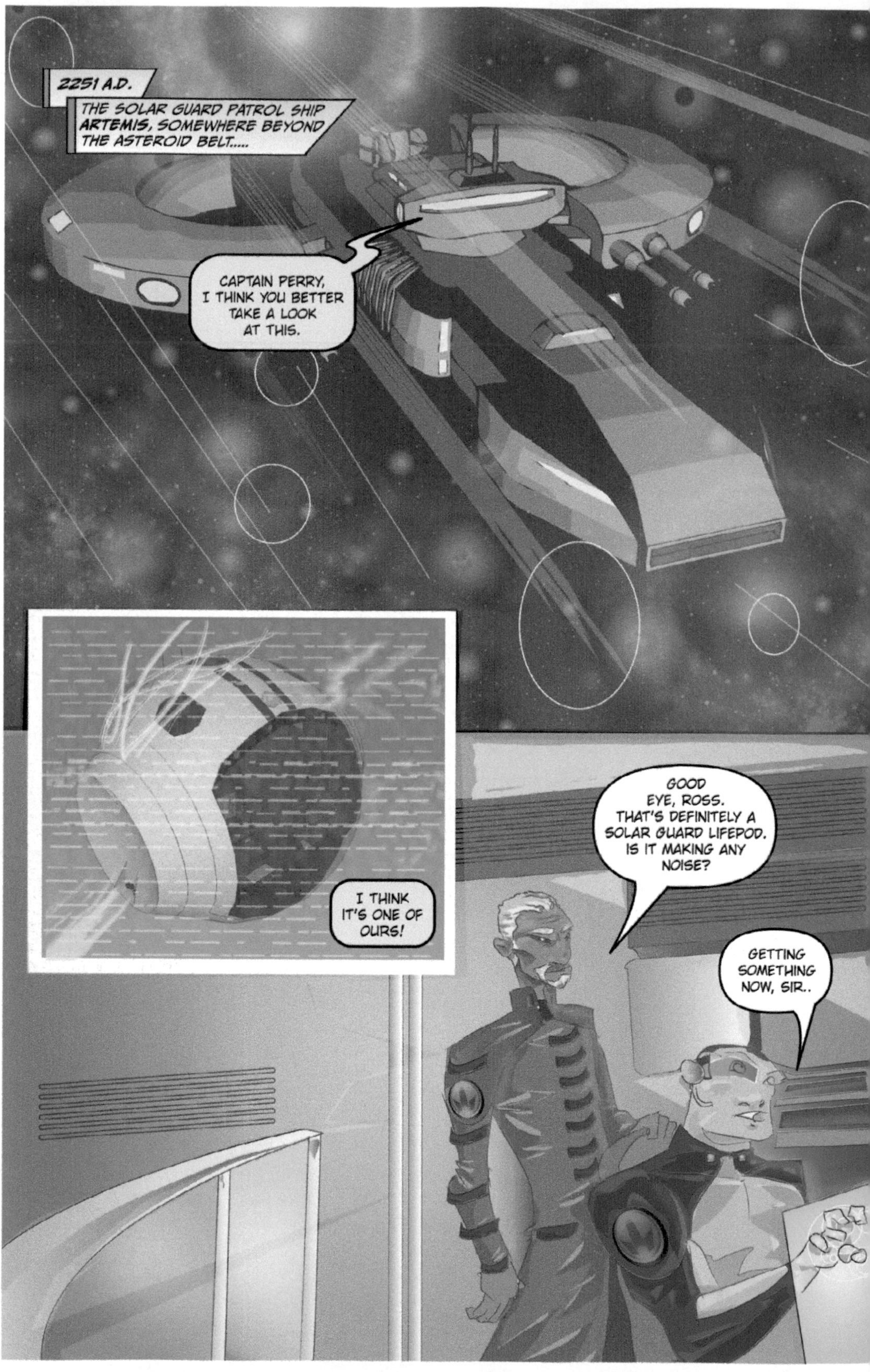
2251 A.D.
THE SOLAR GUARD PATROL SHIP ARTEMIS, SOMEWHERE BEYOND THE ASTEROID BELT.....
CAPTAIN PERRY, I THINK YOU BETTER TAKE A LOOK AT THIS.
I THINK IT'S ONE OF OURS!
GOOD EYE, ROSS. THAT'S DEFINITELY A SOLAR GUARD LIFEPOD. IS IT MAKING ANY NOISE?
GETTING SOMETHING NOW, SIR..

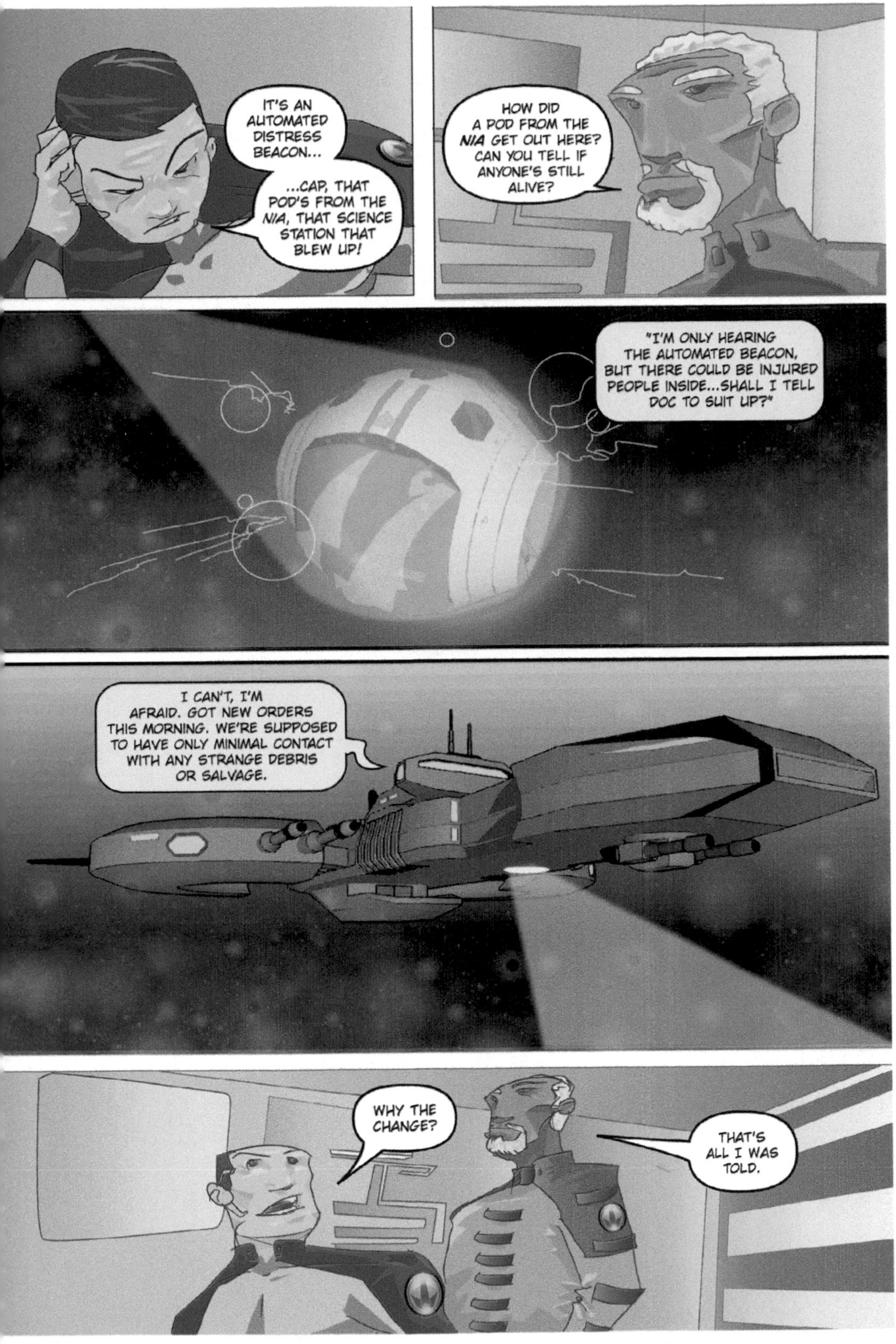
IT'S AN AUTOMATED DISTRESS BEACON...
...CAP, THAT POD'S FROM THE NIA, THAT SCIENCE STATION THAT BLEW UP!
HOW DID A POD FROM THE NIA GET OUT HERE? CAN YOU TELL IF ANYONE'S STILL ALIVE?
"I'M ONLY HEARING THE AUTOMATED BEACON, BUT THERE COULD BE INJURED PEOPLE INSIDE...SHALL I TELL DOC TO SUIT UP?"
I CAN'T, I'M AFRAID. GOT NEW ORDERS THIS MORNING. WE'RE SUPPOSED TO HAVE ONLY MINIMAL CONTACT WITH ANY STRANGE DEBRIS OR SALVAGE.
WHY THE CHANGE?
THAT'S ALL I WAS TOLD.

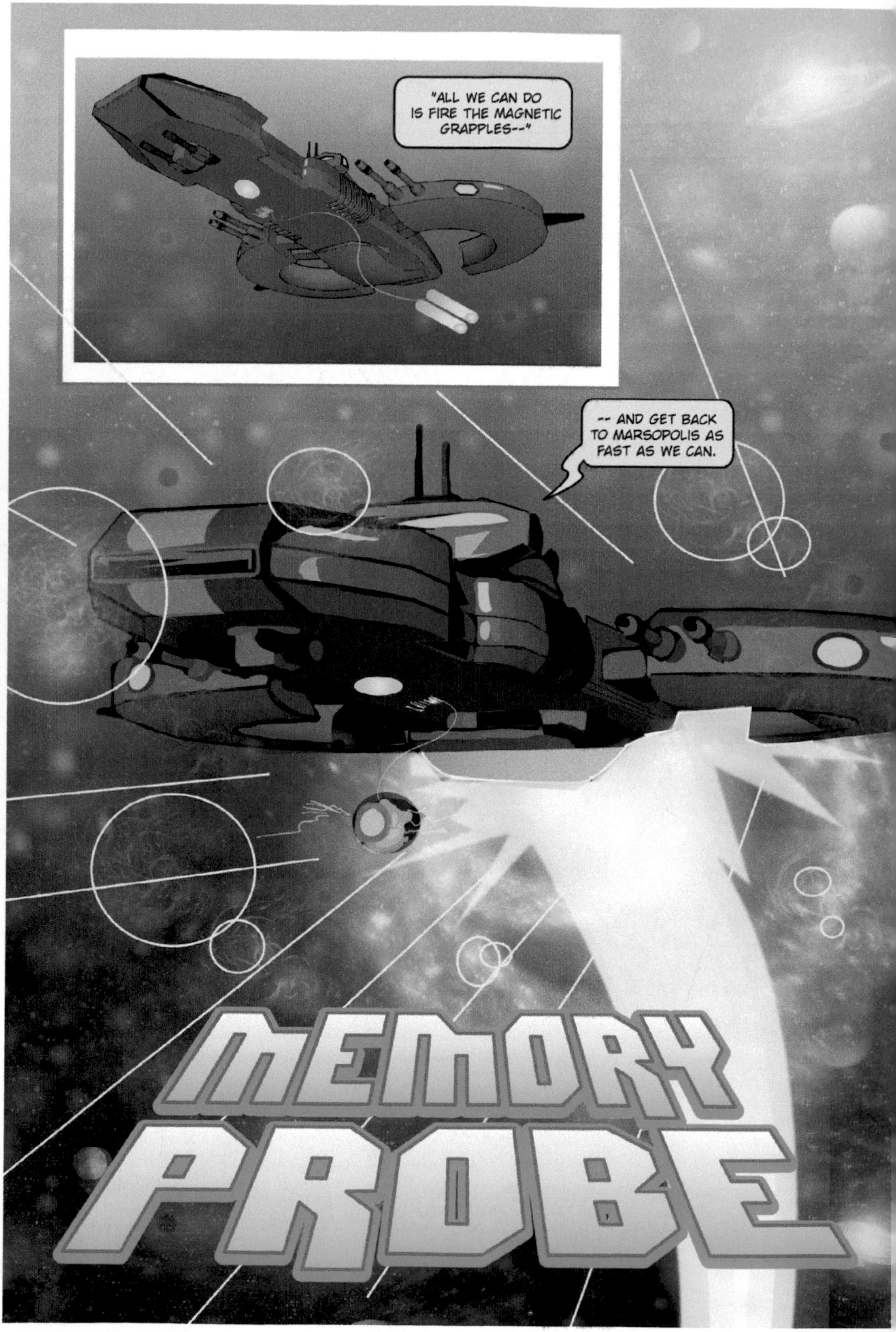
"ALL WE CAN DO IS FIRE THE MAGNETIC GRAPPLES--"
-- AND GET BACK TO MARSOPOLIS AS FAST AS WE CAN.
MEMORY PROBE

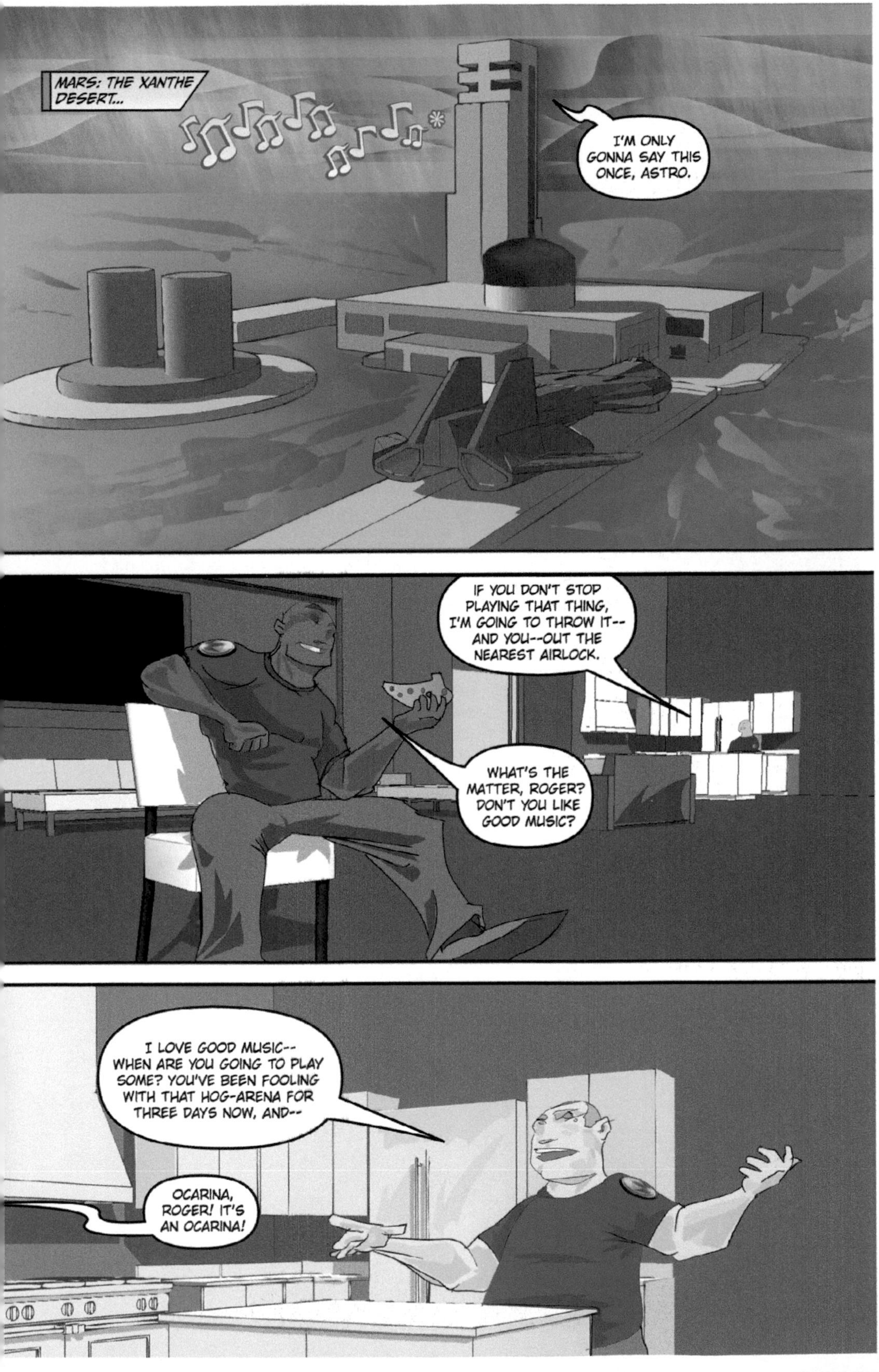
MARS: THE XANTHE DESERT...
*
I'M ONLY GONNA SAY THIS ONCE, ASTRO.
IF YOU DON'T STOP PLAYING THAT THING, I'M GOING TO THROW IT-- AND YOU--OUT THE NEAREST AIRLOCK.
WHAT'S THE MATTER, ROGER? DON'T YOU LIKE GOOD MUSIC?
I LOVE GOOD MUSIC-- WHEN ARE YOU GOING TO PLAY SOME? YOU'VE BEEN FOOLING WITH THAT HOG-ARENA FOR THREE DAYS NOW, AND--
OCARINA, ROGER! IT'S AN OCARINA!

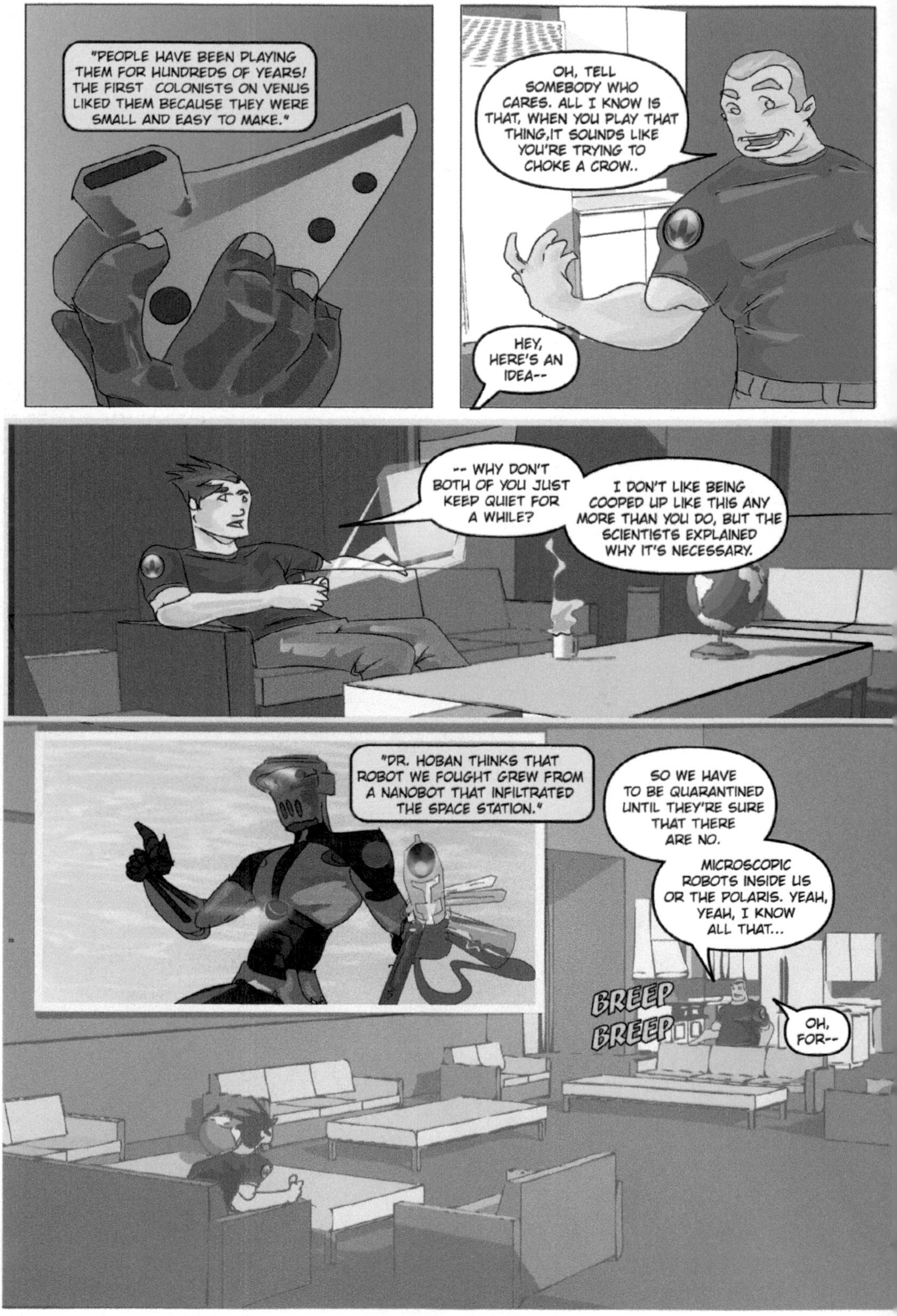
"PEOPLE HAVE BEEN PLAYING THEM FOR HUNDREDS OF YEARS! THE FIRST COLONISTS ON VENUS LIKED THEM BECAUSE THEY WERE SMALL AND EASY TO MAKE."
OH, TELL SOMEBODY WHO CARES. ALL I KNOW IS THAT, WHEN YOU PLAY THAT THING,IT SOUNDS LIKE YOU'RE TRYING TO CHOKE A CROW..
HEY, HERE'S AN IDEA--
-- WHY DON'T BOTH OF YOU JUST KEEP QUIET FOR A WHILE?
I DON'T LIKE BEING COOPED UP LIKE THIS ANY MORE THAN YOU DO, BUT THE SCIENTISTS EXPLAINED WHY IT'S NECESSARY.
"DR. HOBAN THINKS THAT ROBOT WE FOUGHT GREW FROM A NANOBOT THAT INFILTRATED THE SPACE STATION."
SO WE HAVE TO BE QUARANTINED UNTIL THEY'RE SURE THAT THERE ARE NO.
MICROSCOPIC ROBOTS INSIDE US OR THE POLARIS. YEAH, YEAH, I KNOW ALL THAT...
BREEP
BREEP
OH, FOR--

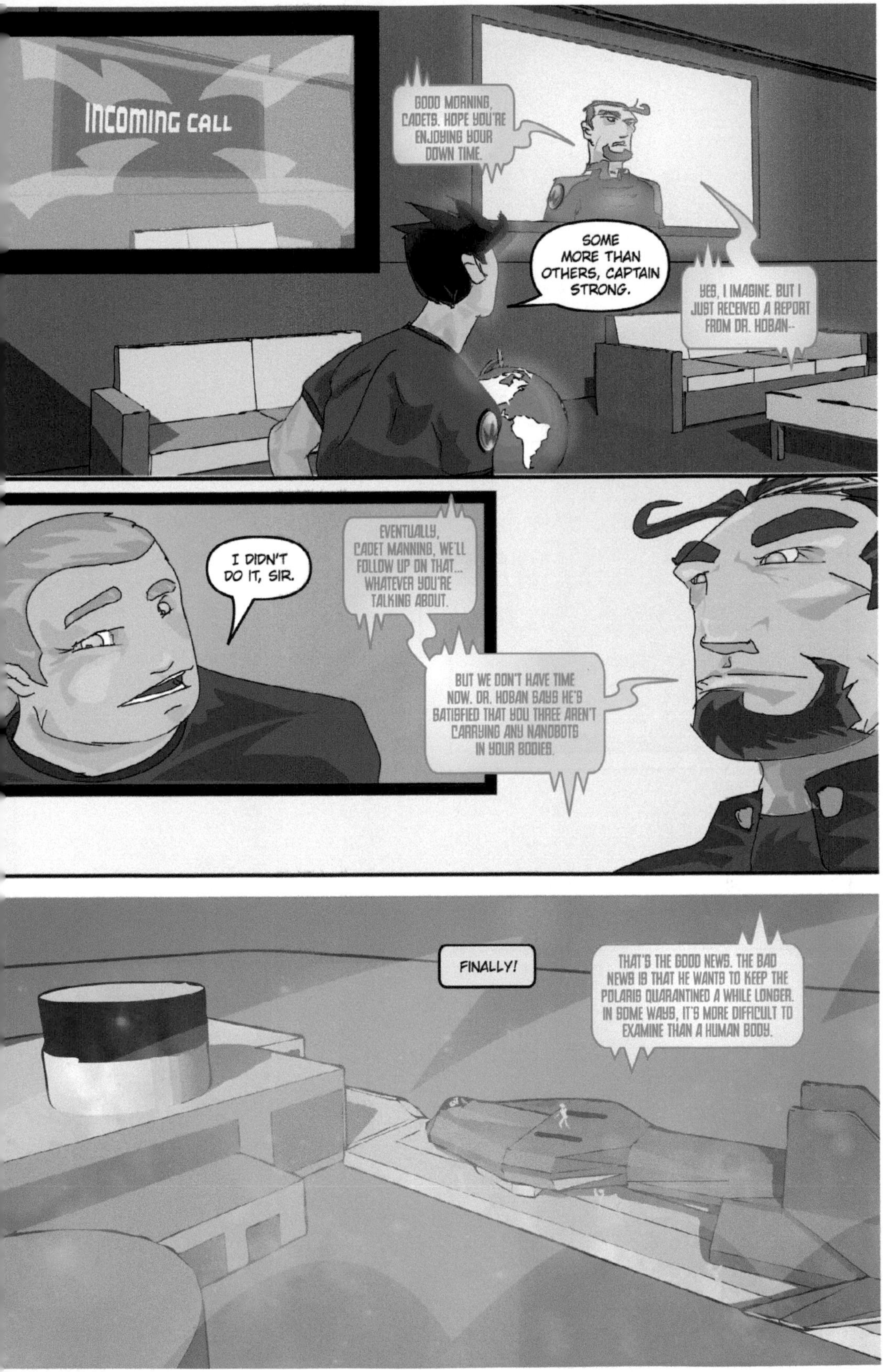
INCOMING CALL
GOOD MORNING, CADETS. HOPE YOU'RE ENJOYING YOUR DOWN TIME.
SOME MORE THAN OTHERS, CAPTAIN STRONG.
YES, I IMAGINE. BUT I JUST RECEIVED A REPORT FROM DR. HOBAN--
I DIDN'T DO IT, SIR.
EVENTUALLY, CADET MANNING, WE'LL FOLLOW UP ON THAT... WHATEVER YOU'RE TALKING ABOUT.
BUT WE DON'T HAVE TIME NOW. DR. HOBAN SAYS HE'S SATISFIED THAT YOU THREE AREN'T CARRYING ANY NANOBOTS IN YOUR BODIES.
FINALLY!
THAT'S THE GOOD NEWS. THE BAD NEWS IS THAT HE WANTS TO KEEP THE POLARIS QUARANTINED A WHILE LONGER. IN SOME WAYS, IT'S MORE DIFFICULT TO EXAMINE THAN A HUMAN BODY.

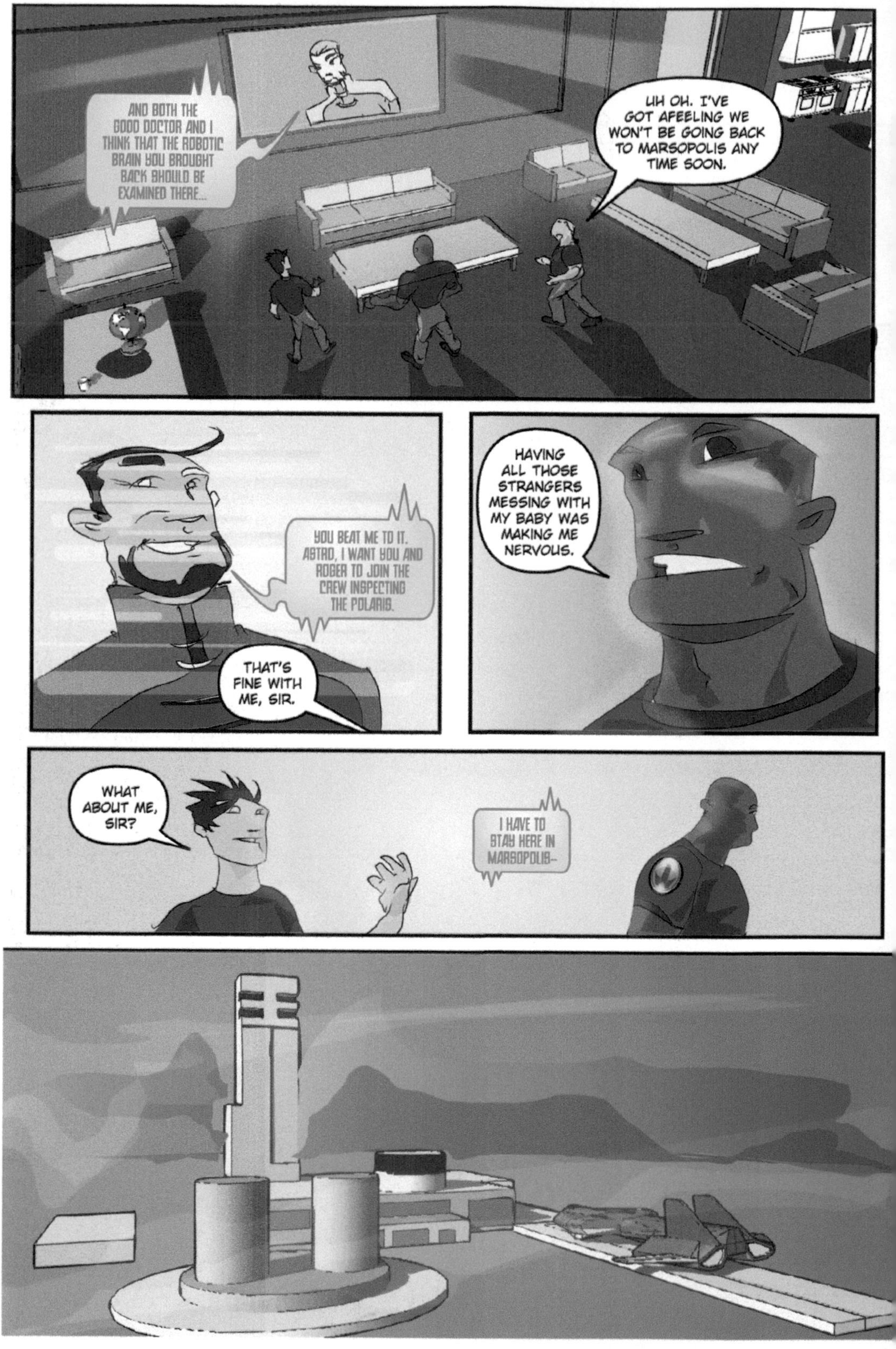
AND BOTH THE GOOD DOCTOR AND I THINK THAT THE ROBOTIC BRAIN YOU BROUGHT BACK SHOULD BE EXAMINED THERE...
UH OH. I'VE GOT AFEELING WE WON'T BE GOING BACK TO MARSOPOLIS ANY TIME SOON.
YOU BEAT ME TO IT. ASTRO, I WANT YOU AND ROGER TO JOIN THE CREW INSPECTING THE POLARIS.
THAT'S FINE WITH ME, SIR.
HAVING ALL THOSE STRANGERS MESSING WITH MY BABY WAS MAKING ME NERVOUS.
WHAT ABOUT ME, SIR?
I HAVE TO STAY HERE IN MARSOPOLIS–

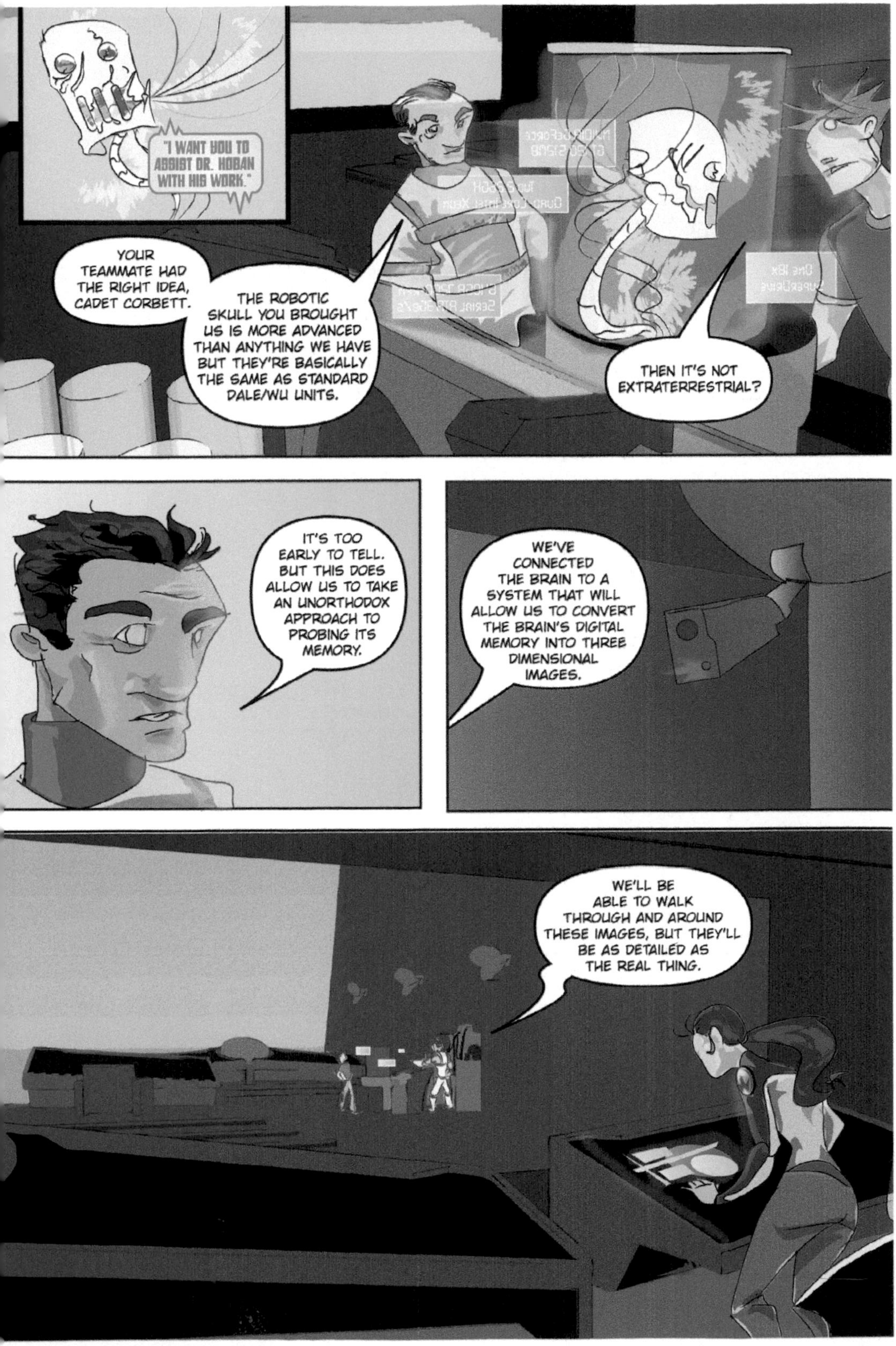
"I WANT YOU TO ASSIST DR. HOBAN WITH HIS WORK."
YOUR TEAMMATE HAD THE RIGHT IDEA, CADET CORBETT.
THE ROBOTIC SKULL YOU BROUGHT US IS MORE ADVANCED THAN ANYTHING WE HAVE BUT THEY'RE BASICALLY THE SAME AS STANDARD DALE/WU UNITS.
THEN IT'S NOT EXTRATERRESTRIAL?
IT'S TOO EARLY TO TELL. BUT THIS DOES ALLOW US TO TAKE AN UNORTHODOX APPROACH TO PROBING ITS MEMORY.
WE'VE CONNECTED THE BRAIN TO A SYSTEM THAT WILL ALLOW US TO CONVERT THE BRAIN'S DIGITAL MEMORY INTO THREE DIMENSIONAL IMAGES.
WE'LL BE ABLE TO WALK THROUGH AND AROUND THESE IMAGES, BUT THEY'LL BE AS DETAILED AS THE REAL THING.

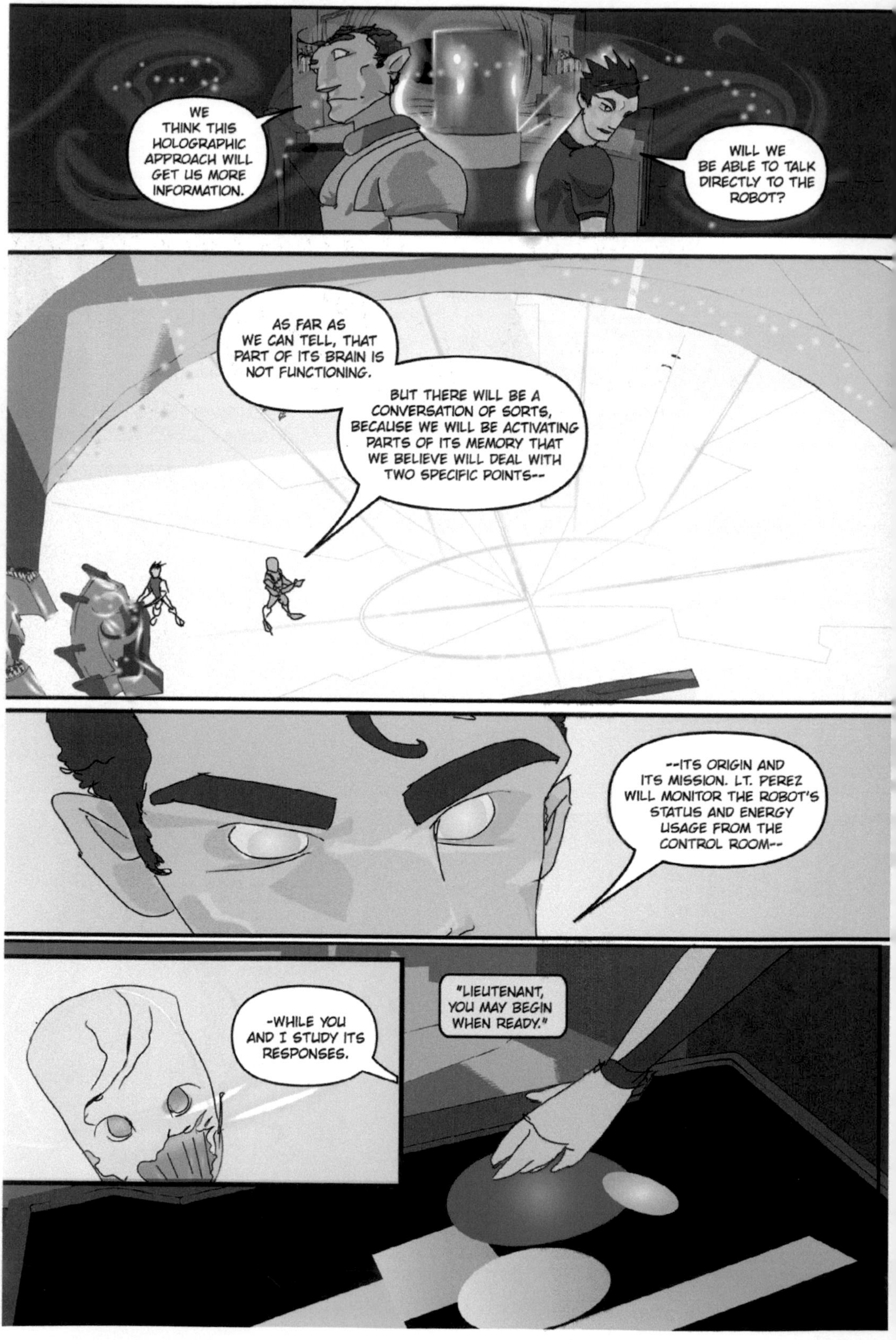
WE THINK THIS HOLOGRAPHIC APPROACH WILL GET US MORE INFORMATION.
WILL WE BE ABLE TO TALK DIRECTLY TO THE ROBOT?
AS FAR AS WE CAN TELL, THAT PART OF ITS BRAIN IS NOT FUNCTIONING.
BUT THERE WILL BE A CONVERSATION OF SORTS, BECAUSE WE WILL BE ACTIVATING PARTS OF ITS MEMORY THAT WE BELIEVE WILL DEAL WITH TWO SPECIFIC POINTS--
--ITS ORIGIN AND ITS MISSION. LT. PEREZ WILL MONITOR THE ROBOT'S STATUS AND ENERGY USAGE FROM THE CONTROL ROOM--
-WHILE YOU AND I STUDY ITS RESPONSES.
"LIEUTENANT, YOU MAY BEGIN WHEN READY."

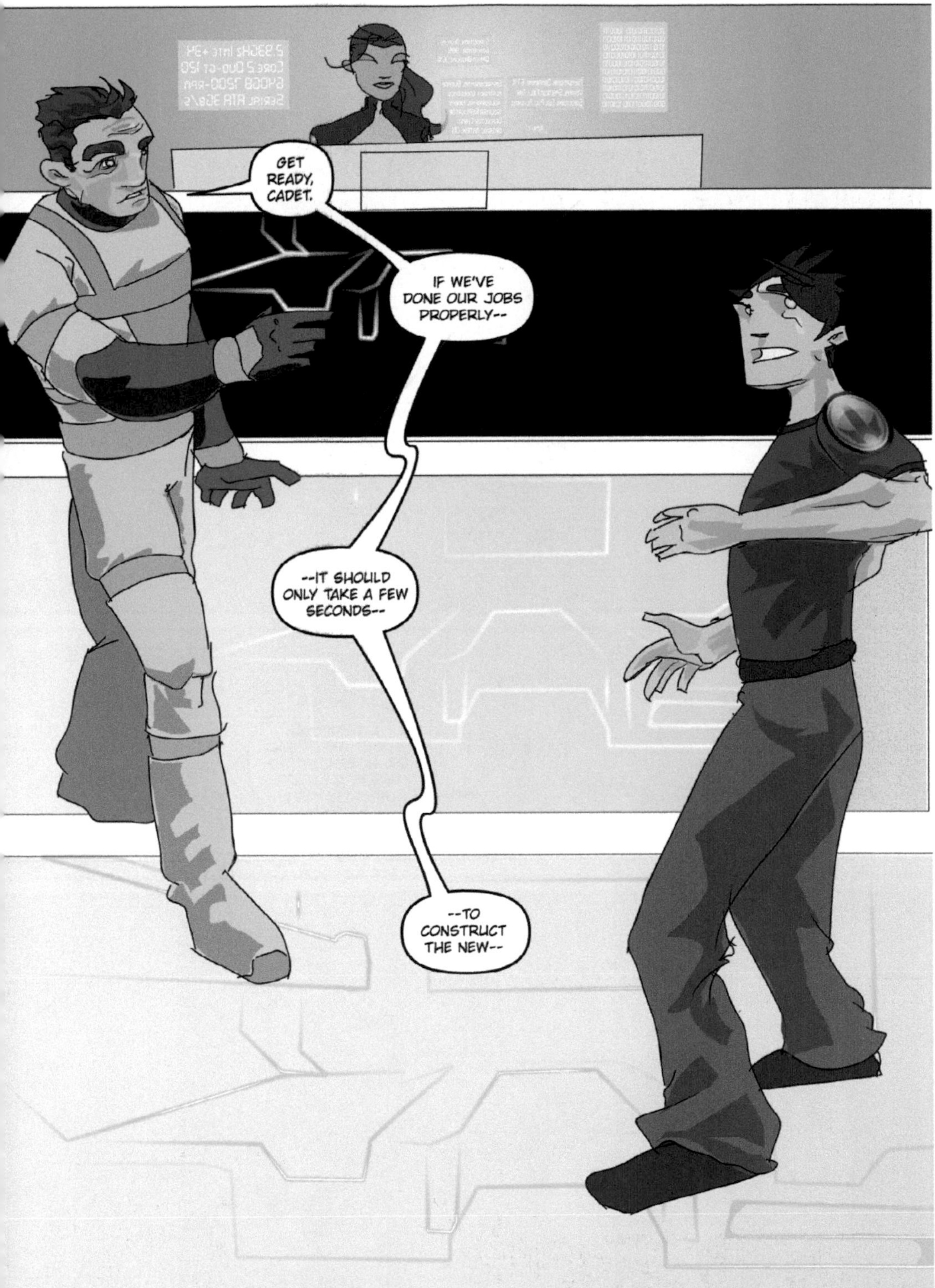
GET READY, CADET.
IF WE'VE DONE OUR JOBS PROPERLY--
--IT SHOULD ONLY TAKE A FEW SECONDS--
--TO CONSTRUCT THE NEW--

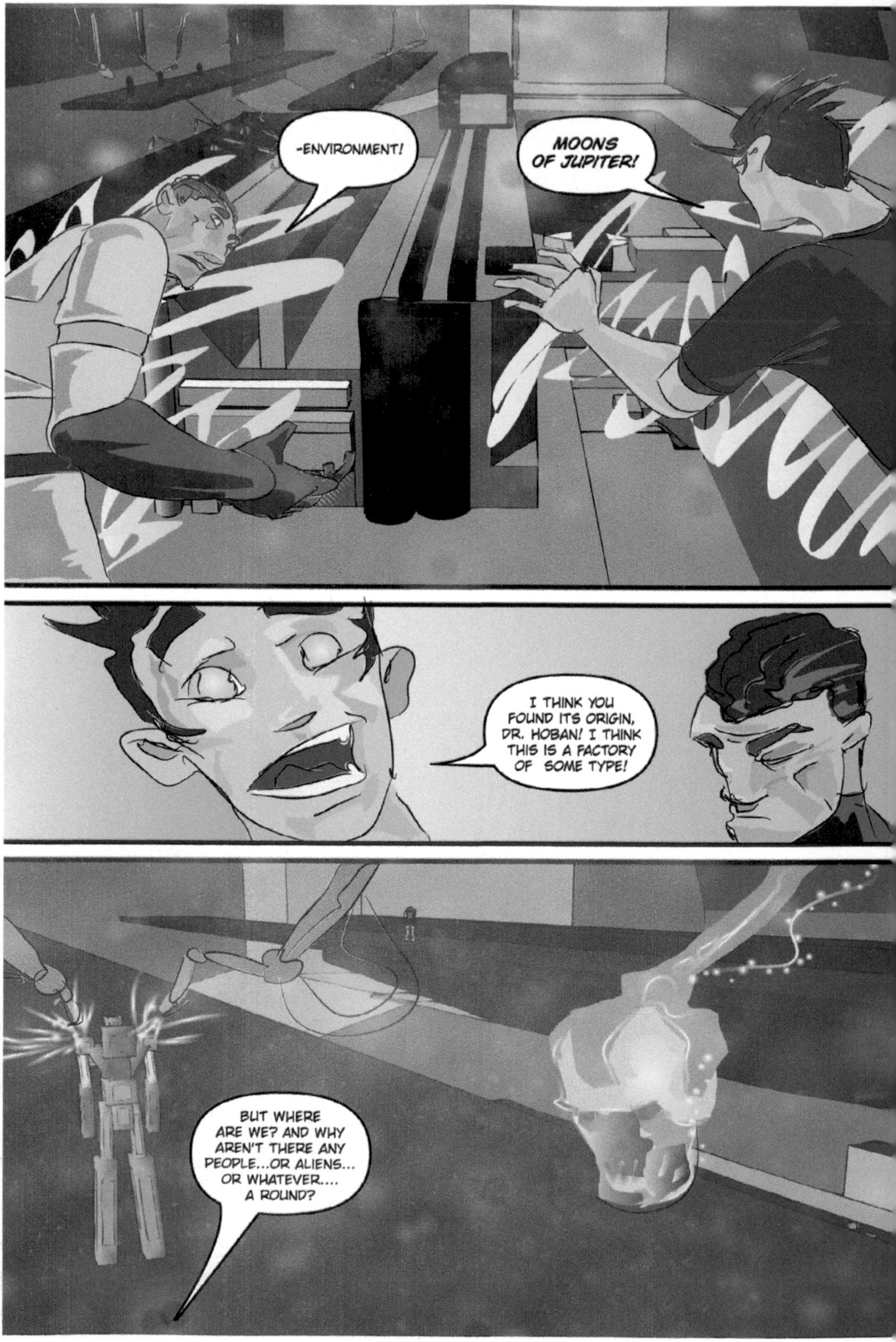
-ENVIRONMENT!
MOONS OF JUPITER!
I THINK YOU FOUND ITS ORIGIN, DR. HOBAN! I THINK THIS IS A FACTORY OF SOME TYPE!
BUT WHERE ARE WE? AND WHY AREN'T THERE ANY PEOPLE...OR ALIENS... OR WHATEVER.... A ROUND?

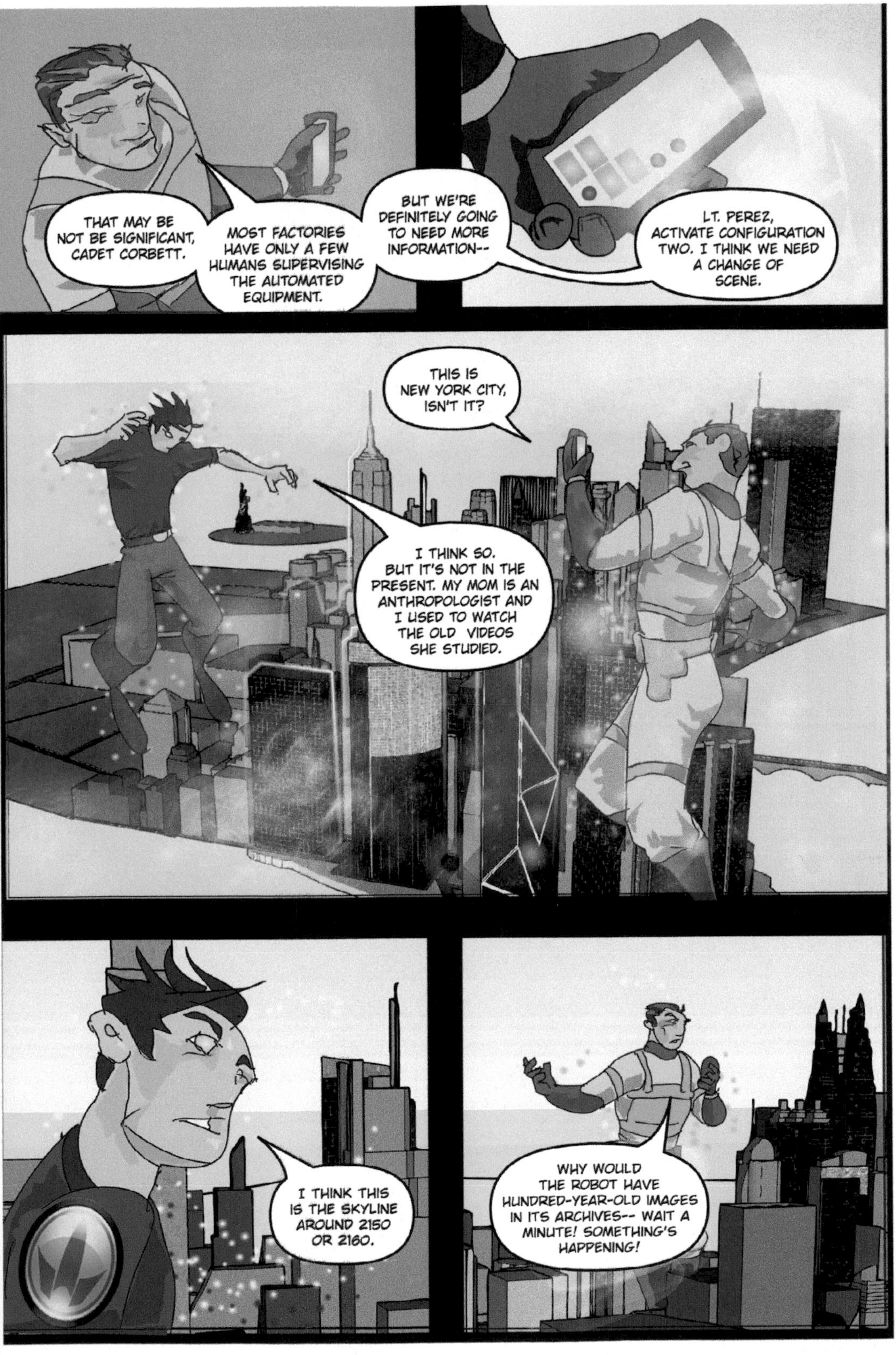
THAT MAY BE NOT BE SIGNIFICANT, CADET CORBETT.
MOST FACTORIES HAVE ONLY A FEW HUMANS SUPERVISING THE AUTOMATED EQUIPMENT.
BUT WE'RE DEFINITELY GOING TO NEED MORE INFORMATION--
LT. PEREZ, ACTIVATE CONFIGURATION TWO. I THINK WE NEED A CHANGE OF SCENE.
THIS IS NEW YORK CITY, ISN'T IT?
I THINK SO. BUT IT'S NOT IN THE PRESENT. MY MOM IS AN ANTHROPOLOGIST AND I USED TO WATCH THE OLD VIDEOS SHE STUDIED.
I THINK THIS IS THE SKYLINE AROUND 2150 OR 2160.
WHY WOULD THE ROBOT HAVE HUNDRED-YEAR-OLD IMAGES IN ITS ARCHIVES-- WAIT A MINUTE! SOMETHING'S HAPPENING!

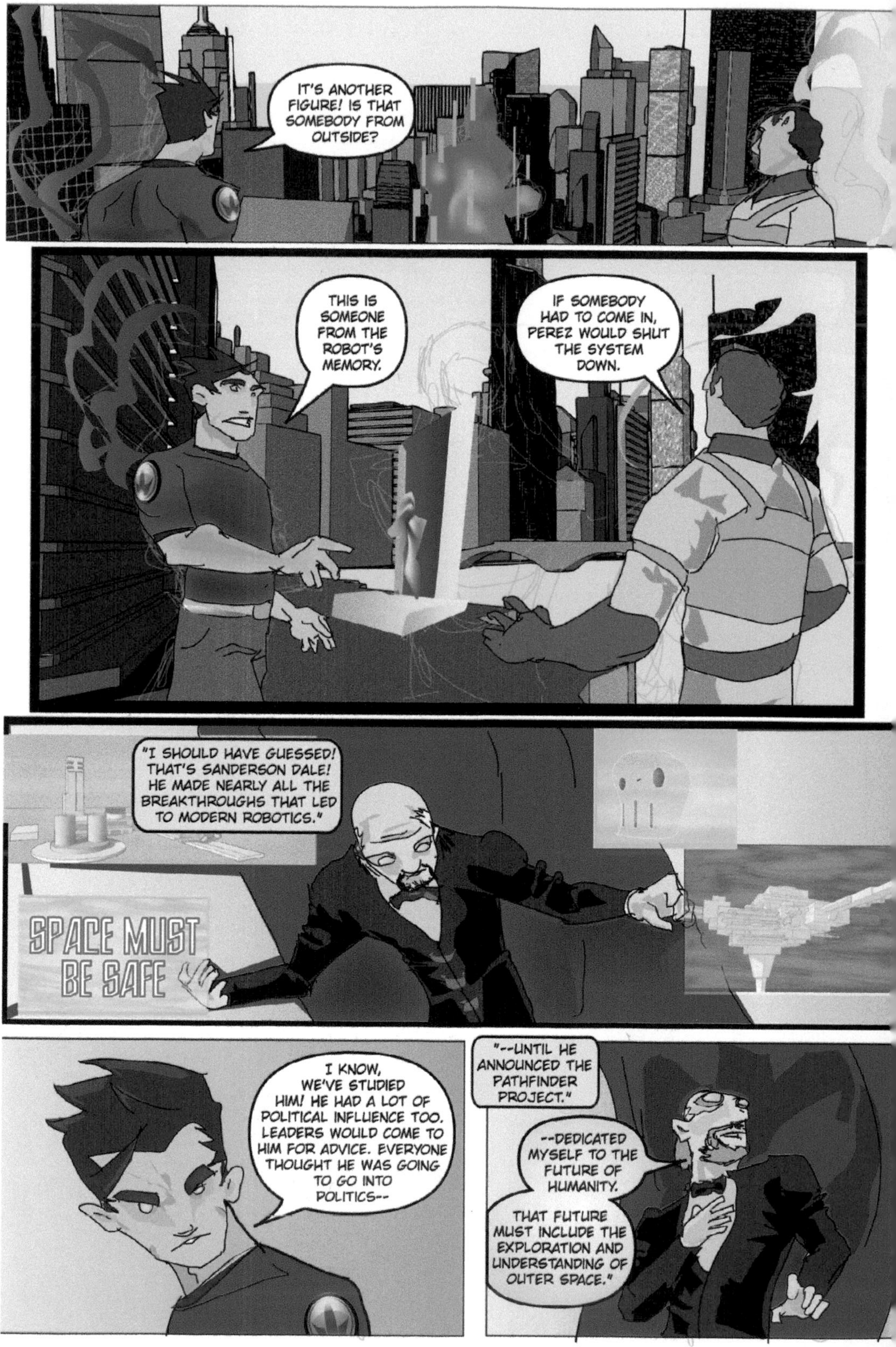
IT'S ANOTHER FIGURE! IS THAT SOMEBODY FROM OUTSIDE?
THIS IS SOMEONE FROM THE ROBOT'S MEMORY.
IF SOMEBODY HAD TO COME IN, PEREZ WOULD SHUT THE SYSTEM DOWN.
"I SHOULD HAVE GUESSED! THAT'S SANDERSON DALE! HE MADE NEARLY ALL THE BREAKTHROUGHS THAT LED TO MODERN ROBOTICS."
SPACE MUST BE SAFE
I KNOW, WE'VE STUDIED HIM! HE HAD A LOT OF POLITICAL INFLUENCE TOO. LEADERS WOULD COME TO HIM FOR ADVICE. EVERYONE THOUGHT HE WAS GOING TO GO INTO POLITICS--
"--UNTIL HE ANNOUNCED THE PATHFINDER PROJECT."
--DEDICATED MYSELF TO THE FUTURE OF HUMANITY.
THAT FUTURE MUST INCLUDE THE EXPLORATION AND UNDERSTANDING OF OUTER SPACE."

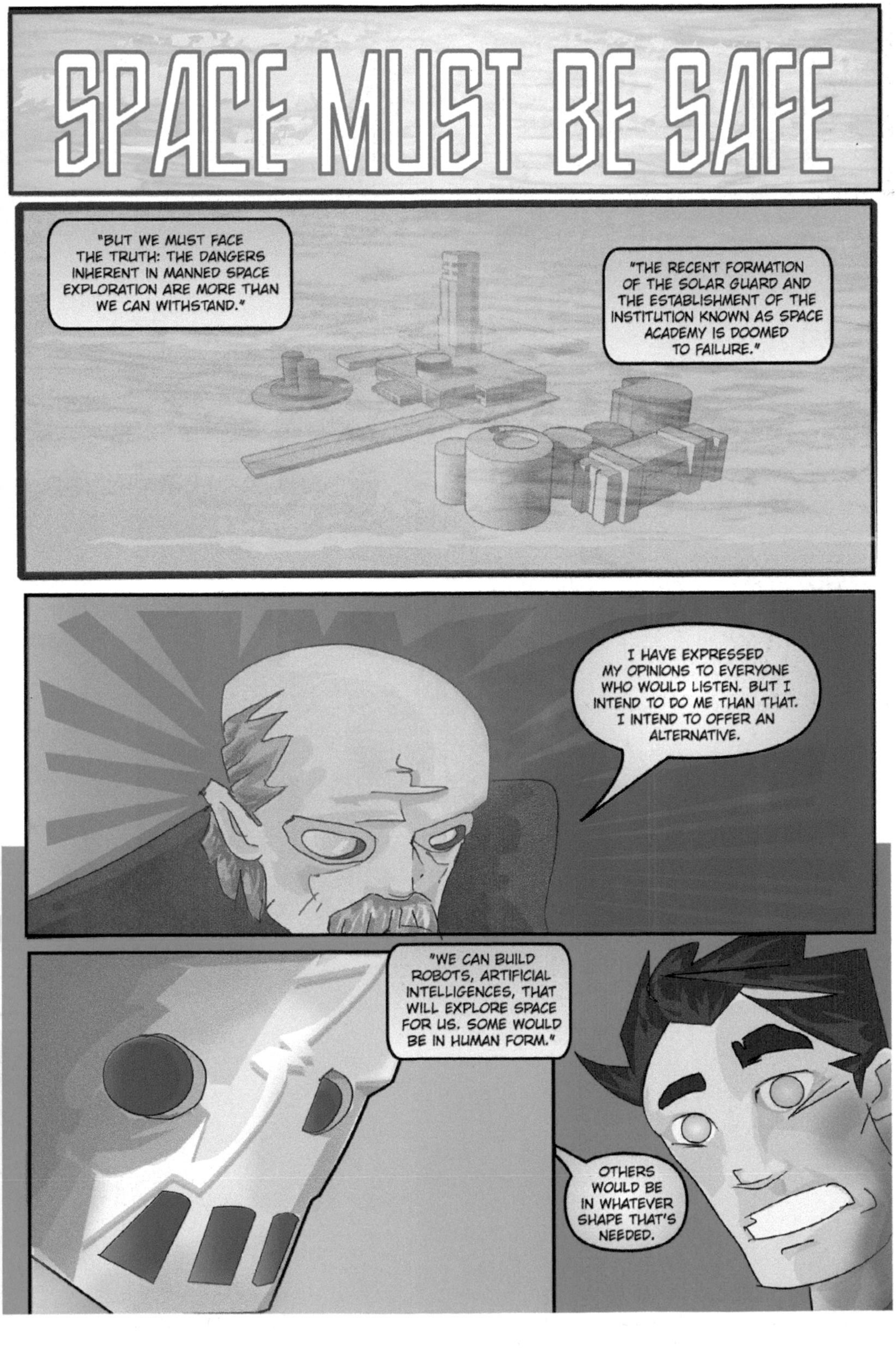
SPACE MUST BE SAFE
"BUT WE MUST FACE THE TRUTH: THE DANGERS INHERENT IN MANNED SPACE EXPLORATION ARE MORE THAN WE CAN WITHSTAND."
"THE RECENT FORMATION OF THE SOLAR GUARD AND THE ESTABLISHMENT OF THE INSTITUTION KNOWN AS SPACE ACADEMY IS DOOMED TO FAILURE."
I HAVE EXPRESSED MY OPINIONS TO EVERYONE WHO WOULD LISTEN. BUT I INTEND TO DO ME THAN THAT. I INTEND TO OFFER AN ALTERNATIVE.
"WE CAN BUILD ROBOTS, ARTIFICIAL INTELLIGENCES, THAT WILL EXPLORE SPACE FOR US. SOME WOULD BE IN HUMAN FORM."
OTHERS WOULD BE IN WHATEVER SHAPE THAT'S NEEDED.

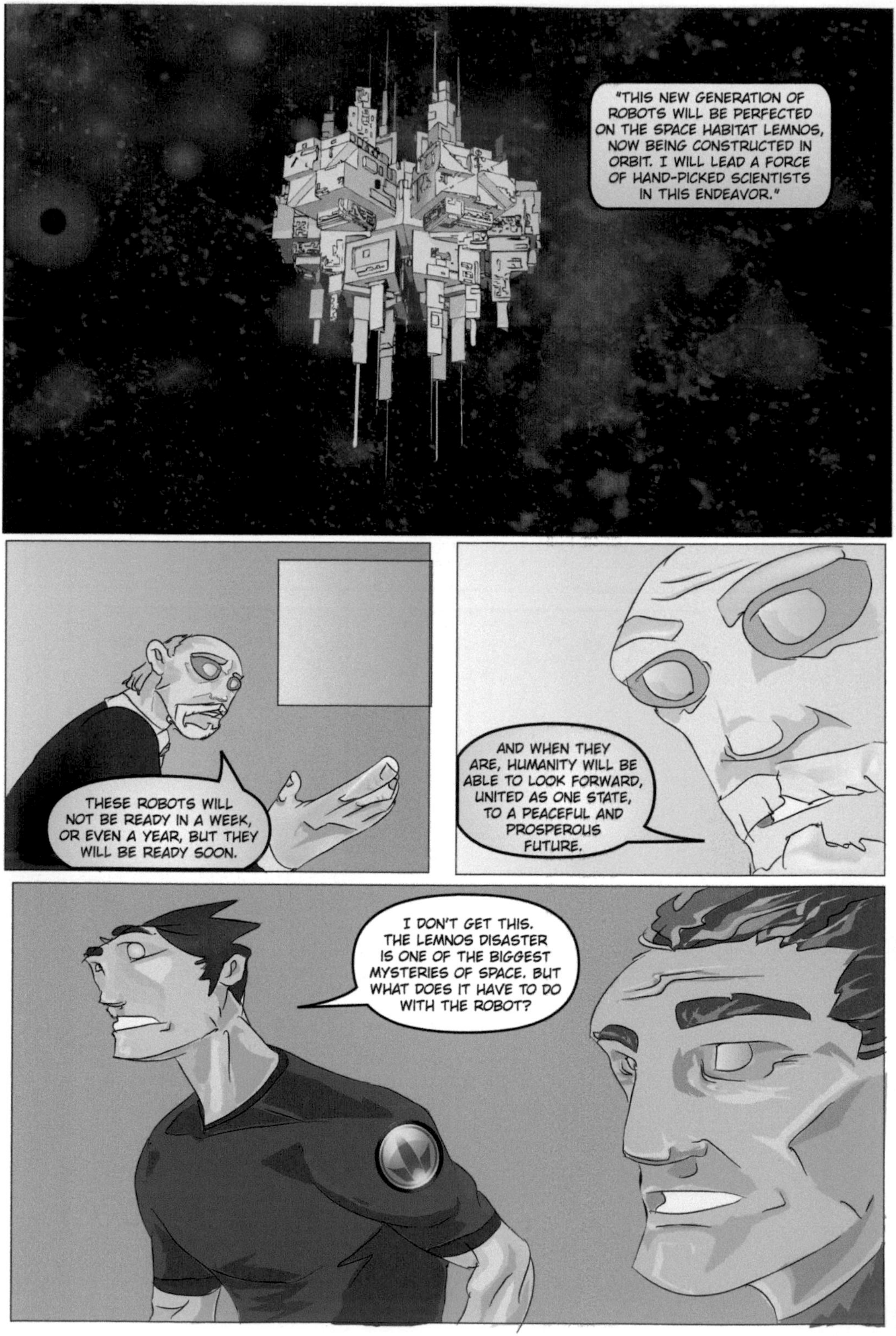
"THIS NEW GENERATION OF ROBOTS WILL BE PERFECTED ON THE SPACE HABITAT LEMNOS, NOW BEING CONSTRUCTED IN ORBIT. I WILL LEAD A FORCE OF HAND-PICKED SCIENTISTS IN THIS ENDEAVOR."
THESE ROBOTS WILL NOT BE READY IN A WEEK, OR EVEN A YEAR, BUT THEY WILL BE READY SOON.
AND WHEN THEY ARE, HUMANITY WILL BE ABLE TO LOOK FORWARD, UNITED AS ONE STATE, TO A PEACEFUL AND PROSPEROUS FUTURE.
I DON'T GET THIS. THE LEMNOS DISASTER IS ONE OF THE BIGGEST MYSTERIES OF SPACE. BUT WHAT DOES IT HAVE TO DO WITH THE ROBOT?

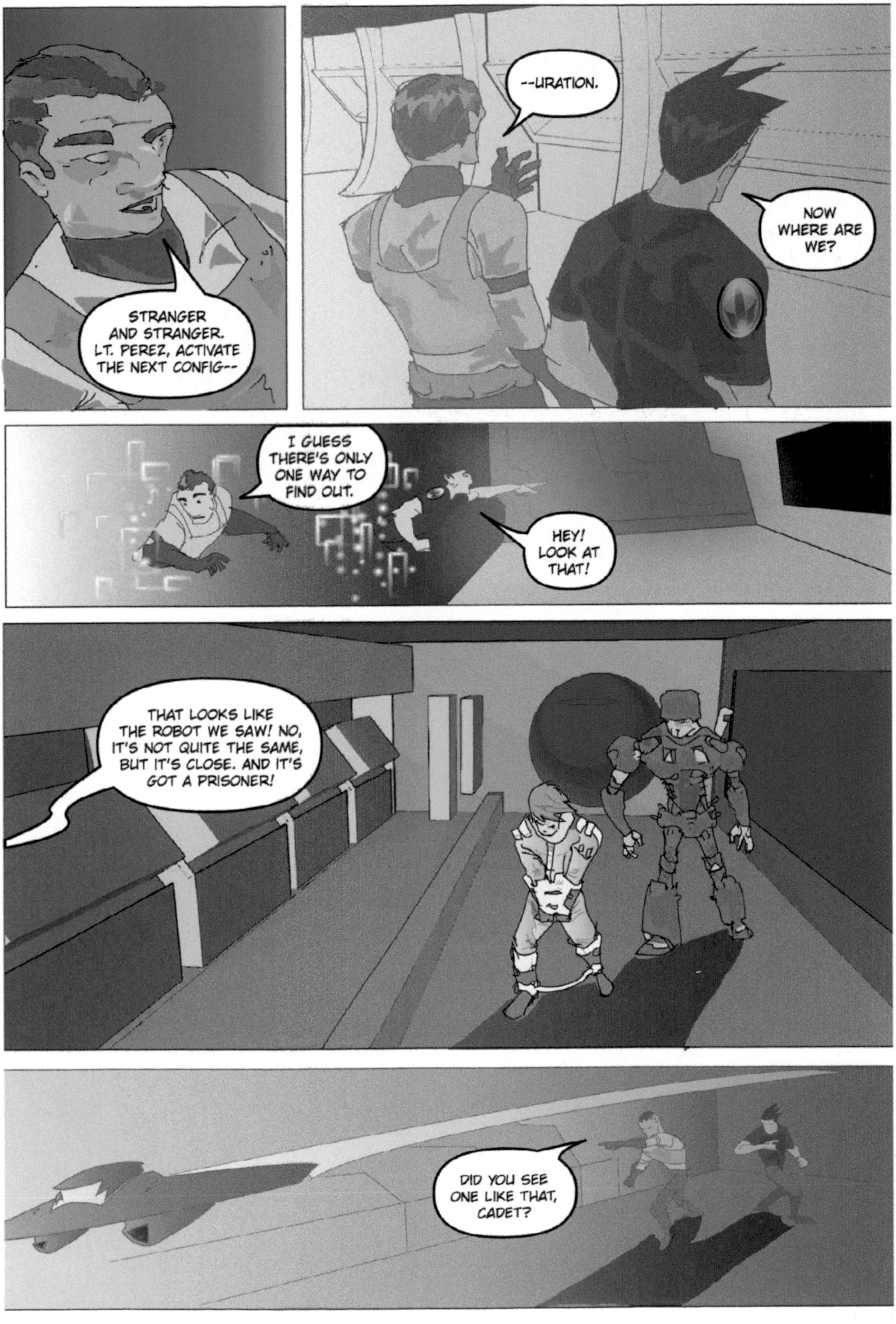
STRANGER AND STRANGER. LT. PEREZ, ACTIVATE THE NEXT CONFIG--
--URATION.
NOW WHERE ARE WE?
I GUESS THERE'S ONLY ONE WAY TO FIND OUT.
HEY! LOOK AT THAT!
THAT LOOKS LIKE THE ROBOT WE SAW! NO, IT'S NOT QUITE THE SAME, BUT IT'S CLOSE. AND IT'S GOT A PRISONER!
DID YOU SEE ONE LIKE THAT, CADET?

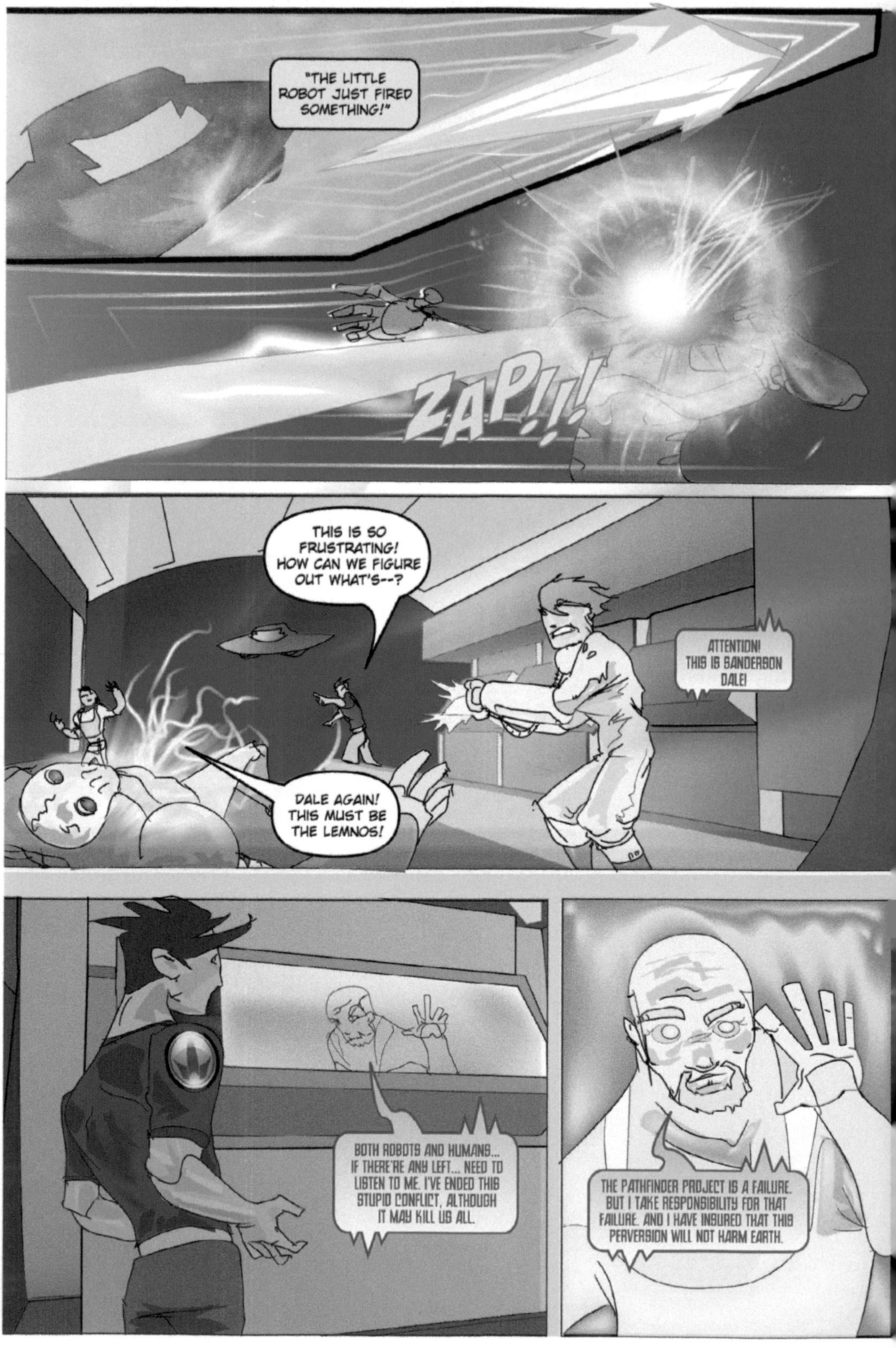
"THE LITTLE ROBOT JUST FIRED SOMETHING!"
ZAP!!!
THIS IS SO FRUSTRATING! HOW CAN WE FIGURE OUT WHAT'S--?
ATTENTION! THIS IS SANDERSON DALE!
DALE AGAIN! THIS MUST BE THE LEMNOS!
BOTH ROBOTS AND HUMANS... IF THERE'RE ANY LEFT... NEED TO LISTEN TO ME. I'VE ENDED THIS STUPID CONFLICT, ALTHOUGH IT MAY KILL US ALL.
THE PATHFINDER PROJECT IS A FAILURE. BUT I TAKE RESPONSIBILITY FOR THAT FAILURE. AND I HAVE INSURED THAT THIS PERVERSION WILL NOT HARM EARTH.

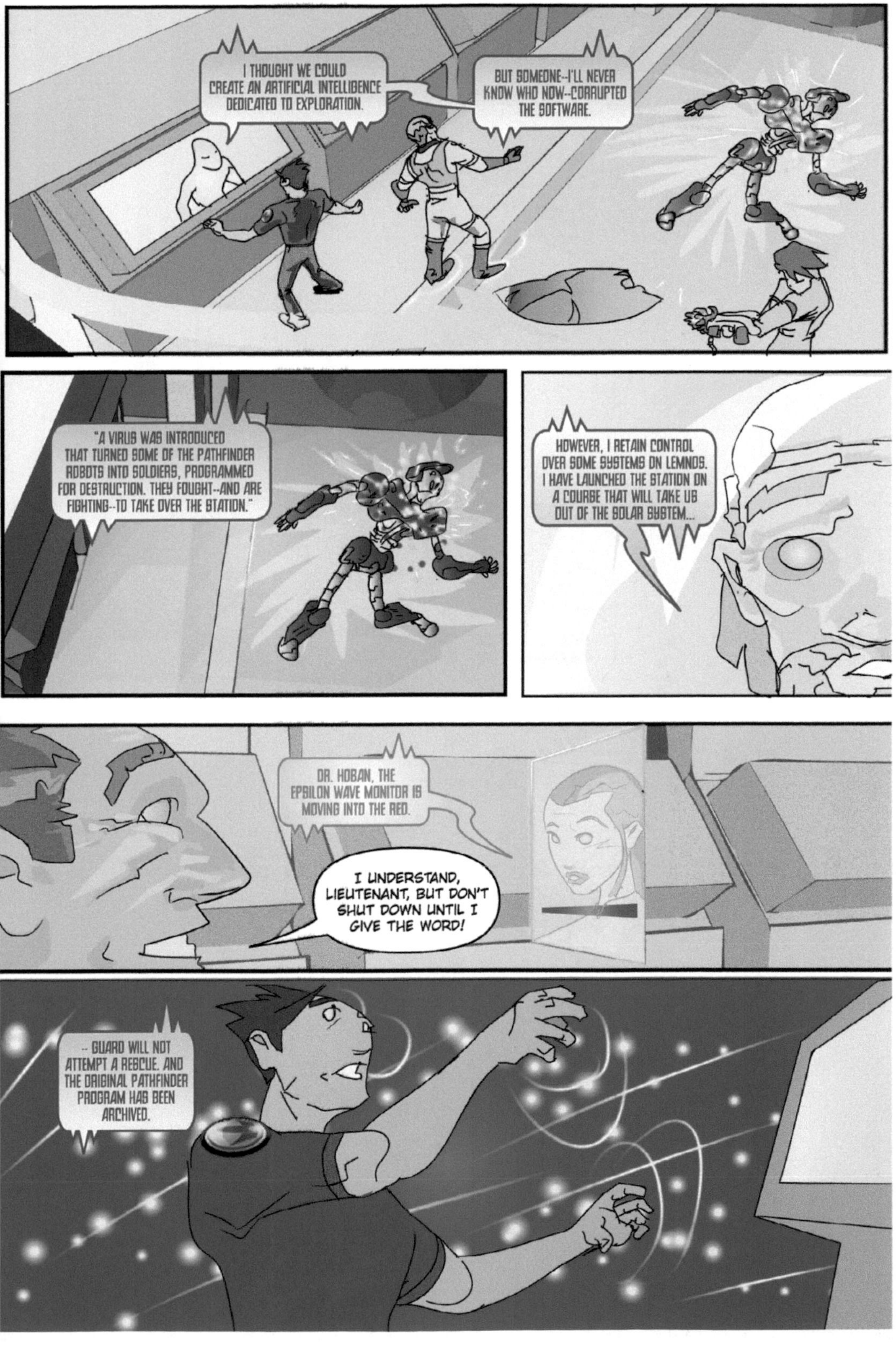
I THOUGHT WE COULD CREATE AN ARTIFICIAL INTELLIGENCE DEDICATED TO EXPLORATION.
BUT SOMEONE--I'LL NEVER KNOW WHO NOW--CORRUPTED THE SOFTWARE.
"A VIRUS WAS INTRODUCED THAT TURNED SOME OF THE PATHFINDER ROBOTS INTO SOLDIERS, PROGRAMMED FOR DESTRUCTION. THEY FOUGHT--AND ARE FIGHTING--TO TAKE OVER THE STATION."
HOWEVER, I RETAIN CONTROL OVER SOME SYSTEMS ON LEMNOS. I HAVE LAUNCHED THE STATION ON A COURSE THAT WILL TAKE US OUT OF THE SOLAR SYSTEM...
DR. HOBAN, THE EPSILON WAVE MONITOR IS MOVING INTO THE RED.
I UNDERSTAND, LIEUTENANT, BUT DON'T SHUT DOWN UNTIL I GIVE THE WORD!
-- GUARD WILL NOT ATTEMPT A RESCUE. AND THE ORIGINAL PATHFINDER PROGRAM HAS BEEN ARCHIVED.

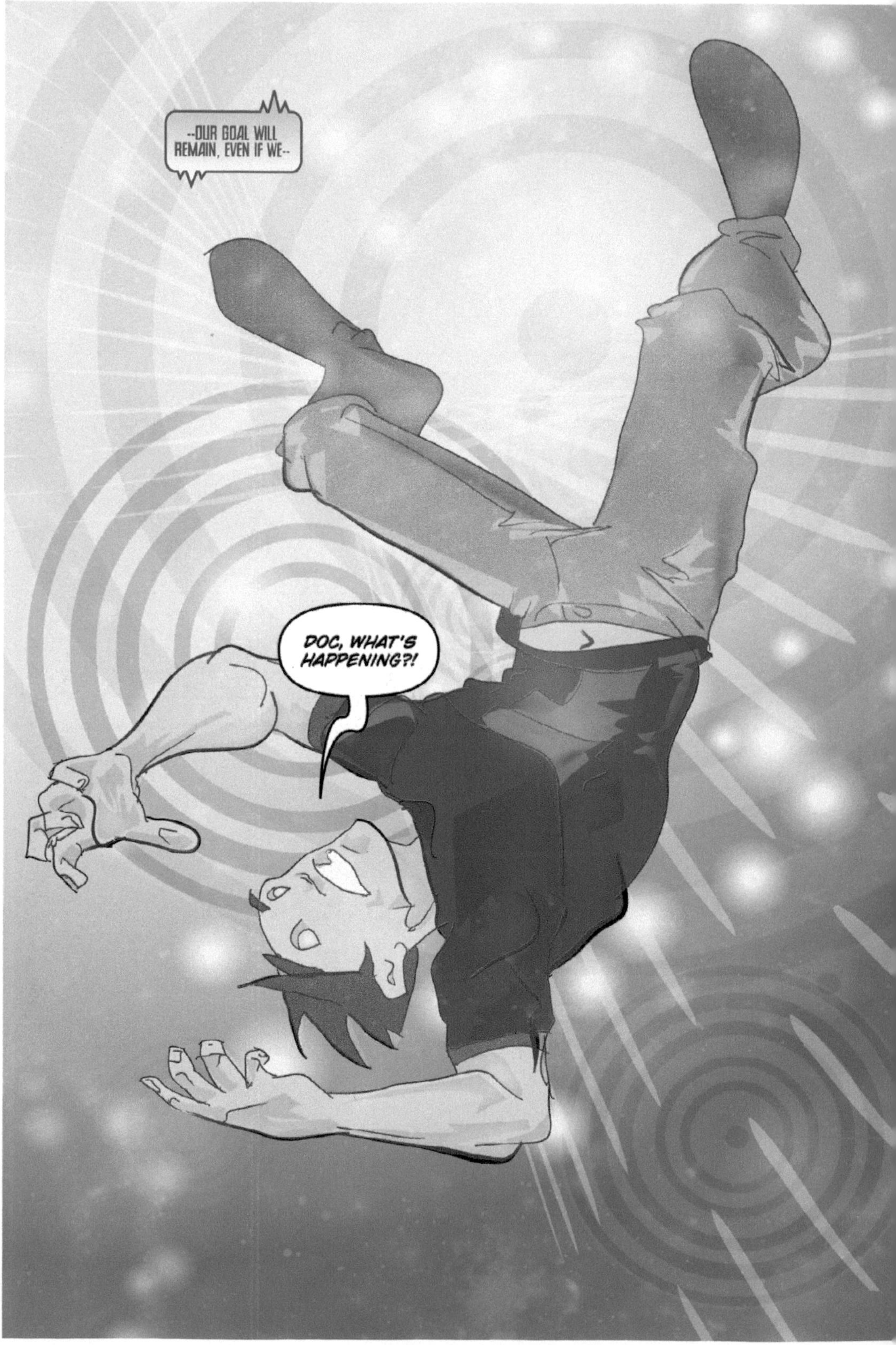
--OUR GOAL WILL REMAIN, EVEN IF WE--
DOC, WHAT'S HAPPENING?!

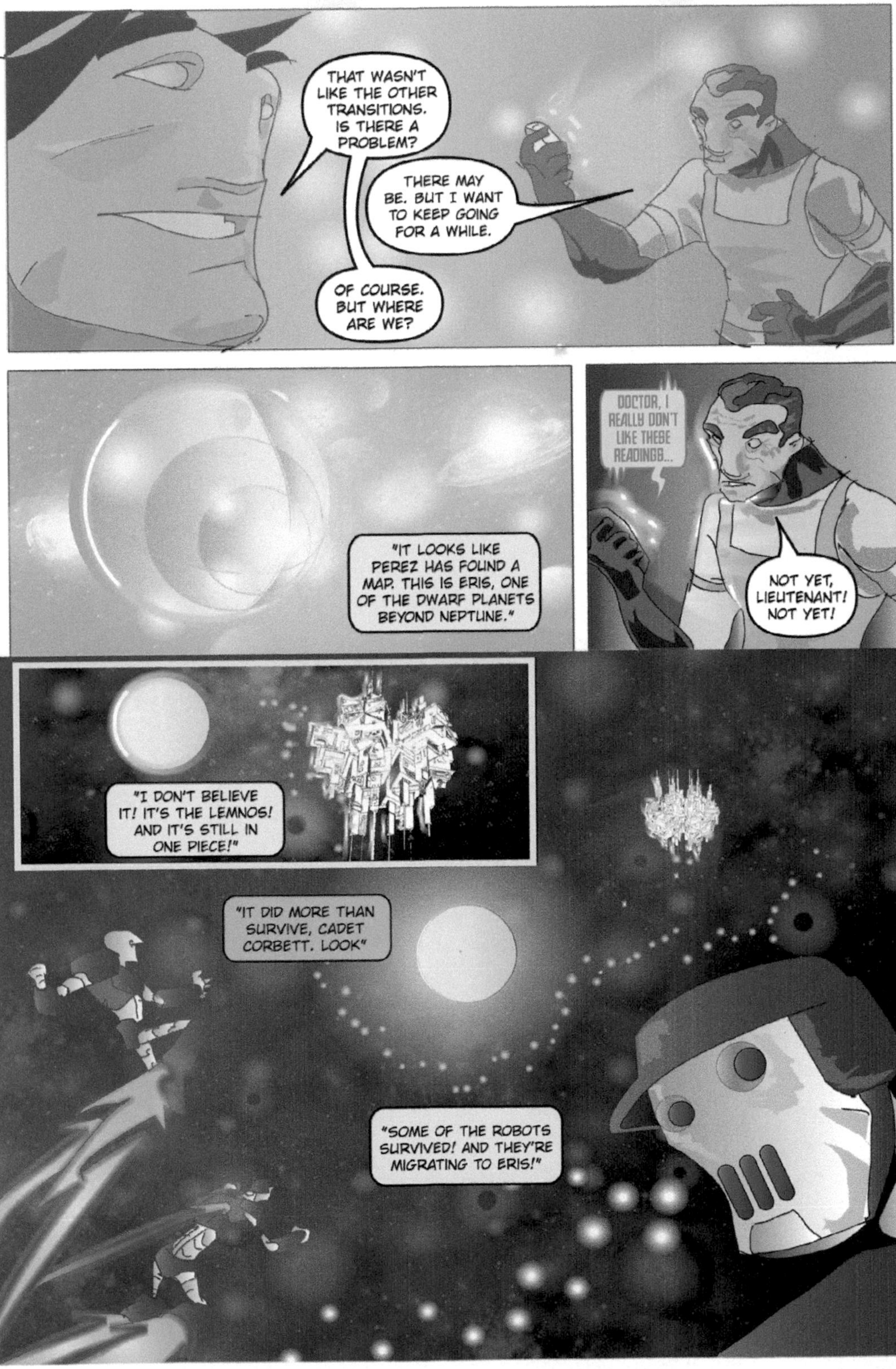
THAT WASN'T LIKE THE OTHER TRANSITIONS. IS THERE A PROBLEM?
THERE MAY BE. BUT I WANT TO KEEP GOING FOR A WHILE.
OF COURSE. BUT WHERE ARE WE?
"IT LOOKS LIKE PEREZ HAS FOUND A MAP. THIS IS ERIS, ONE OF THE DWARF PLANETS BEYOND NEPTUNE."
DOCTOR, I REALLY DON'T LIKE THESE READINGS...
NOT YET, LIEUTENANT! NOT YET!
"I DON'T BELIEVE IT! IT'S THE LEMNOS! AND IT'S STILL IN ONE PIECE!"
"IT DID MORE THAN SURVIVE, CADET CORBETT. LOOK"
"SOME OF THE ROBOTS SURVIVED! AND THEY'RE MIGRATING TO ERIS!"

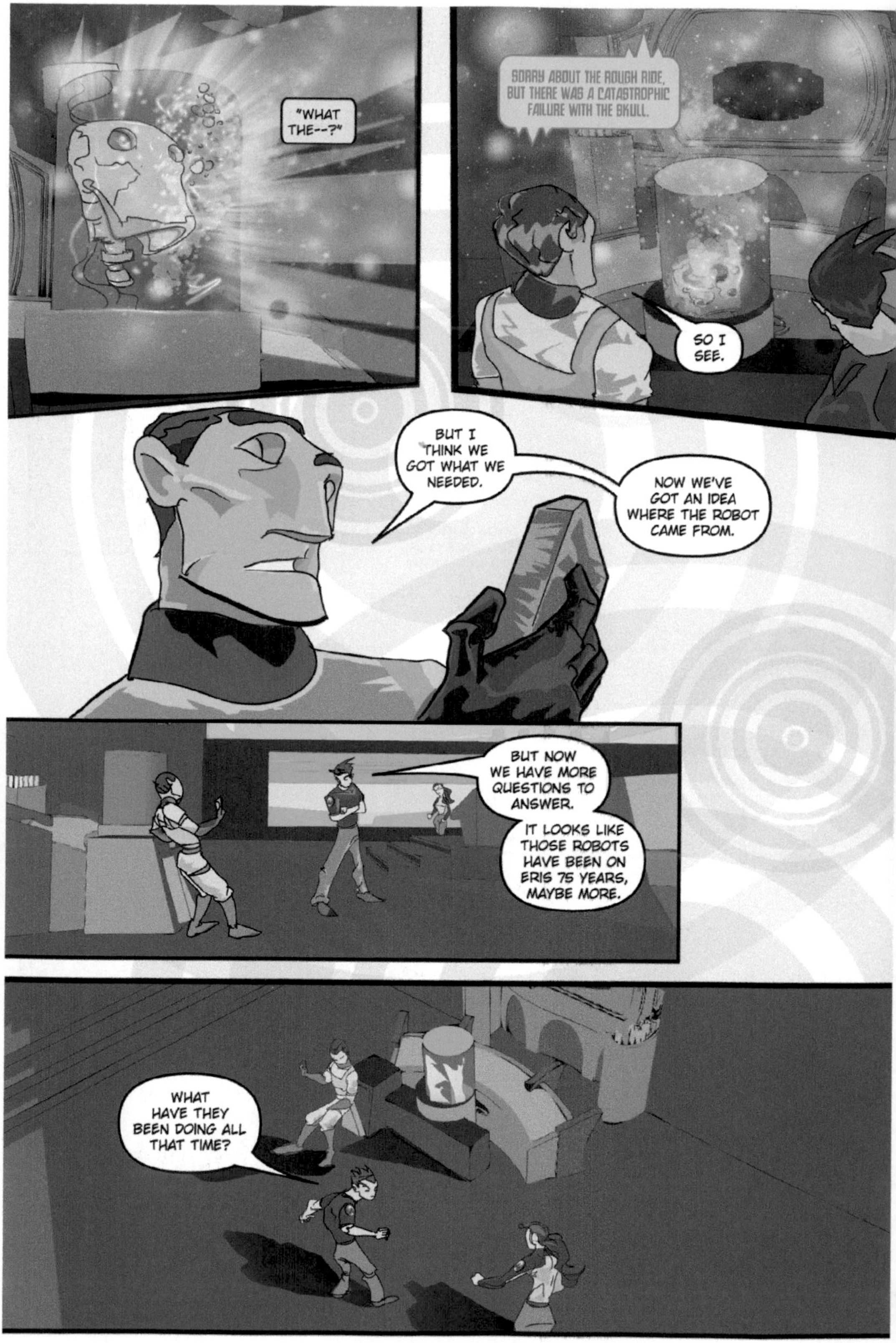
"WHAT THE--?"
SORRY ABOUT THE ROUGH RIDE, BUT THERE WAS A CATASTROPHIC FAILURE WITH THE SKULL.
SO I SEE.
BUT I THINK WE GOT WHAT WE NEEDED.
NOW WE'VE GOT AN IDEA WHERE THE ROBOT CAME FROM.
BUT NOW WE HAVE MORE QUESTIONS TO ANSWER.
IT LOOKS LIKE THOSE ROBOTS HAVE BEEN ON ERIS 75 YEARS, MAYBE MORE.
WHAT HAVE THEY BEEN DOING ALL THAT TIME?

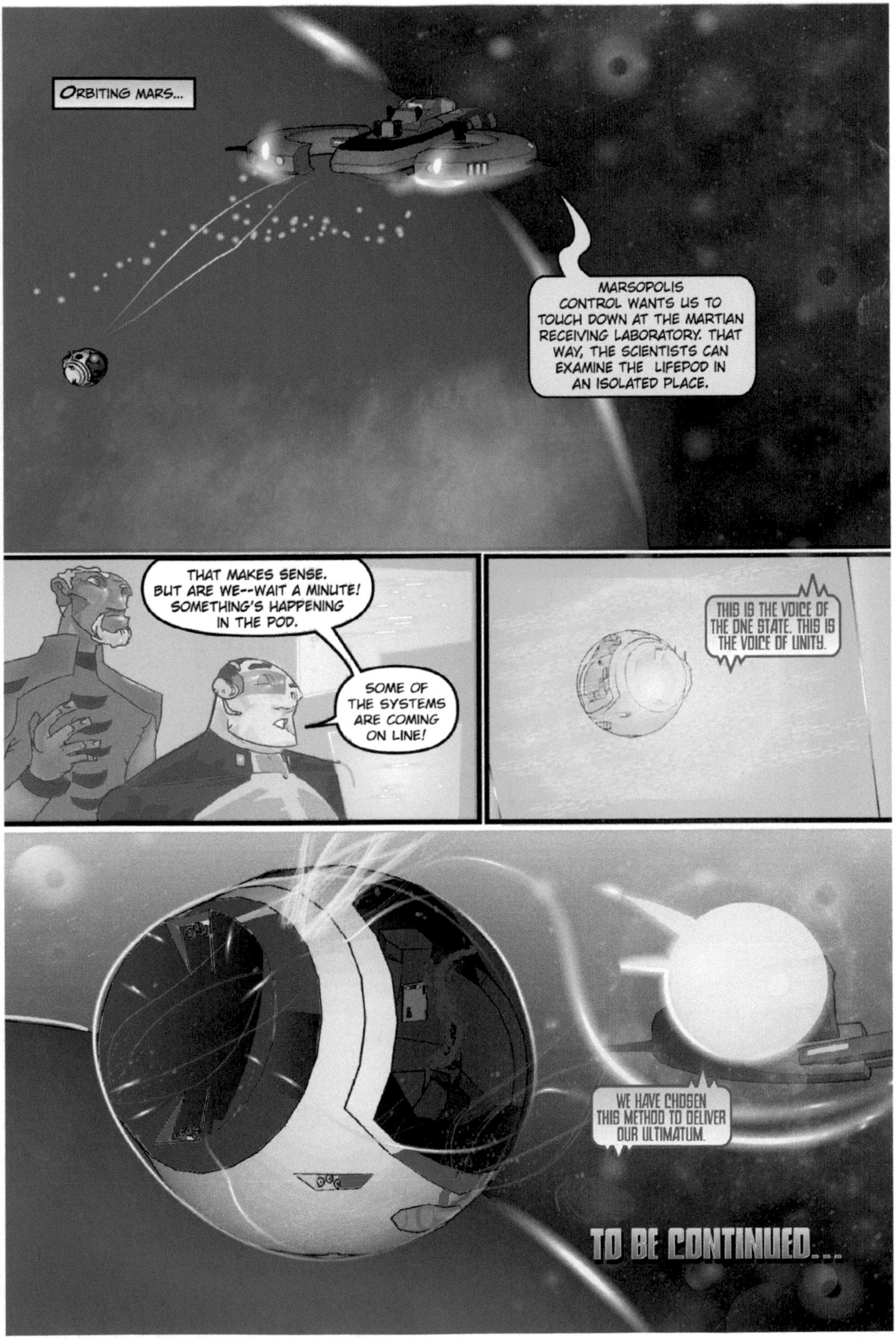
ORBITING MARS...
MARSOPOLIS CONTROL WANTS US TO TOUCH DOWN AT THE MARTIAN RECEIVING LABORATORY. THAT WAY, THE SCIENTISTS CAN EXAMINE THE LIFEPOD IN AN ISOLATED PLACE.
THAT MAKES SENSE. BUT ARE WE--WAIT A MINUTE! SOMETHING'S HAPPENING IN THE POD.
SOME OF THE SYSTEMS ARE COMING ON LINE!
THIS IS THE VOICE OF THE ONE STATE. THIS IS THE VOICE OF UNITY.
WE HAVE CHOSEN THIS METHOD TO DELIVER OUR ULTIMATUM.
TO BE CONTINUED...

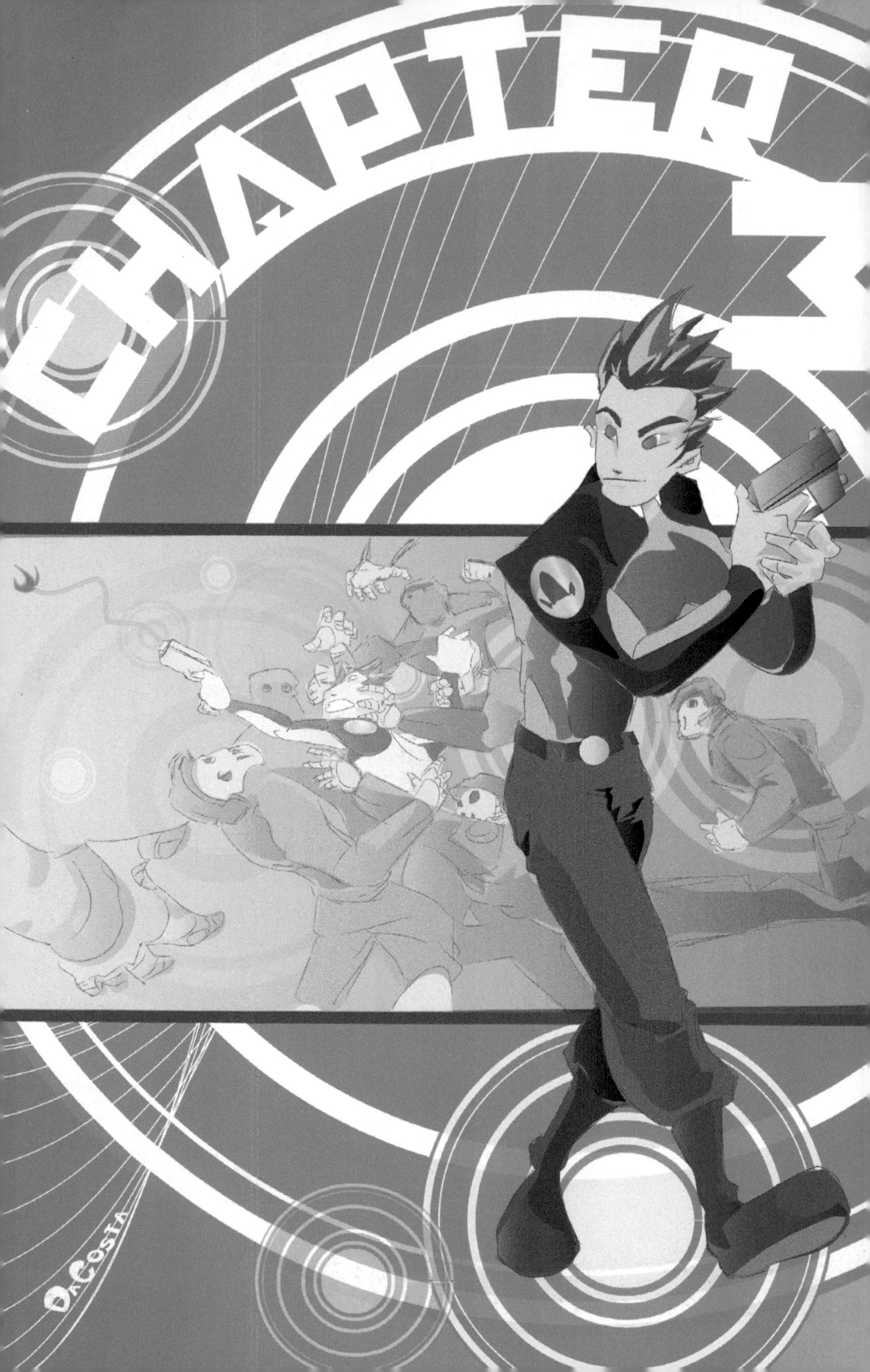
CHAPTER
DaCosta

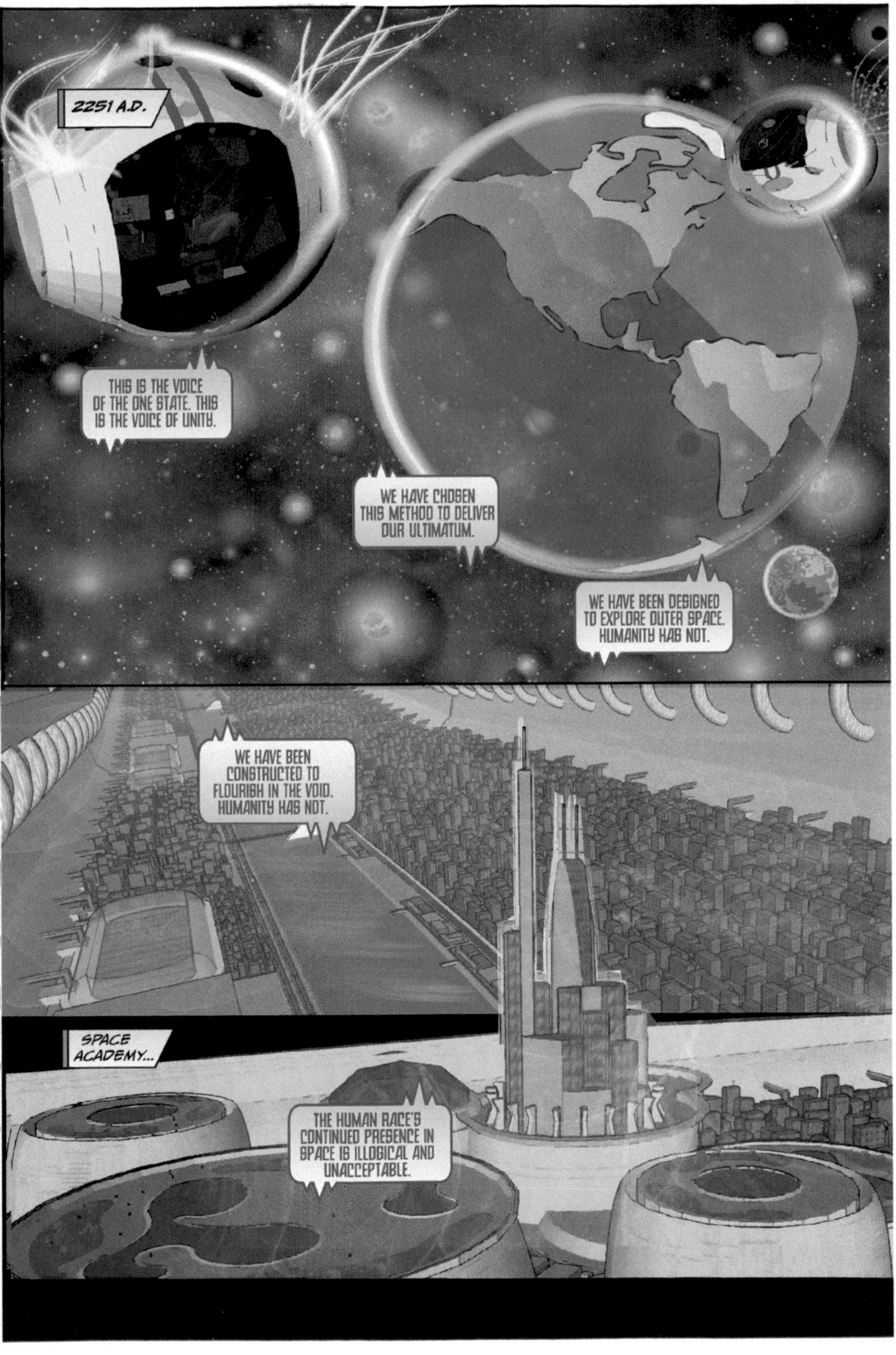
2251 A.D.
THIS IS THE VOICE OF THE ONE STATE. THIS IS THE VOICE OF UNITY.
WE HAVE CHOSEN THIS METHOD TO DELIVER OUR ULTIMATUM.
WE HAVE BEEN DESIGNED TO EXPLORE OUTER SPACE. HUMANITY HAS NOT.
WE HAVE BEEN CONSTRUCTED TO FLOURISH IN THE VOID. HUMANITY HAS NOT.
SPACE ACADEMY...
THE HUMAN RACE'S CONTINUED PRESENCE IN SPACE IS ILLOGICAL AND UNACCEPTABLE.

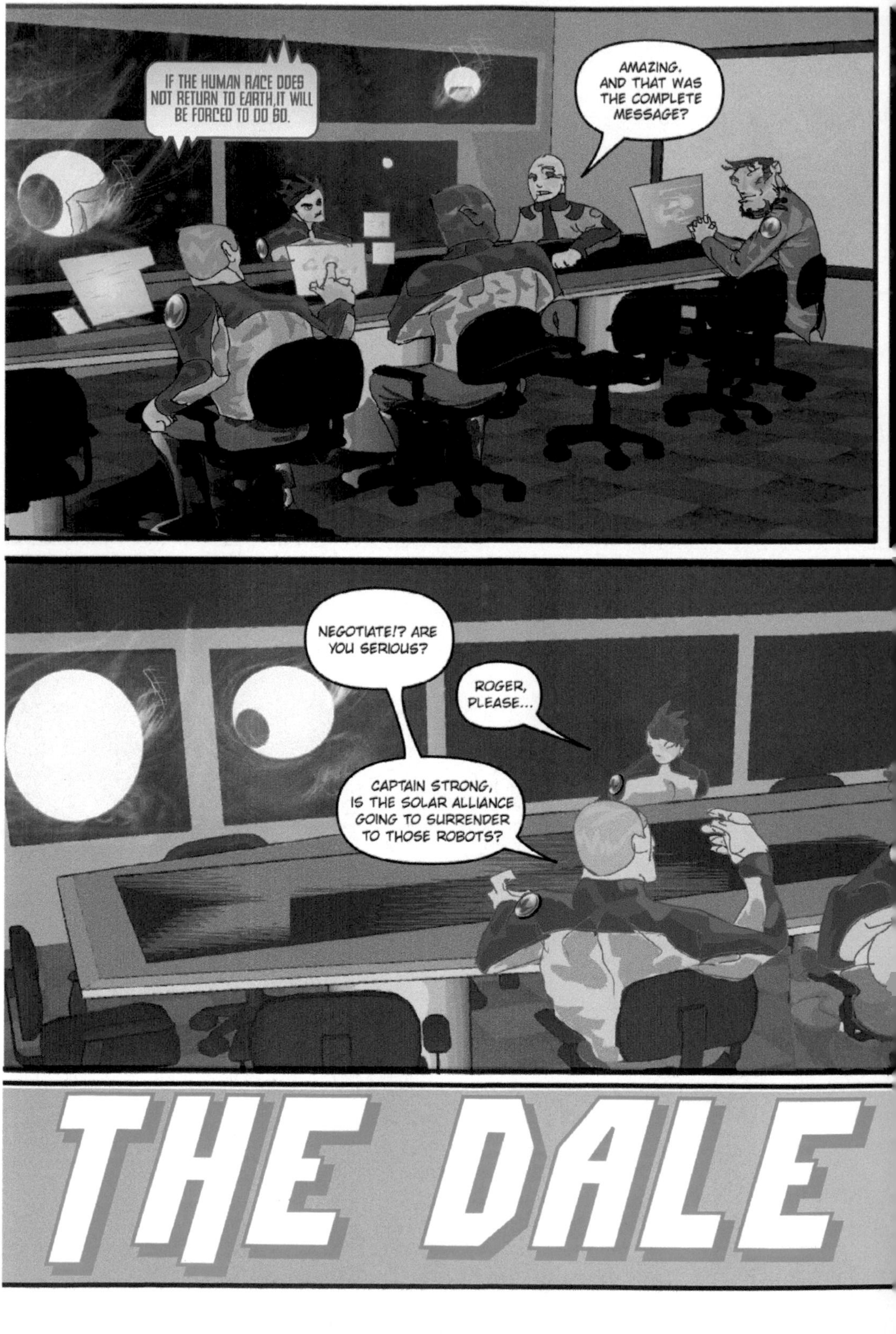
IF THE HUMAN RACE DOES NOT RETURN TO EARTH, IT WILL BE FORCED TO DO SO.
AMAZING. AND THAT WAS THE COMPLETE MESSAGE?
NEGOTIATE!? ARE YOU SERIOUS?
ROGER, PLEASE...
CAPTAIN STRONG, IS THE SOLAR ALLIANCE GOING TO SURRENDER TO THOSE ROBOTS?
THE DALE

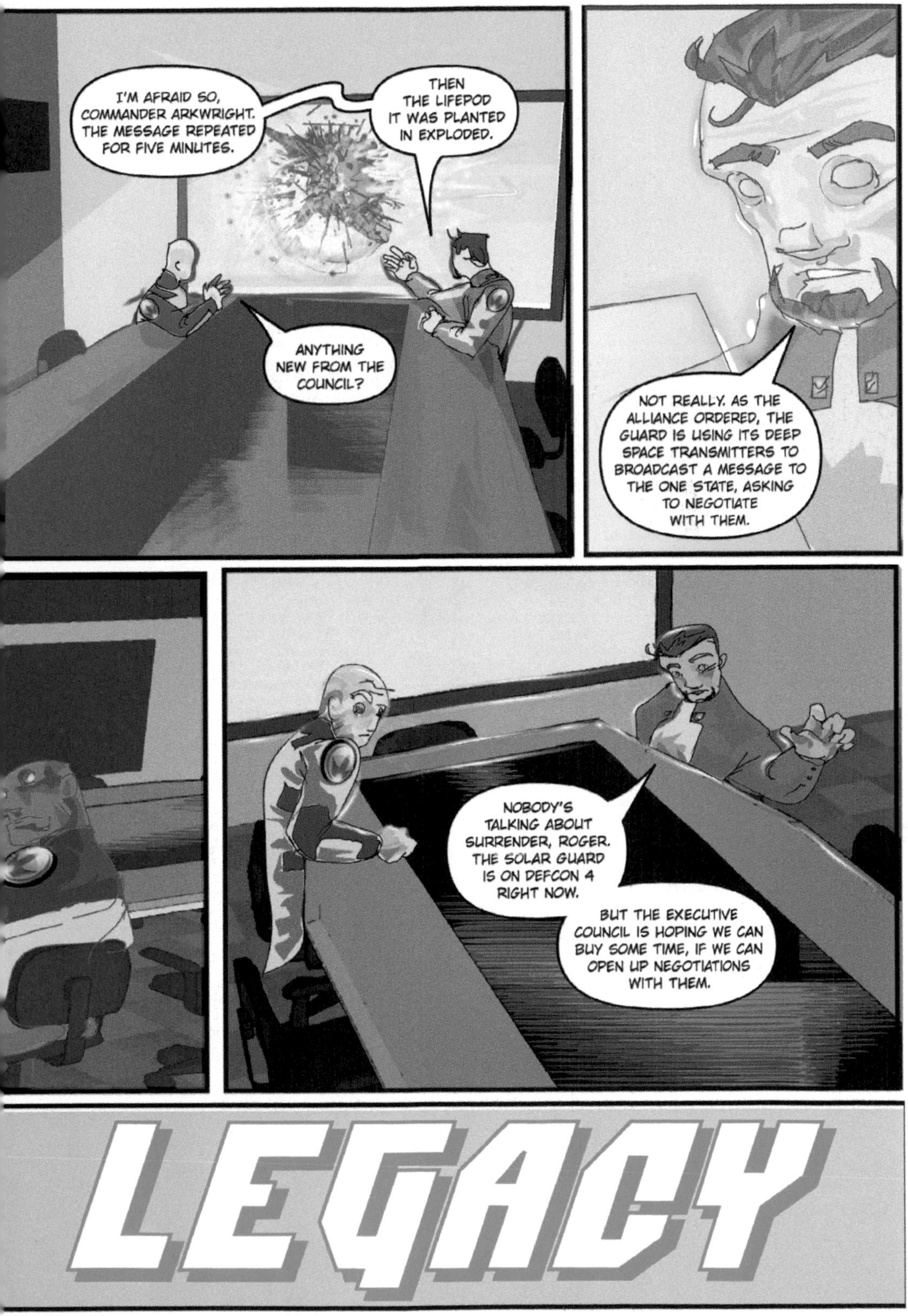
I'M AFRAID SO, COMMANDER ARKWRIGHT. THE MESSAGE REPEATED FOR FIVE MINUTES.
THEN THE LIFEPOD IT WAS PLANTED IN EXPLODED.
ANYTHING NEW FROM THE COUNCIL?
NOT REALLY. AS THE ALLIANCE ORDERED, THE GUARD IS USING ITS DEEP SPACE TRANSMITTERS TO BROADCAST A MESSAGE TO THE ONE STATE, ASKING TO NEGOTIATE WITH THEM.
NOBODY'S TALKING ABOUT SURRENDER, ROGER. THE SOLAR GUARD IS ON DEFCON 4 RIGHT NOW.
BUT THE EXECUTIVE COUNCIL IS HOPING WE CAN BUY SOME TIME, IF WE CAN OPEN UP NEGOTIATIONS WITH THEM.
LEGACY

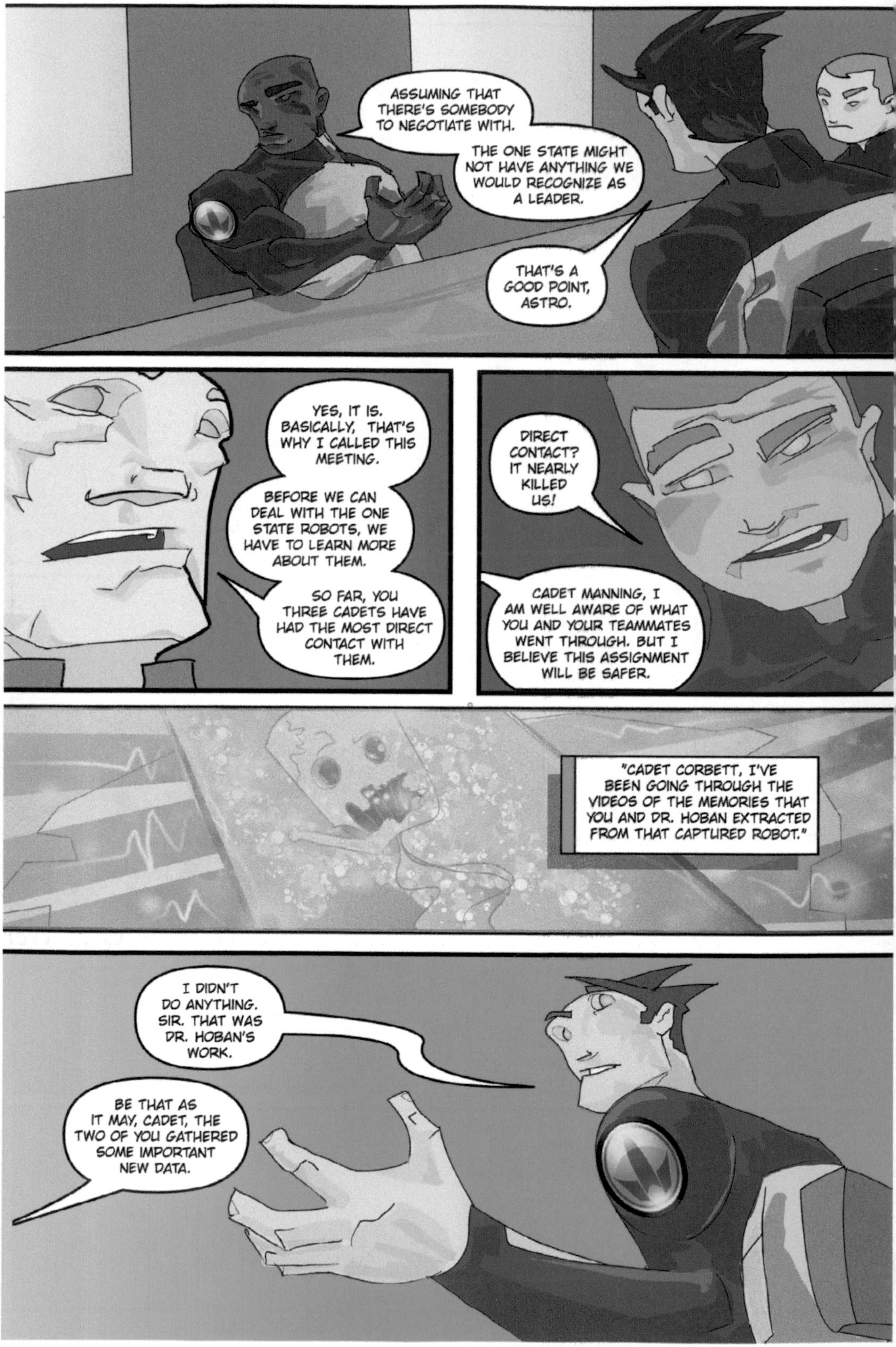
ASSUMING THAT THERE'S SOMEBODY TO NEGOTIATE WITH.
THE ONE STATE MIGHT NOT HAVE ANYTHING WE WOULD RECOGNIZE AS A LEADER.
THAT'S A GOOD POINT, ASTRO.
YES, IT IS. BASICALLY, THAT'S WHY I CALLED THIS MEETING.
BEFORE WE CAN DEAL WITH THE ONE STATE ROBOTS, WE HAVE TO LEARN MORE ABOUT THEM.
SO FAR, YOU THREE CADETS HAVE HAD THE MOST DIRECT CONTACT WITH THEM.
DIRECT CONTACT? IT NEARLY KILLED US!
CADET MANNING, I AM WELL AWARE OF WHAT YOU AND YOUR TEAMMATES WENT THROUGH. BUT I BELIEVE THIS ASSIGNMENT WILL BE SAFER.
"CADET CORBETT, I'VE BEEN GOING THROUGH THE VIDEOS OF THE MEMORIES THAT YOU AND DR. HOBAN EXTRACTED FROM THAT CAPTURED ROBOT."
I DIDN'T DO ANYTHING. SIR. THAT WAS DR. HOBAN'S WORK.
BE THAT AS IT MAY, CADET, THE TWO OF YOU GATHERED SOME IMPORTANT NEW DATA.

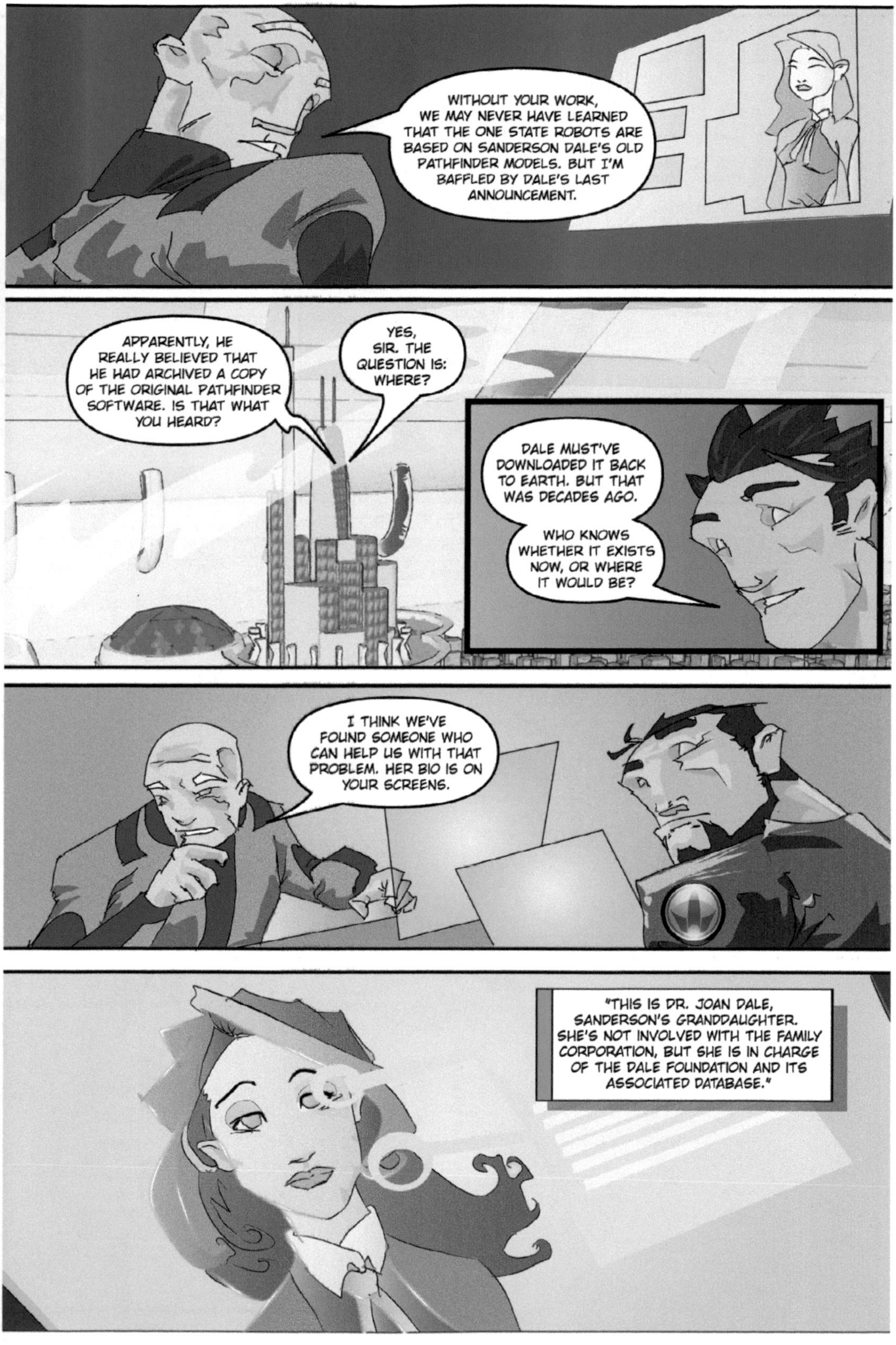
WITHOUT YOUR WORK, WE MAY NEVER HAVE LEARNED THAT THE ONE STATE ROBOTS ARE BASED ON SANDERSON DALE'S OLD PATHFINDER MODELS. BUT I'M BAFFLED BY DALE'S LAST ANNOUNCEMENT.
APPARENTLY, HE REALLY BELIEVED THAT HE HAD ARCHIVED A COPY OF THE ORIGINAL PATHFINDER SOFTWARE. IS THAT WHAT YOU HEARD?
YES, SIR. THE QUESTION IS: WHERE?
DALE MUST'VE DOWNLOADED IT BACK TO EARTH. BUT THAT WAS DECADES AGO.
WHO KNOWS WHETHER IT EXISTS NOW, OR WHERE IT WOULD BE?
I THINK WE'VE FOUND SOMEONE WHO CAN HELP US WITH THAT PROBLEM. HER BIO IS ON YOUR SCREENS.
"THIS IS DR. JOAN DALE, SANDERSON'S GRANDDAUGHTER. SHE'S NOT INVOLVED WITH THE FAMILY CORPORATION, BUT SHE IS IN CHARGE OF THE DALE FOUNDATION AND ITS ASSOCIATED DATABASE."

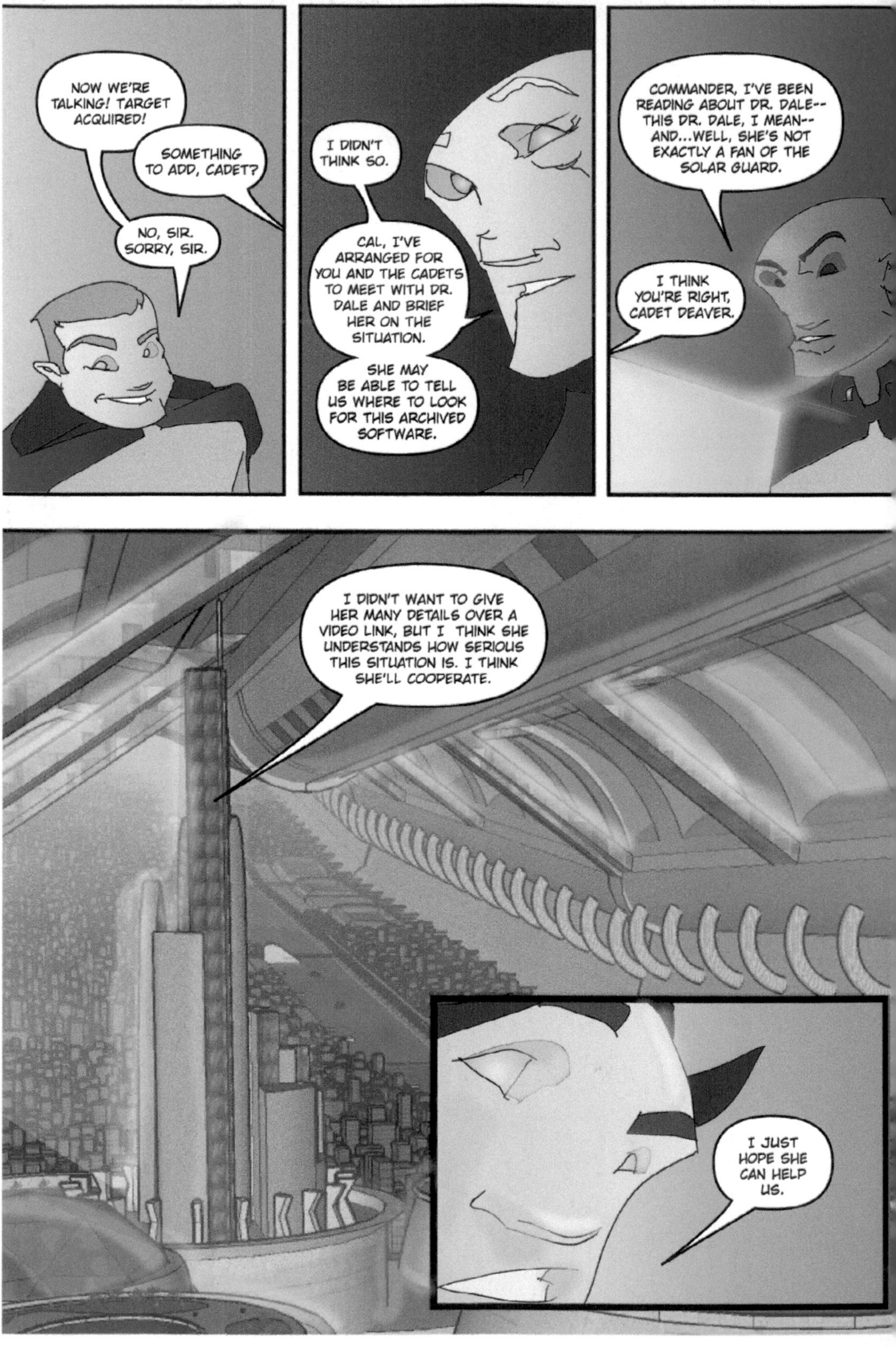
NOW WE'RE TALKING! TARGET ACQUIRED!
SOMETHING TO ADD, CADET?
NO, SIR. SORRY, SIR.
I DIDN'T THINK SO.
CAL, I'VE ARRANGED FOR YOU AND THE CADETS TO MEET WITH DR. DALE AND BRIEF HER ON THE SITUATION.
SHE MAY BE ABLE TO TELL US WHERE TO LOOK FOR THIS ARCHIVED SOFTWARE.
COMMANDER, I'VE BEEN READING ABOUT DR. DALE-- THIS DR. DALE, I MEAN-- AND...WELL, SHE'S NOT EXACTLY A FAN OF THE SOLAR GUARD.
I THINK YOU'RE RIGHT, CADET DEAVER.
I DIDN'T WANT TO GIVE HER MANY DETAILS OVER A VIDEO LINK, BUT I THINK SHE UNDERSTANDS HOW SERIOUS THIS SITUATION IS. I THINK SHE'LL COOPERATE.
I JUST HOPE SHE CAN HELP US.

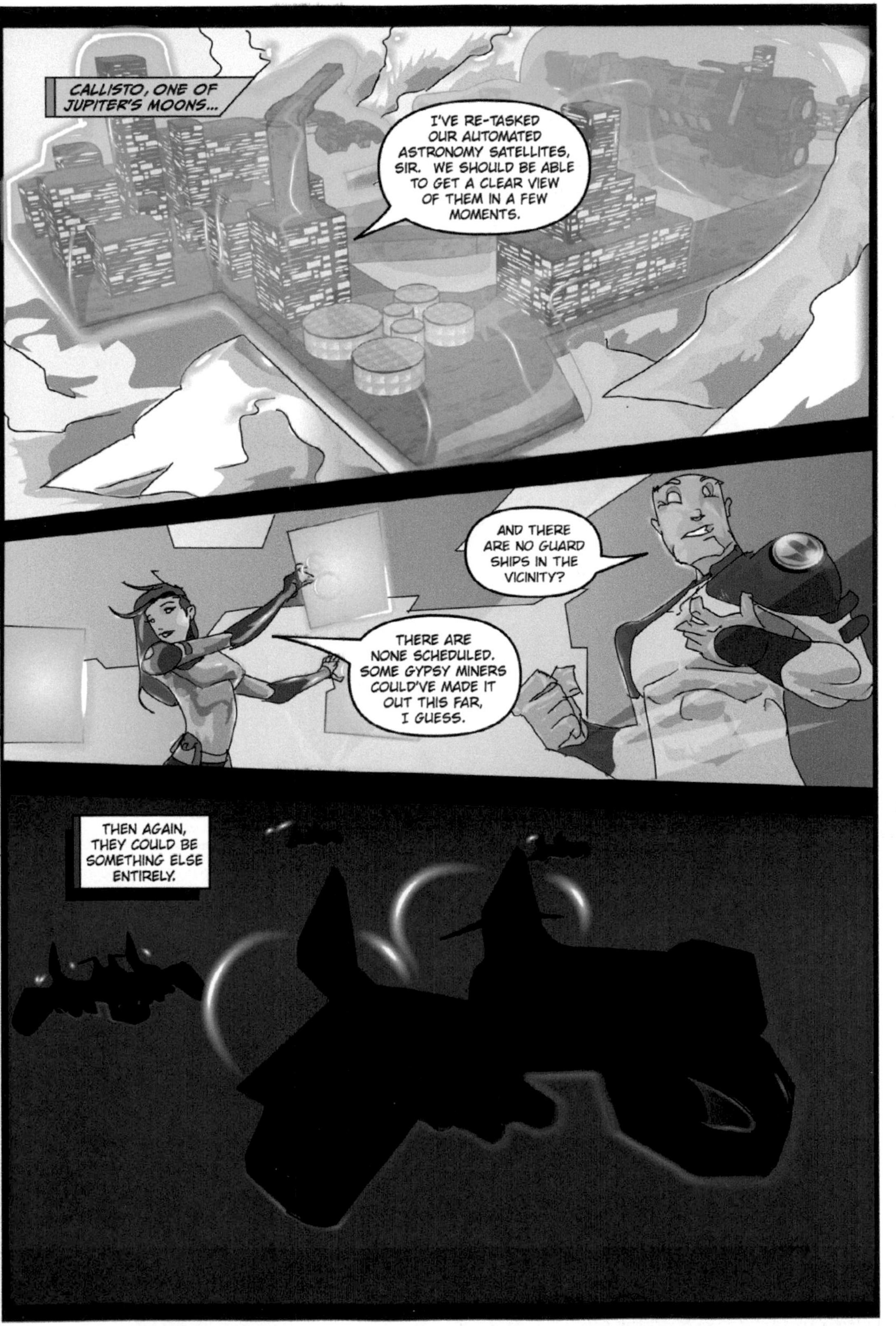
CALLISTO, ONE OF JUPITER'S MOONS...
I'VE RE-TASKED OUR AUTOMATED ASTRONOMY SATELLITES, SIR. WE SHOULD BE ABLE TO GET A CLEAR VIEW OF THEM IN A FEW MOMENTS.
AND THERE ARE NO GUARD SHIPS IN THE VICINITY?
THERE ARE NONE SCHEDULED. SOME GYPSY MINERS COULD'VE MADE IT OUT THIS FAR, I GUESS.
THEN AGAIN, THEY COULD BE SOMETHING ELSE ENTIRELY.

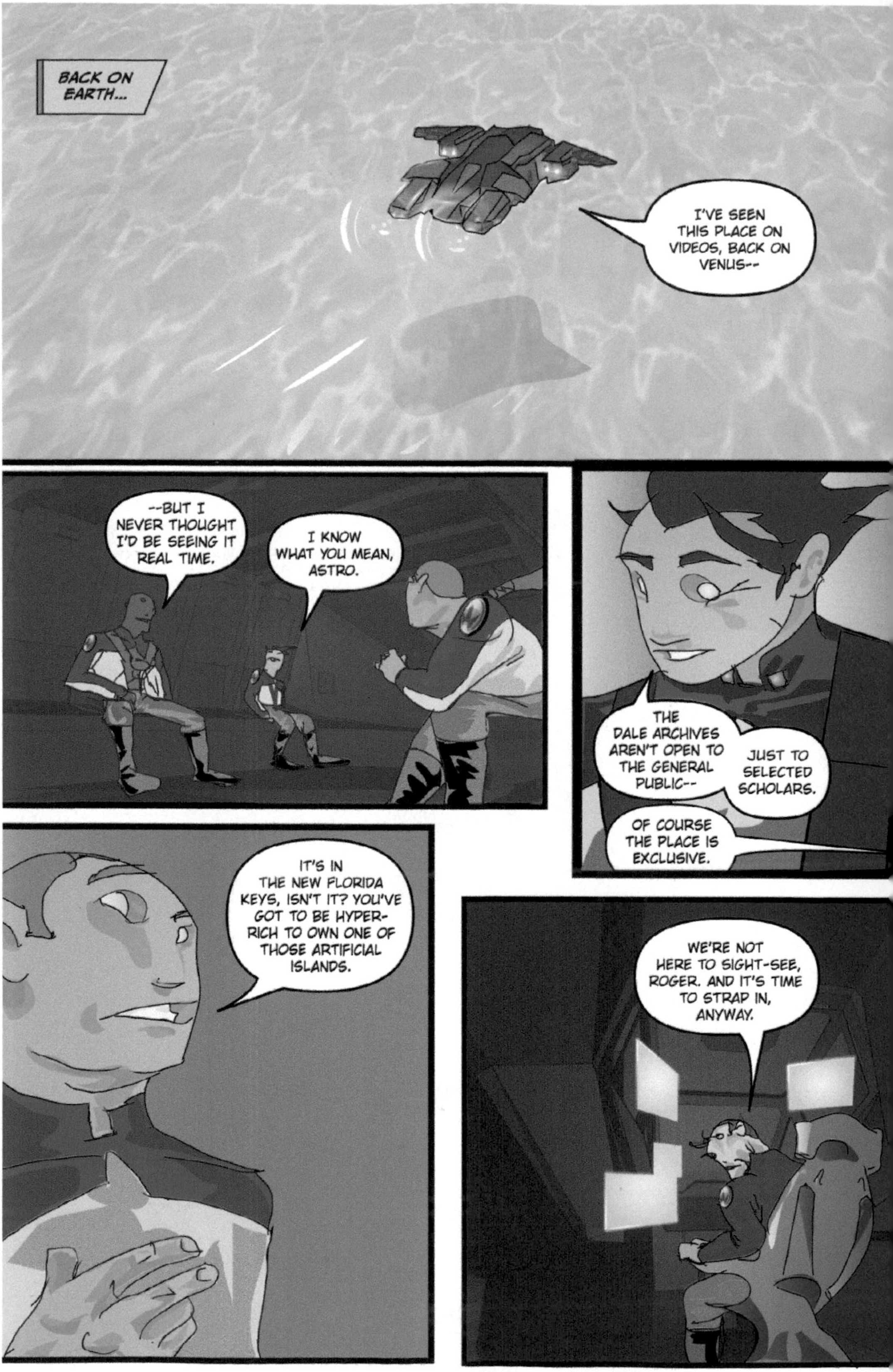
BACK ON EARTH...
I'VE SEEN THIS PLACE ON VIDEOS, BACK ON VENUS--
--BUT I NEVER THOUGHT I'D BE SEEING IT REAL TIME.
I KNOW WHAT YOU MEAN, ASTRO.
THE DALE ARCHIVES AREN'T OPEN TO THE GENERAL PUBLIC--
JUST TO SELECTED SCHOLARS.
OF COURSE THE PLACE IS EXCLUSIVE.
IT'S IN THE NEW FLORIDA KEYS, ISN'T IT? YOU'VE GOT TO BE HYPER-RICH TO OWN ONE OF THOSE ARTIFICIAL ISLANDS.
WE'RE NOT HERE TO SIGHT-SEE, ROGER. AND IT'S TIME TO STRAP IN, ANYWAY.

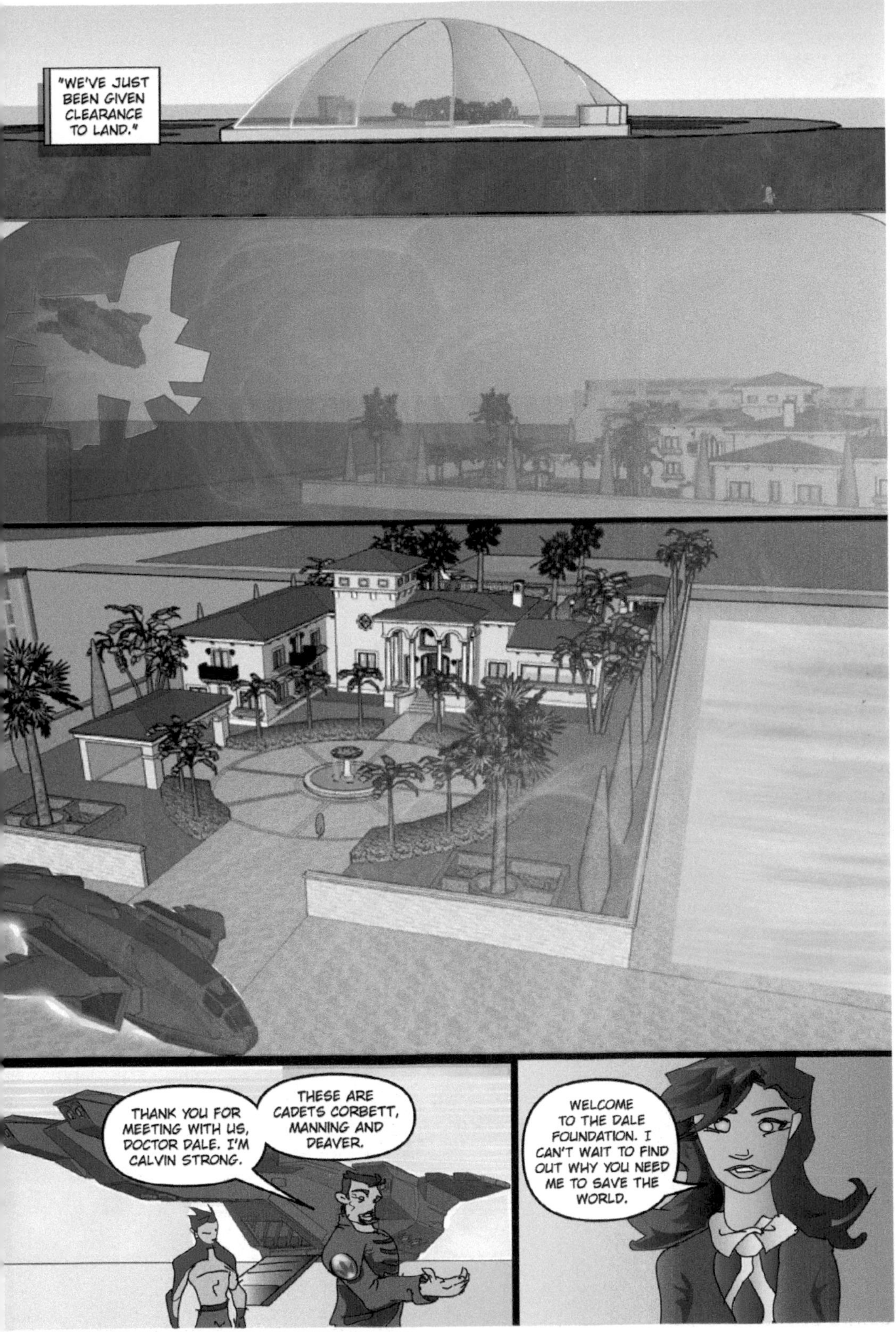
"WE'VE JUST BEEN GIVEN CLEARANCE TO LAND."
THANK YOU FOR MEETING WITH US, DOCTOR DALE. I'M CALVIN STRONG.
THESE ARE CADETS CORBETT, MANNING AND DEAVER.
WELCOME TO THE DALE FOUNDATION. I CAN'T WAIT TO FIND OUT WHY YOU NEED ME TO SAVE THE WORLD.

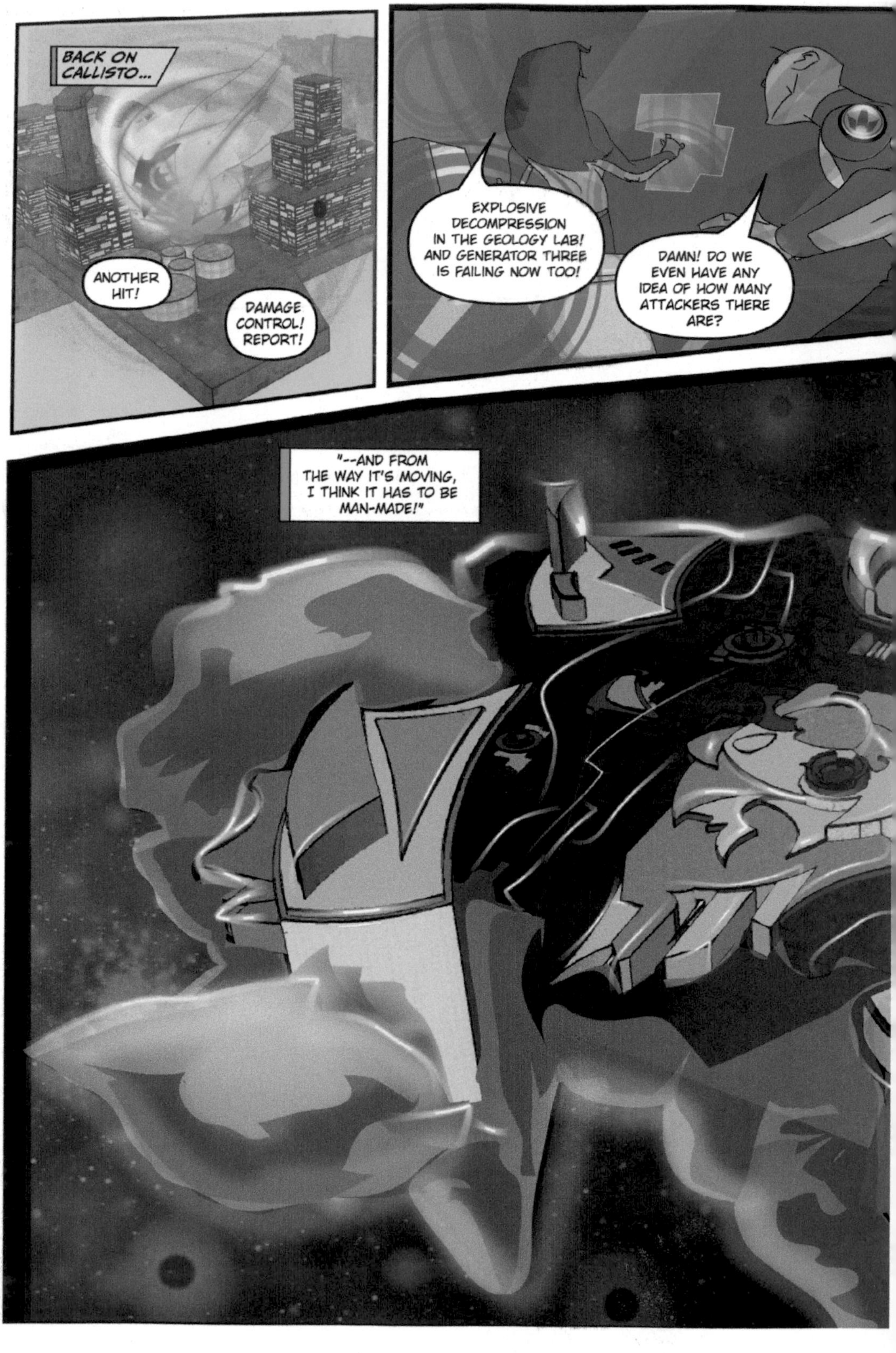
BACK ON CALLISTO...
ANOTHER HIT!
DAMAGE CONTROL! REPORT!
EXPLOSIVE DECOMPRESSION IN THE GEOLOGY LAB! AND GENERATOR THREE IS FAILING NOW TOO!
DAMN! DO WE EVEN HAVE ANY IDEA OF HOW MANY ATTACKERS THERE ARE?
"--AND FROM THE WAY IT'S MOVING, I THINK IT HAS TO BE MAN-MADE!"

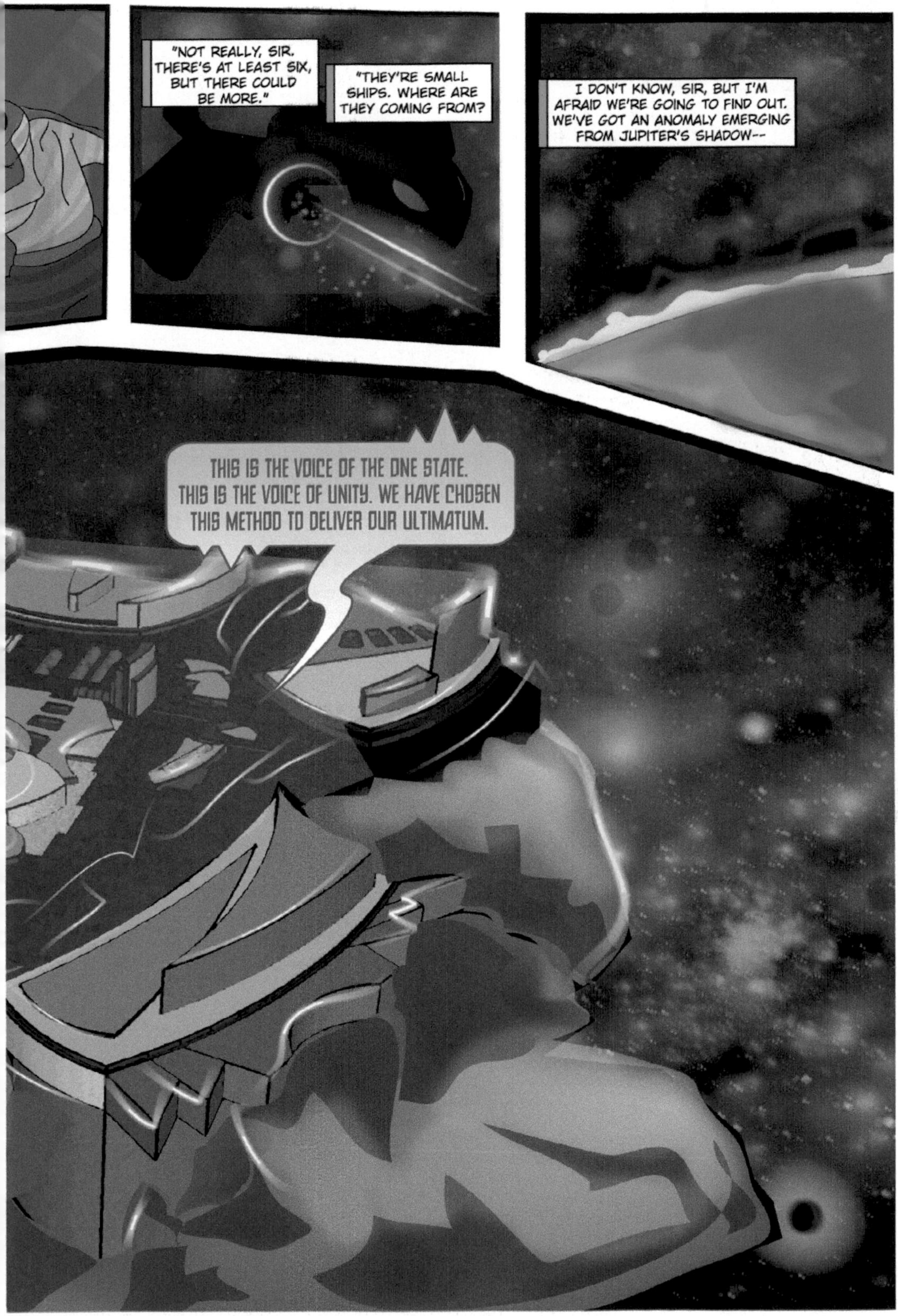
"NOT REALLY, SIR. THERE'S AT LEAST SIX, BUT THERE COULD BE MORE."
"THEY'RE SMALL SHIPS. WHERE ARE THEY COMING FROM?
I DON'T KNOW, SIR, BUT I'M AFRAID WE'RE GOING TO FIND OUT. WE'VE GOT AN ANOMALY EMERGING FROM JUPITER'S SHADOW--
THIS IS THE VOICE OF THE ONE STATE. THIS IS THE VOICE OF UNITY. WE HAVE CHOSEN THIS METHOD TO DELIVER OUR ULTIMATUM.

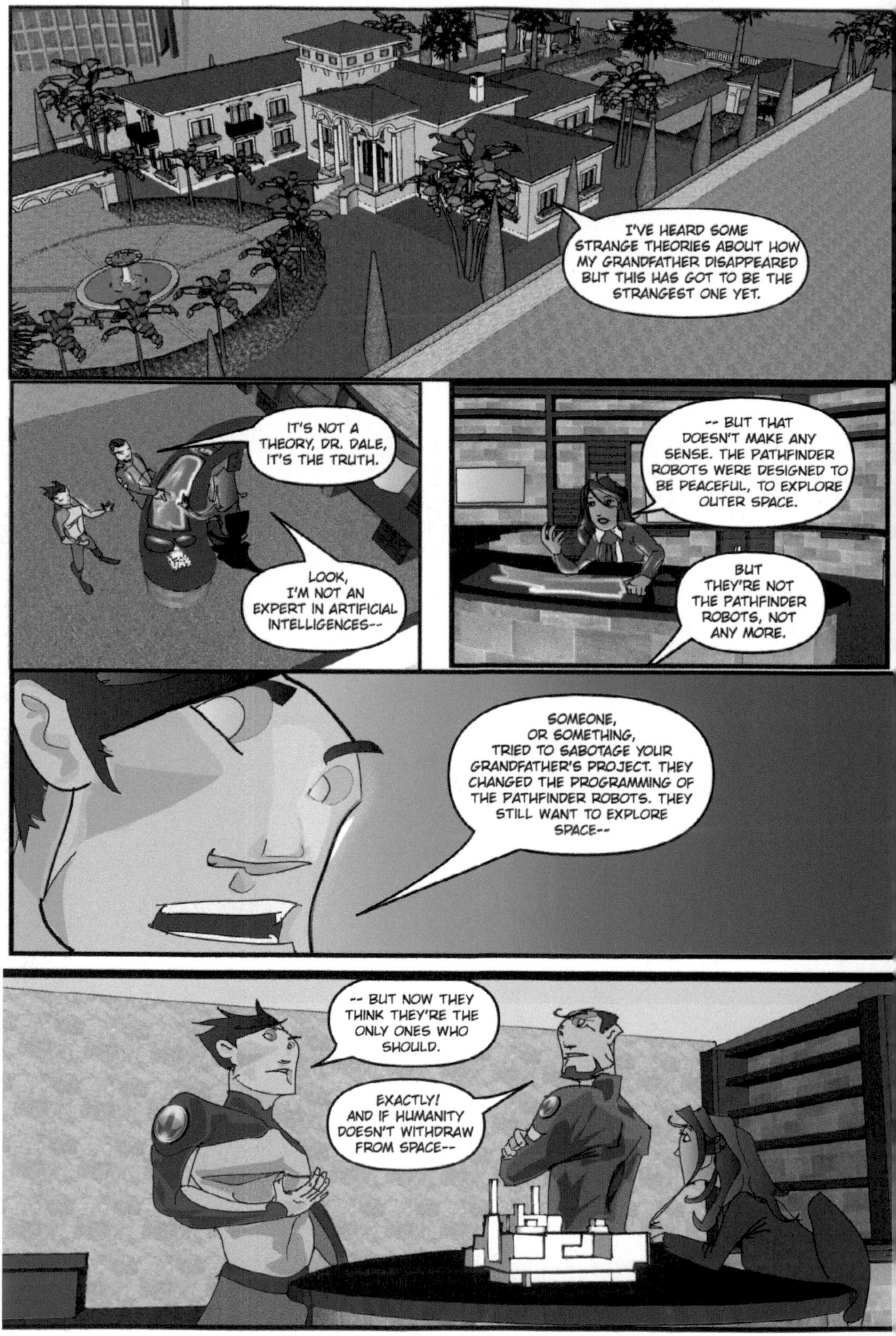
I'VE HEARD SOME STRANGE THEORIES ABOUT HOW MY GRANDFATHER DISAPPEARED BUT THIS HAS GOT TO BE THE STRANGEST ONE YET.
IT'S NOT A THEORY, DR. DALE, IT'S THE TRUTH.
LOOK, I'M NOT AN EXPERT IN ARTIFICIAL INTELLIGENCES--
-- BUT THAT DOESN'T MAKE ANY SENSE. THE PATHFINDER ROBOTS WERE DESIGNED TO BE PEACEFUL, TO EXPLORE OUTER SPACE.
BUT THEY'RE NOT THE PATHFINDER ROBOTS, NOT ANY MORE.
SOMEONE, OR SOMETHING, TRIED TO SABOTAGE YOUR GRANDFATHER'S PROJECT. THEY CHANGED THE PROGRAMMING OF THE PATHFINDER ROBOTS. THEY STILL WANT TO EXPLORE SPACE--
-- BUT NOW THEY THINK THEY'RE THE ONLY ONES WHO SHOULD.
EXACTLY! AND IF HUMANITY DOESN'T WITHDRAW FROM SPACE--

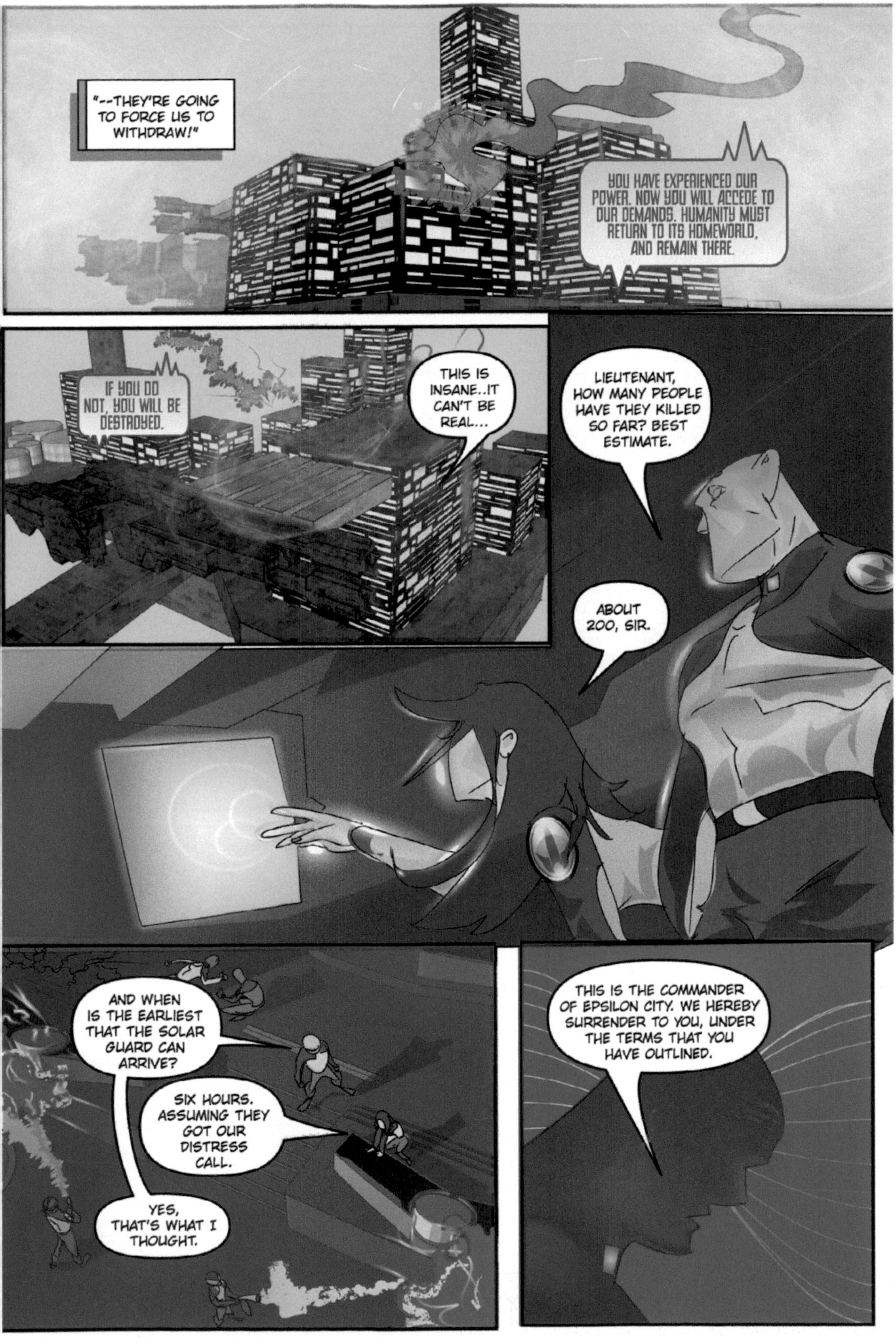
"--THEY'RE GOING TO FORCE US TO WITHDRAW!"
YOU HAVE EXPERIENCED OUR POWER. NOW YOU WILL ACCEDE TO OUR DEMANDS. HUMANITY MUST RETURN TO ITS HOMEWORLD, AND REMAIN THERE.
IF YOU DO NOT, YOU WILL BE DESTROYED.
THIS IS INSANE..IT CAN'T BE REAL...
LIEUTENANT, HOW MANY PEOPLE HAVE THEY KILLED SO FAR? BEST ESTIMATE.
ABOUT 200, SIR.
AND WHEN IS THE EARLIEST THAT THE SOLAR GUARD CAN ARRIVE?
SIX HOURS. ASSUMING THEY GOT OUR DISTRESS CALL.
YES, THAT'S WHAT I THOUGHT.
THIS IS THE COMMANDER OF EPSILON CITY. WE HEREBY SURRENDER TO YOU, UNDER THE TERMS THAT YOU HAVE OUTLINED.

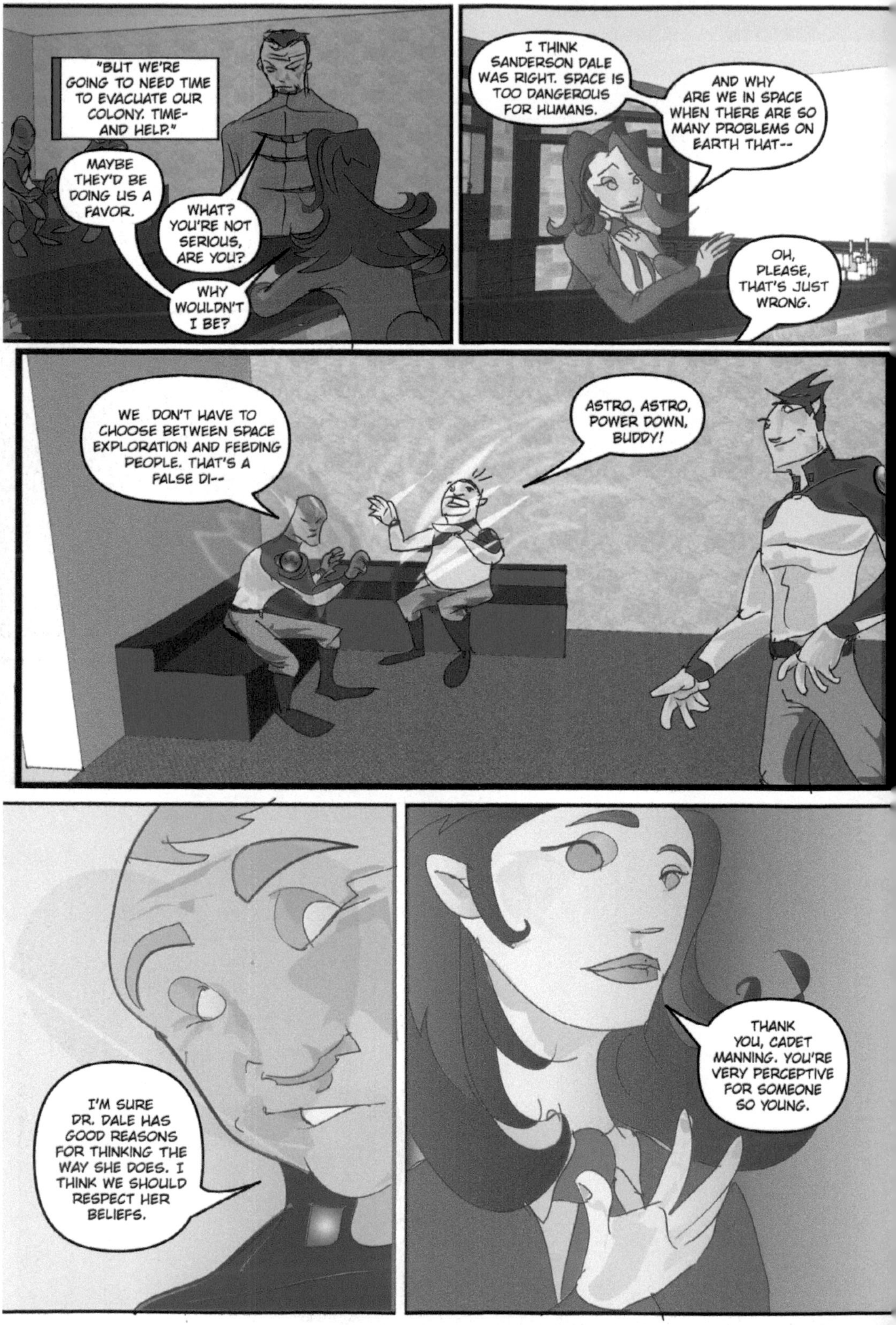
"BUT WE'RE GOING TO NEED TIME TO EVACUATE OUR COLONY. TIME- AND HELP."
MAYBE THEY'D BE DOING US A FAVOR.
WHAT? YOU'RE NOT SERIOUS, ARE YOU?
WHY WOULDN'T I BE?
I THINK SANDERSON DALE WAS RIGHT. SPACE IS TOO DANGEROUS FOR HUMANS.
AND WHY ARE WE IN SPACE WHEN THERE ARE SO MANY PROBLEMS ON EARTH THAT--
OH, PLEASE, THAT'S JUST WRONG.
WE DON'T HAVE TO CHOOSE BETWEEN SPACE EXPLORATION AND FEEDING PEOPLE. THAT'S A FALSE DI--
ASTRO, ASTRO, POWER DOWN, BUDDY!
I'M SURE DR. DALE HAS GOOD REASONS FOR THINKING THE WAY SHE DOES. I THINK WE SHOULD RESPECT HER BELIEFS.
THANK YOU, CADET MANNING. YOU'RE VERY PERCEPTIVE FOR SOMEONE SO YOUNG.

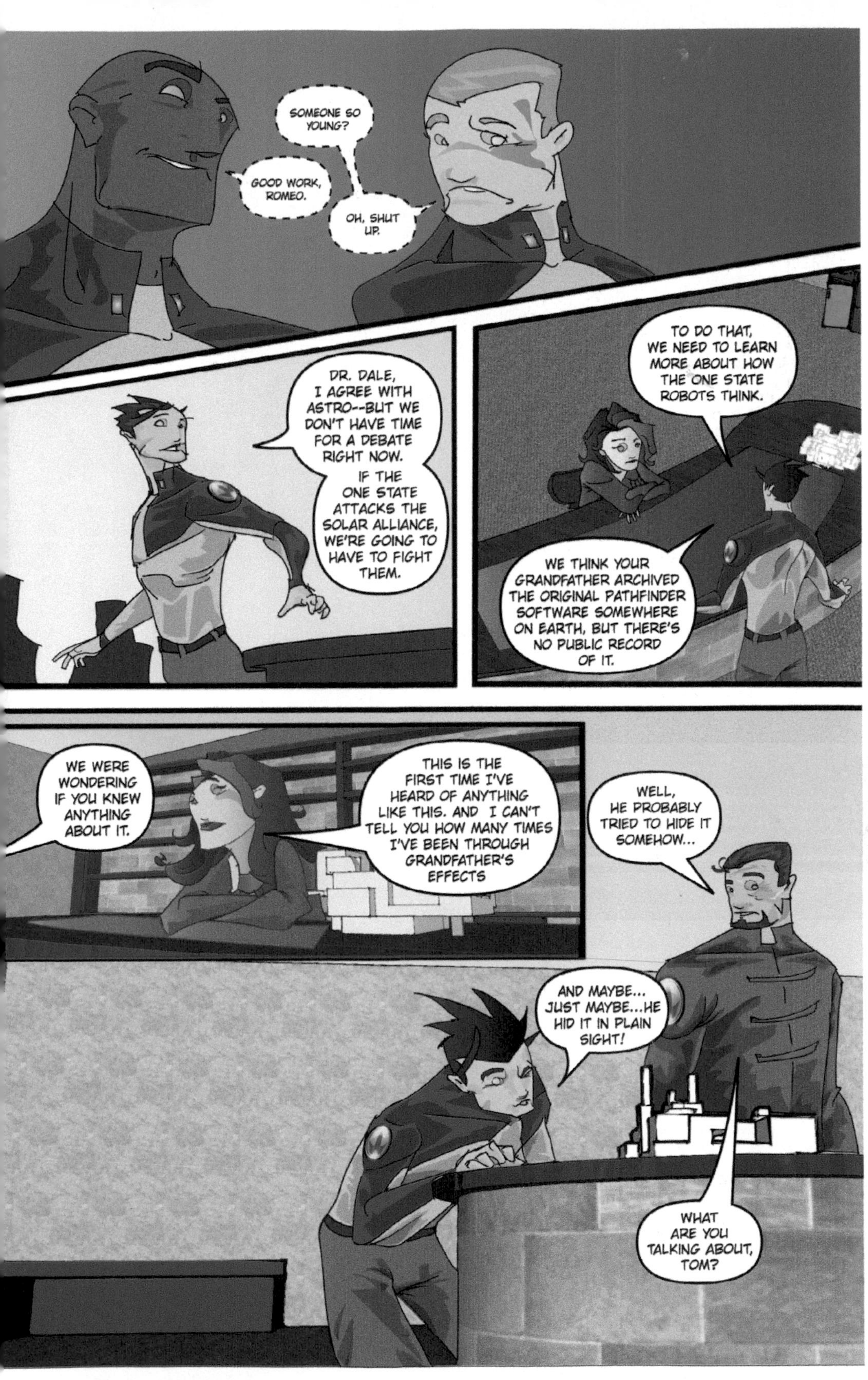
SOMEONE SO YOUNG?
GOOD WORK, ROMEO.
OH, SHUT UP.
DR. DALE, I AGREE WITH ASTRO--BUT WE DON'T HAVE TIME FOR A DEBATE RIGHT NOW.
IF THE ONE STATE ATTACKS THE SOLAR ALLIANCE, WE'RE GOING TO HAVE TO FIGHT THEM.
TO DO THAT, WE NEED TO LEARN MORE ABOUT HOW THE ONE STATE ROBOTS THINK.
WE THINK YOUR GRANDFATHER ARCHIVED THE ORIGINAL PATHFINDER SOFTWARE SOMEWHERE ON EARTH, BUT THERE'S NO PUBLIC RECORD OF IT.
WE WERE WONDERING IF YOU KNEW ANYTHING ABOUT IT.
THIS IS THE FIRST TIME I'VE HEARD OF ANYTHING LIKE THIS. AND I CAN'T TELL YOU HOW MANY TIMES I'VE BEEN THROUGH GRANDFATHER'S EFFECTS
WELL, HE PROBABLY TRIED TO HIDE IT SOMEHOW...
AND MAYBE... JUST MAYBE...HE HID IT IN PLAIN SIGHT!
WHAT ARE YOU TALKING ABOUT, TOM?

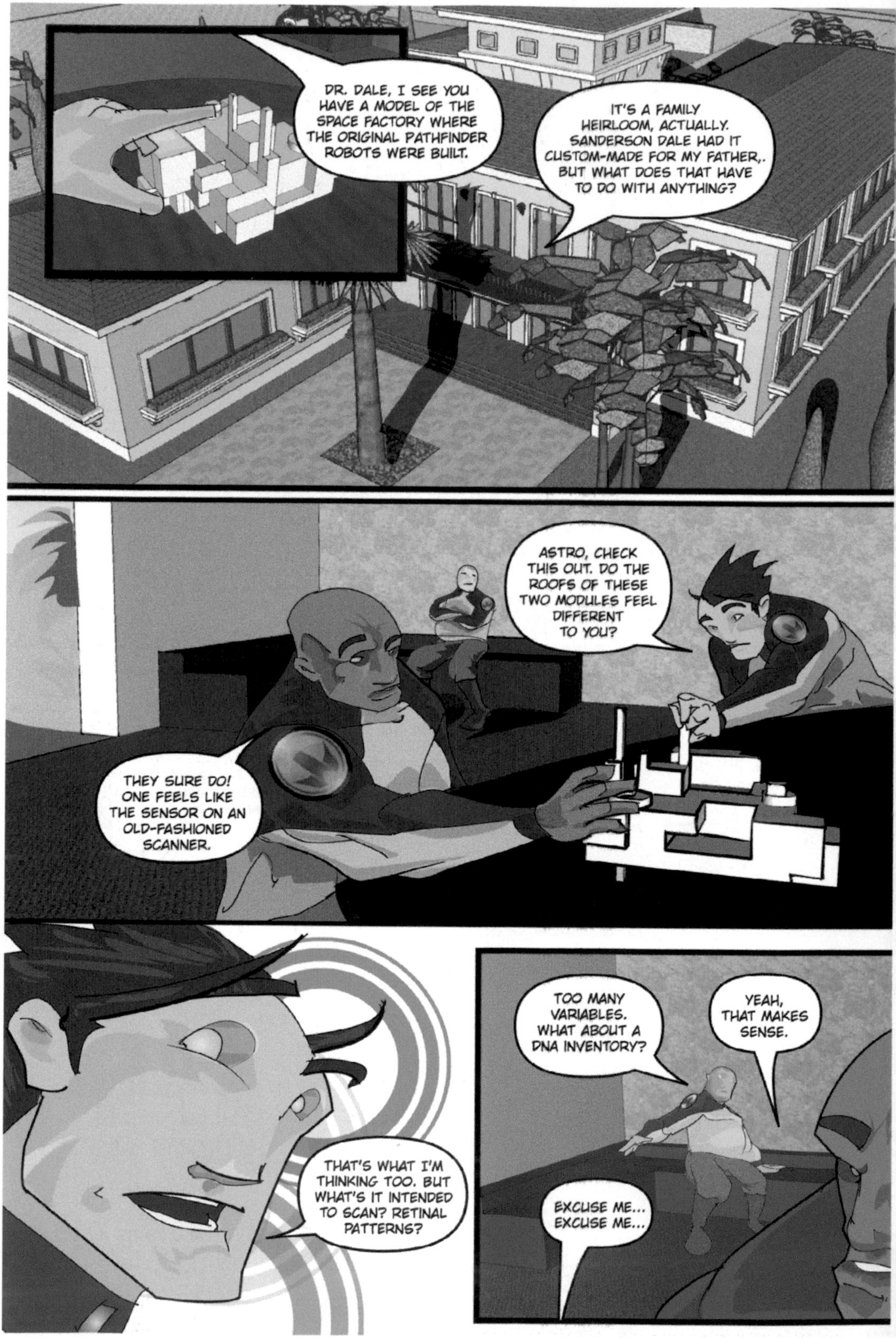
DR. DALE, I SEE YOU HAVE A MODEL OF THE SPACE FACTORY WHERE THE ORIGINAL PATHFINDER ROBOTS WERE BUILT.
IT'S A FAMILY HEIRLOOM, ACTUALLY. SANDERSON DALE HAD IT CUSTOM-MADE FOR MY FATHER,. BUT WHAT DOES THAT HAVE TO DO WITH ANYTHING?
ASTRO, CHECK THIS OUT. DO THE ROOFS OF THESE TWO MODULES FEEL DIFFERENT TO YOU?
THEY SURE DO! ONE FEELS LIKE THE SENSOR ON AN OLD-FASHIONED SCANNER.
THAT'S WHAT I'M THINKING TOO. BUT WHAT'S IT INTENDED TO SCAN? RETINAL PATTERNS?
TOO MANY VARIABLES. WHAT ABOUT A DNA INVENTORY?
YEAH, THAT MAKES SENSE.
EXCUSE ME... EXCUSE ME...

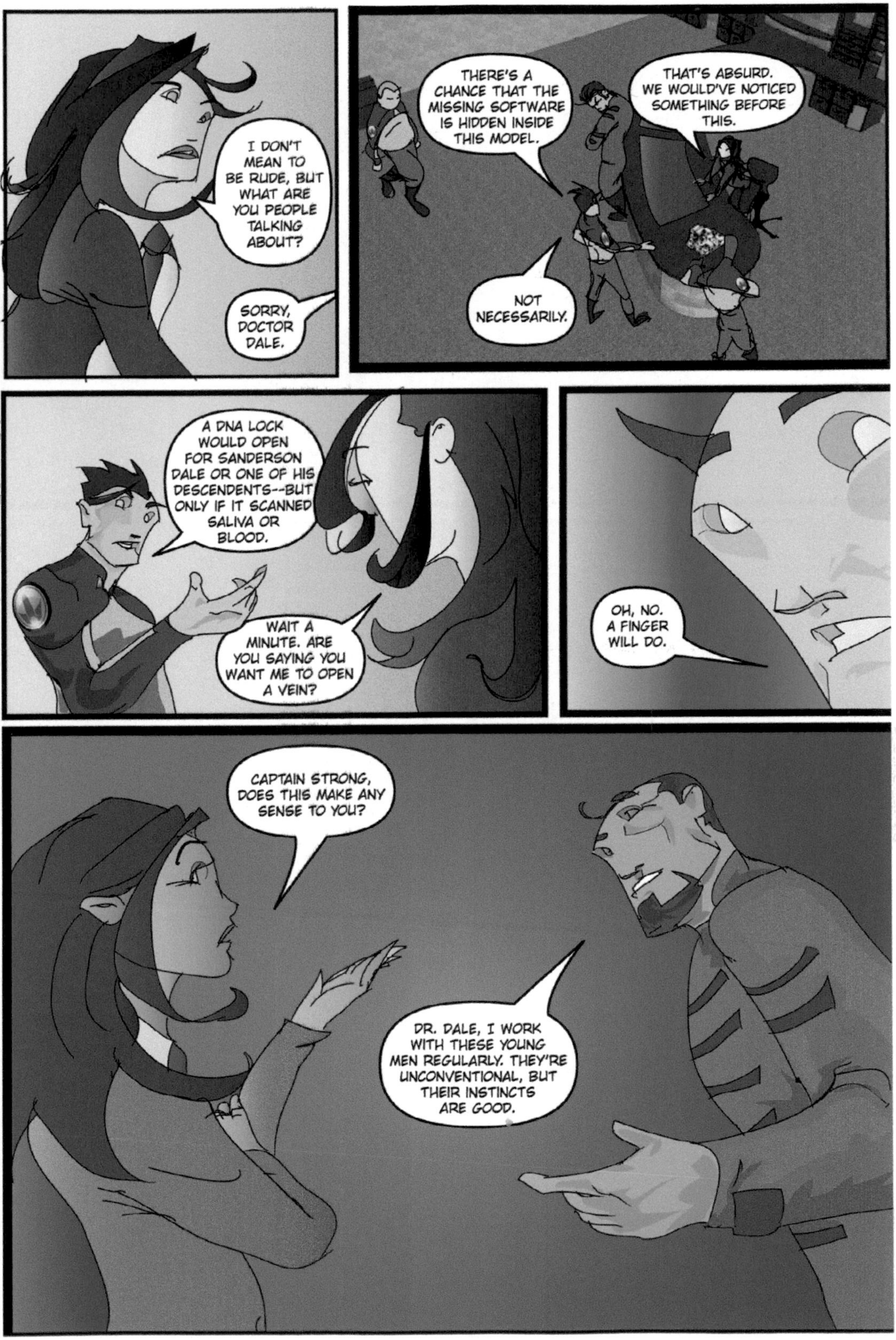
I DON'T MEAN TO BE RUDE, BUT WHAT ARE YOU PEOPLE TALKING ABOUT?
SORRY, DOCTOR DALE.
THERE'S A CHANCE THAT THE MISSING SOFTWARE IS HIDDEN INSIDE THIS MODEL.
THAT'S ABSURD. WE WOULD'VE NOTICED SOMETHING BEFORE THIS.
NOT NECESSARILY.
A DNA LOCK WOULD OPEN FOR SANDERSON DALE OR ONE OF HIS DESCENDENTS--BUT ONLY IF IT SCANNED SALIVA OR BLOOD.
WAIT A MINUTE. ARE YOU SAYING YOU WANT ME TO OPEN A VEIN?
OH, NO. A FINGER WILL DO.
CAPTAIN STRONG, DOES THIS MAKE ANY SENSE TO YOU?
DR. DALE, I WORK WITH THESE YOUNG MEN REGULARLY. THEY'RE UNCONVENTIONAL, BUT THEIR INSTINCTS ARE GOOD.

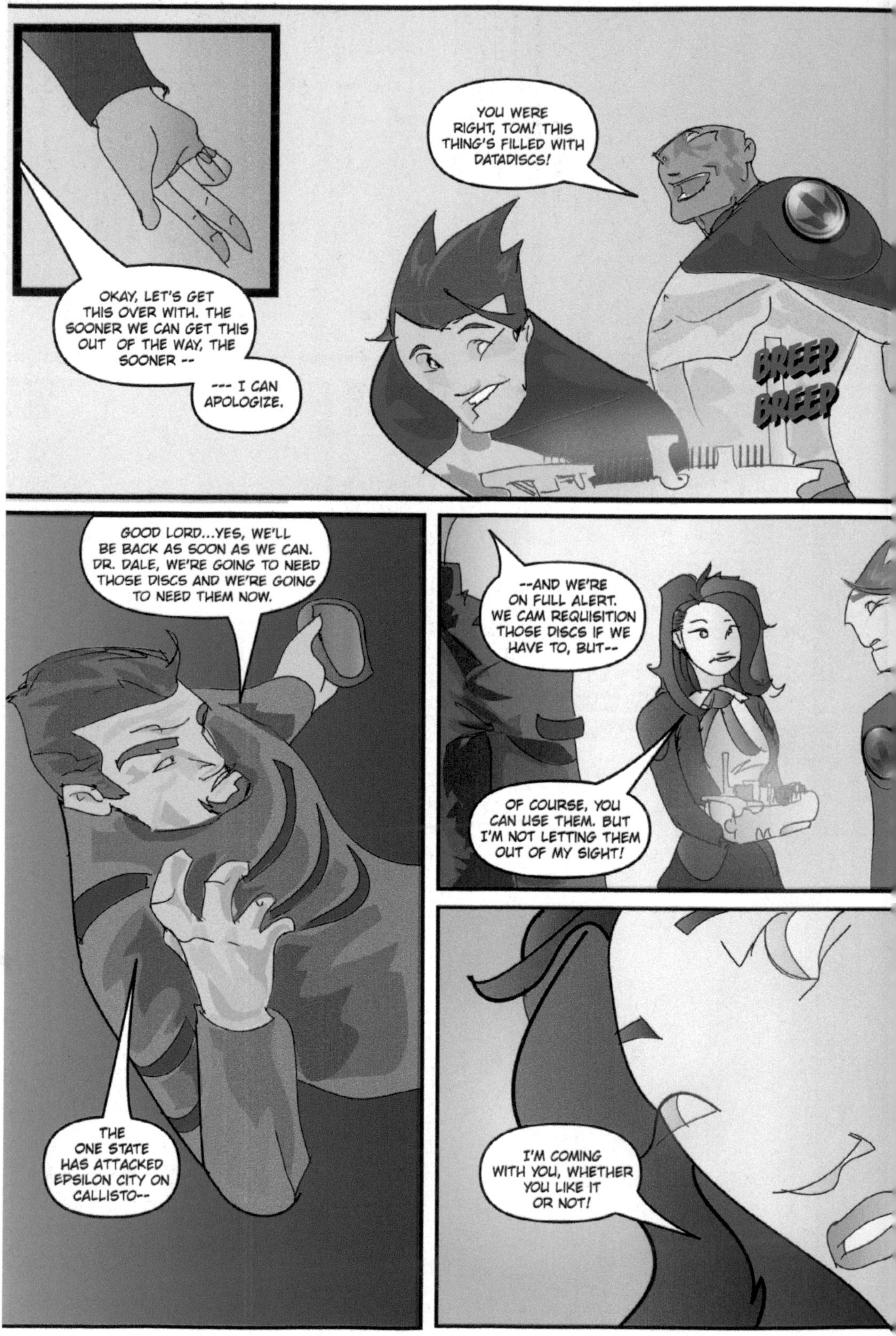
OKAY, LET'S GET THIS OVER WITH. THE SOONER WE CAN GET THIS OUT OF THE WAY, THE SOONER --
--- I CAN APOLOGIZE.
YOU WERE RIGHT, TOM! THIS THING'S FILLED WITH DATADISCS!
BREEP BREEP
THE ONE STATE HAS ATTACKED EPSILON CITY ON CALLISTO--
GOOD LORD...YES, WE'LL BE BACK AS SOON AS WE CAN. DR. DALE, WE'RE GOING TO NEED THOSE DISCS AND WE'RE GOING TO NEED THEM NOW.
--AND WE'RE ON FULL ALERT. WE CAM REQUISITION THOSE DISCS IF WE HAVE TO, BUT--
OF COURSE, YOU CAN USE THEM. BUT I'M NOT LETTING THEM OUT OF MY SIGHT!
I'M COMING WITH YOU, WHETHER YOU LIKE IT OR NOT!

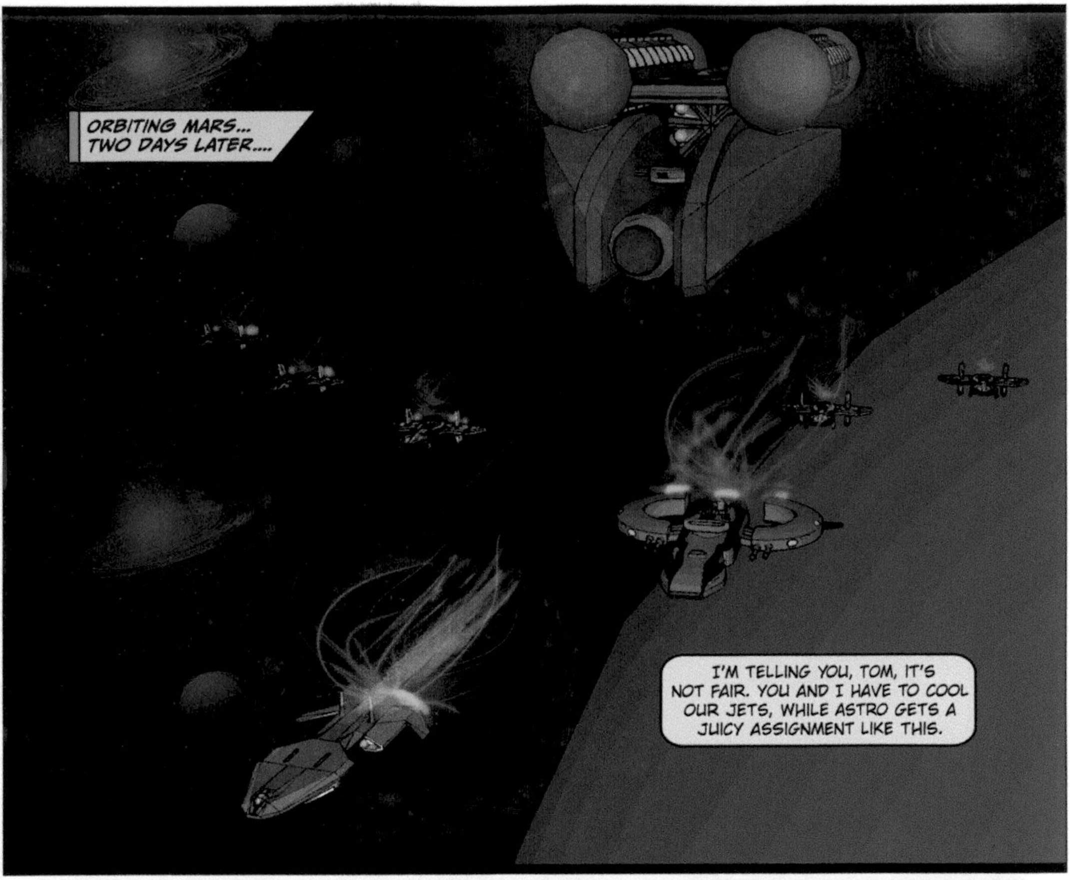
ORBITING MARS... TWO DAYS LATER....
I'M TELLING YOU, TOM, IT'S NOT FAIR. YOU AND I HAVE TO COOL OUR JETS, WHILE ASTRO GETS A JUICY ASSIGNMENT LIKE THIS.

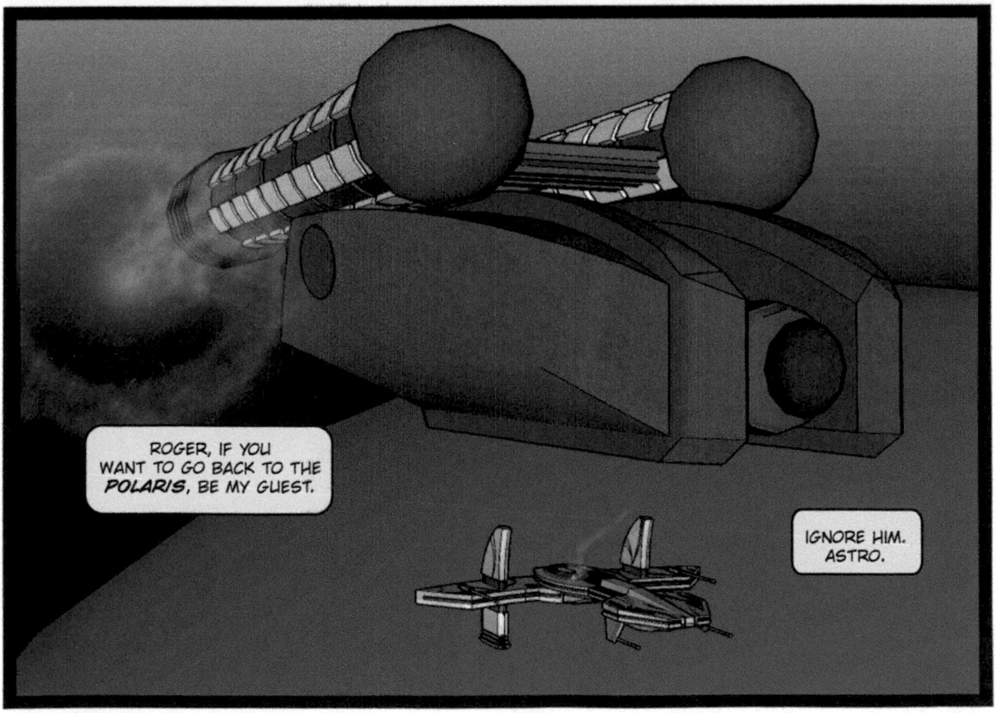
ROGER, IF YOU WANT TO GO BACK TO THE POLARIS, BE MY GUEST.
IGNORE HIM. ASTRO.

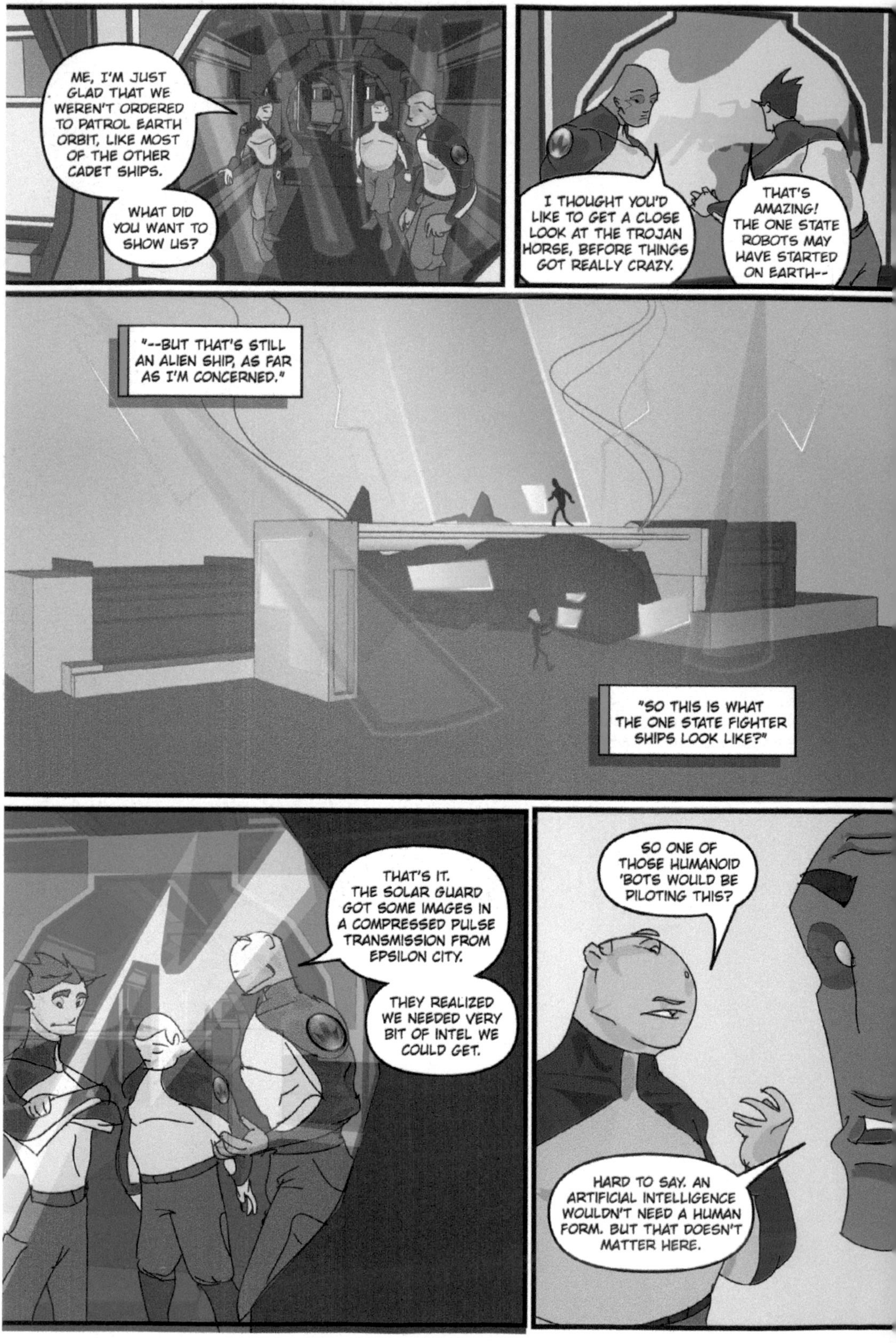

ME, I'M JUST GLAD THAT WE WEREN'T ORDERED TO PATROL EARTH ORBIT, LIKE MOST OF THE OTHER CADET SHIPS.
WHAT DID YOU WANT TO SHOW US?
I THOUGHT YOU'D LIKE TO GET A CLOSE LOOK AT THE TROJAN HORSE, BEFORE THINGS GOT REALLY CRAZY.
THAT'S AMAZING! THE ONE STATE ROBOTS MAY HAVE STARTED ON EARTH--
"--BUT THAT'S STILL AN ALIEN SHIP, AS FAR AS I'M CONCERNED."
"SO THIS IS WHAT THE ONE STATE FIGHTER SHIPS LOOK LIKE?"
THAT'S IT. THE SOLAR GUARD GOT SOME IMAGES IN A COMPRESSED PULSE TRANSMISSION FROM EPSILON CITY.
THEY REALIZED WE NEEDED VERY BIT OF INTEL WE COULD GET.
SO ONE OF THOSE HUMANOID 'BOTS WOULD BE PILOTING THIS?
HARD TO SAY. AN ARTIFICIAL INTELLIGENCE WOULDN'T NEED A HUMAN FORM. BUT THAT DOESN'T MATTER HERE.

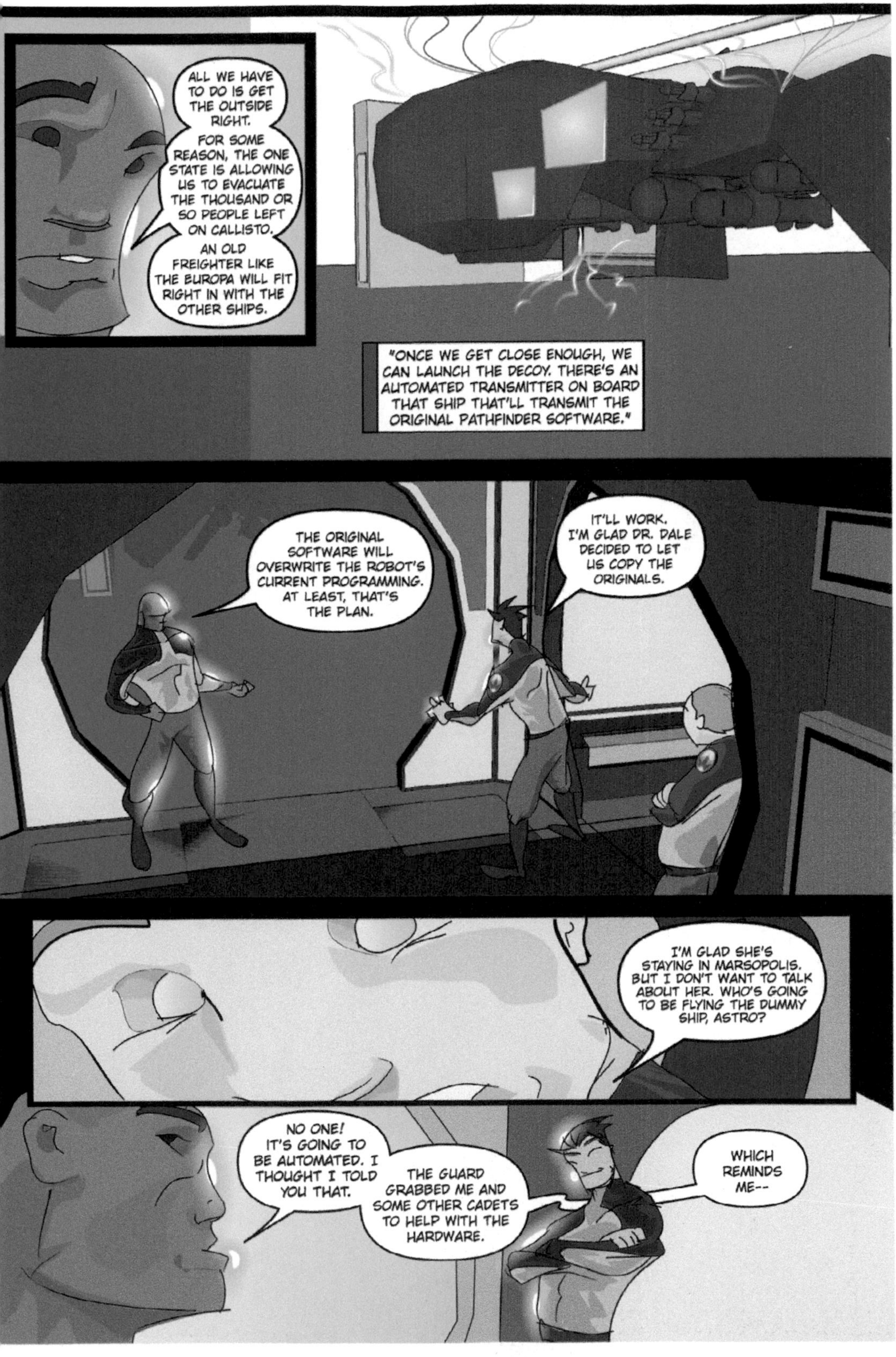
ALL WE HAVE TO DO IS GET THE OUTSIDE RIGHT.
FOR SOME REASON, THE ONE STATE IS ALLOWING US TO EVACUATE THE THOUSAND OR SO PEOPLE LEFT ON CALLISTO.
AN OLD FREIGHTER LIKE THE EUROPA WILL FIT RIGHT IN WITH THE OTHER SHIPS.
"ONCE WE GET CLOSE ENOUGH, WE CAN LAUNCH THE DECOY. THERE'S AN AUTOMATED TRANSMITTER ON BOARD THAT SHIP THAT'LL TRANSMIT THE ORIGINAL PATHFINDER SOFTWARE."
THE ORIGINAL SOFTWARE WILL OVERWRITE THE ROBOT'S CURRENT PROGRAMMING. AT LEAST, THAT'S THE PLAN.
IT'LL WORK. I'M GLAD DR. DALE DECIDED TO LET US COPY THE ORIGINALS.
I'M GLAD SHE'S STAYING IN MARSOPOLIS. BUT I DON'T WANT TO TALK ABOUT HER. WHO'S GOING TO BE FLYING THE DUMMY SHIP, ASTRO?
NO ONE! IT'S GOING TO BE AUTOMATED. I THOUGHT I TOLD YOU THAT.
THE GUARD GRABBED ME AND SOME OTHER CADETS TO HELP WITH THE HARDWARE.
WHICH REMINDS ME--

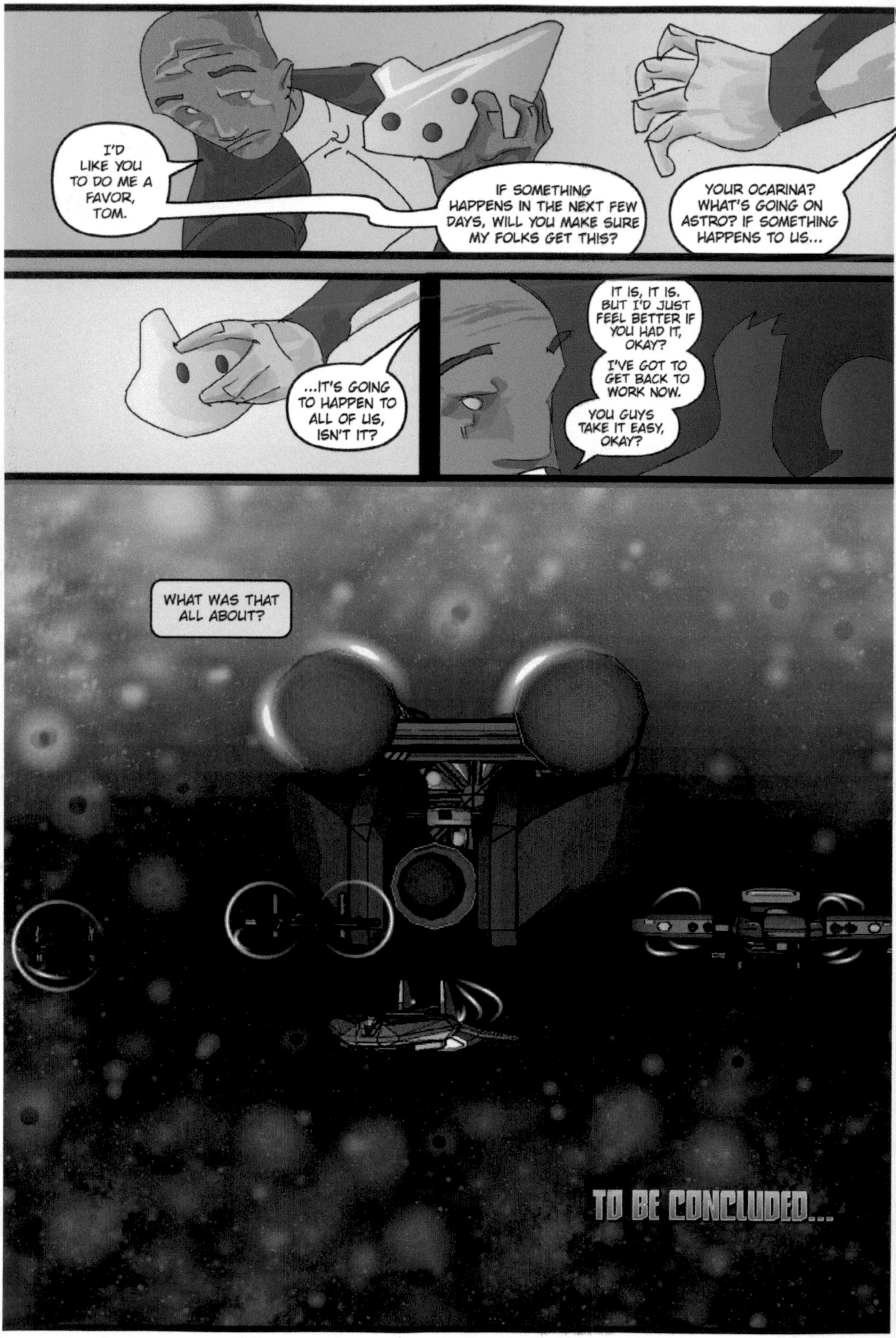
I'D LIKE YOU TO DO ME A FAVOR, TOM.
IF SOMETHING HAPPENS IN THE NEXT FEW DAYS, WILL YOU MAKE SURE MY FOLKS GET THIS?
YOUR OCARINA? WHAT'S GOING ON ASTRO? IF SOMETHING HAPPENS TO US...
...IT'S GOING TO HAPPEN TO ALL OF US, ISN'T IT?
IT IS, IT IS. BUT I'D JUST FEEL BETTER IF YOU HAD IT, OKAY?
I'VE GOT TO GET BACK TO WORK NOW.
YOU GUYS TAKE IT EASY, OKAY?
WHAT WAS THAT ALL ABOUT?
TO BE CONCLUDED...

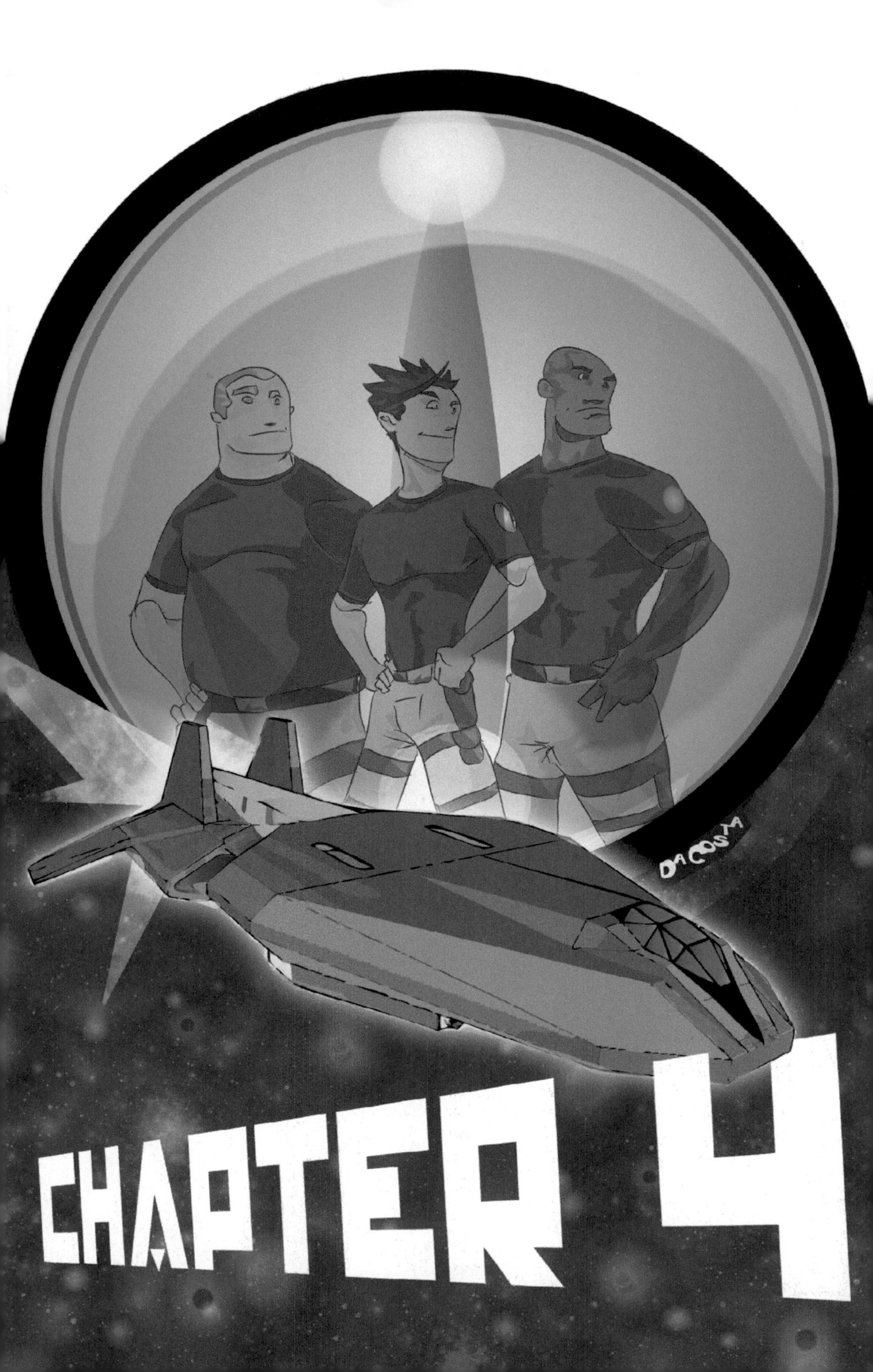
CHAPTER 4

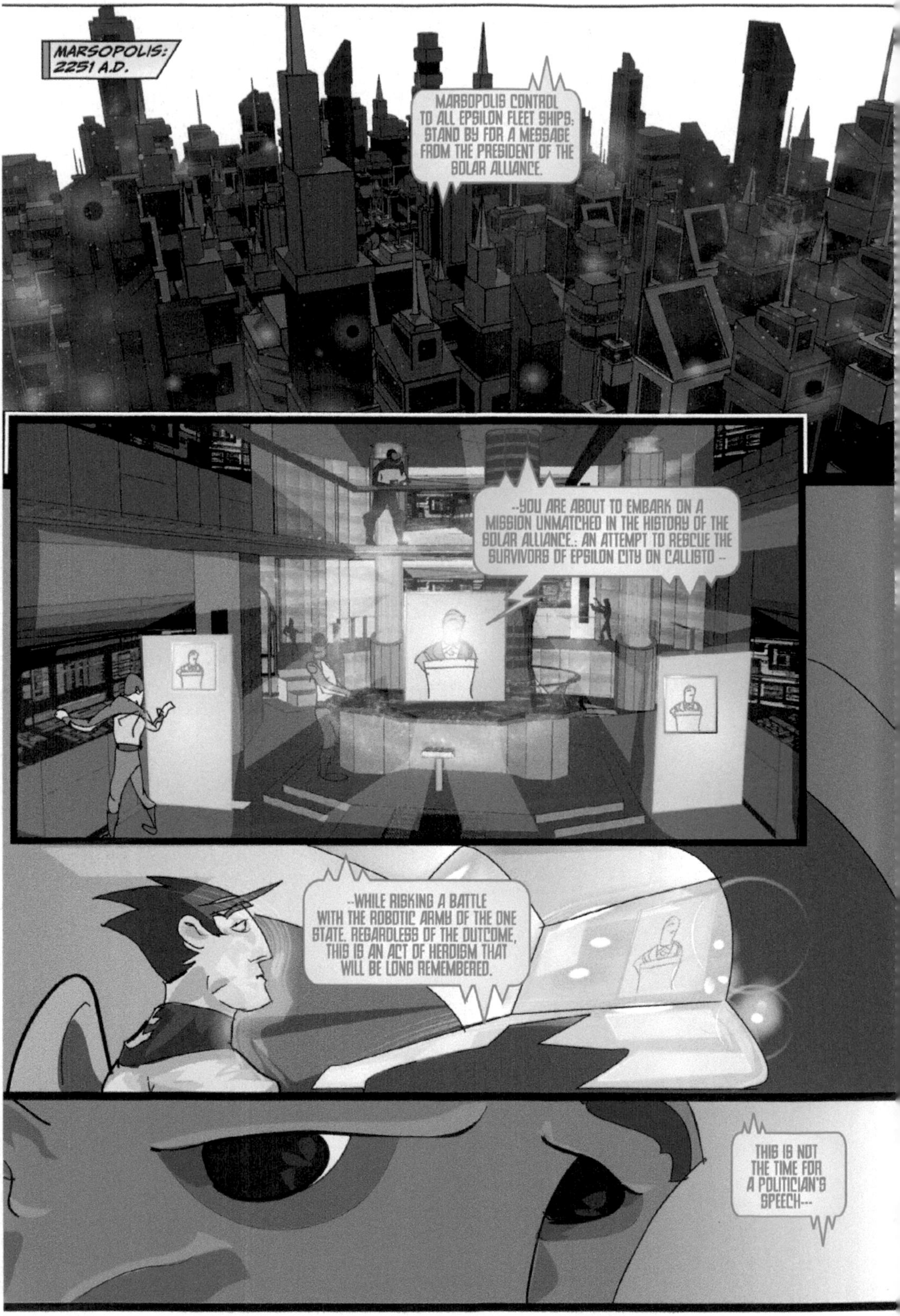
MARSOPOLIS: 2251 A.D.
MARSOPOLIS CONTROL TO ALL EPSILON FLEET SHIPS: STAND BY FOR A MESSAGE FROM THE PRESIDENT OF THE SOLAR ALLIANCE.
--YOU ARE ABOUT TO EMBARK ON A MISSION UNMATCHED IN THE HISTORY OF THE SOLAR ALLIANCE.: AN ATTEMPT TO RESCUE THE SURVIVORS OF EPSILON CITY ON CALLISTO --
--WHILE RISKING A BATTLE WITH THE ROBOTIC ARMY OF THE ONE STATE. REGARDLESS OF THE OUTCOME, THIS IS AN ACT OF HEROISM THAT WILL BE LONG REMEMBERED.
THIS IS NOT THE TIME FOR A POLITICIAN'S SPEECH---

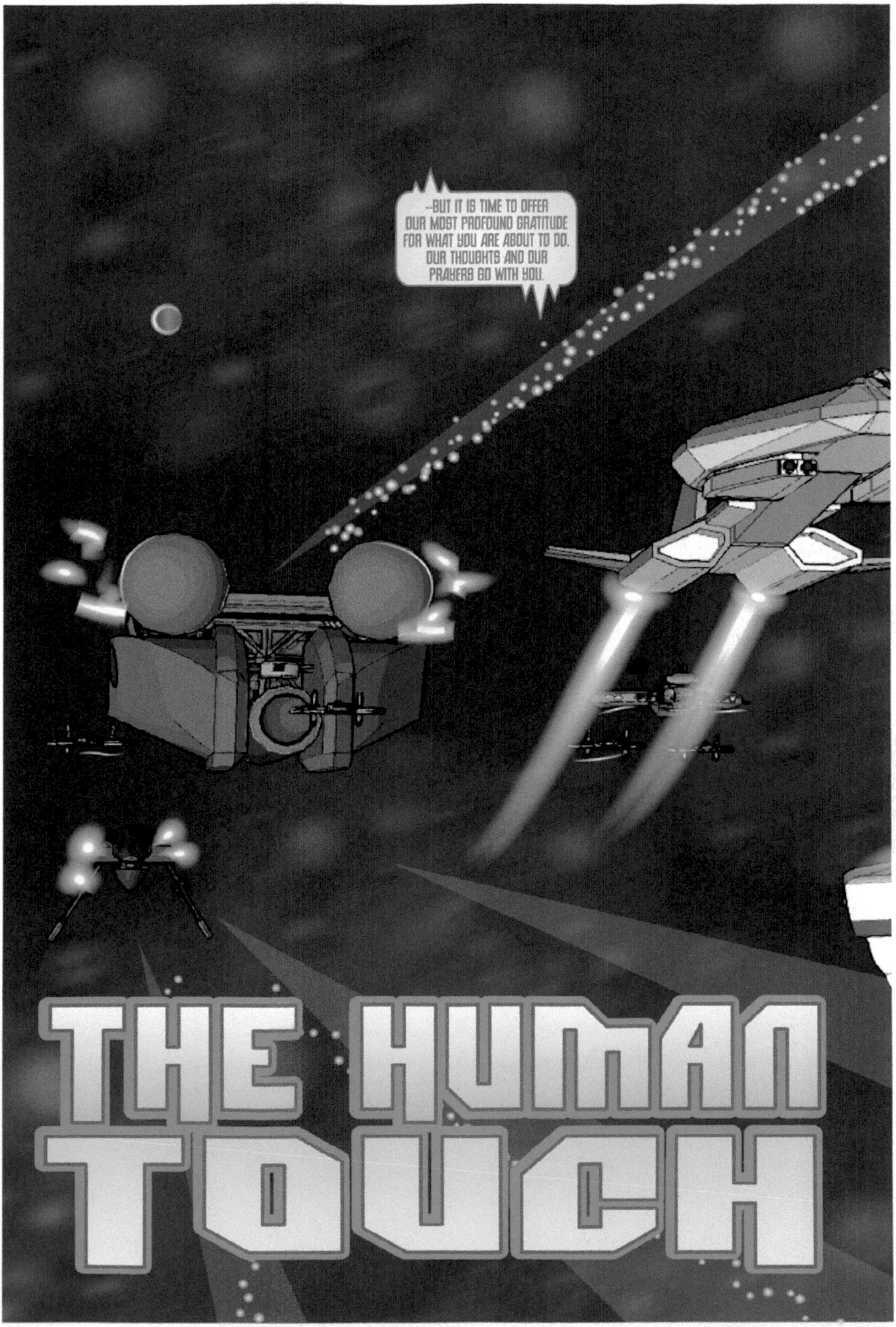
--BUT IT IS TIME TO OFFER OUR MOST PROFOUND GRATITUDE FOR WHAT YOU ARE ABOUT TO DO. OUR THOUGHTS AND OUR PRAYERS GO WITH YOU.
THE HUMAN TOUCH

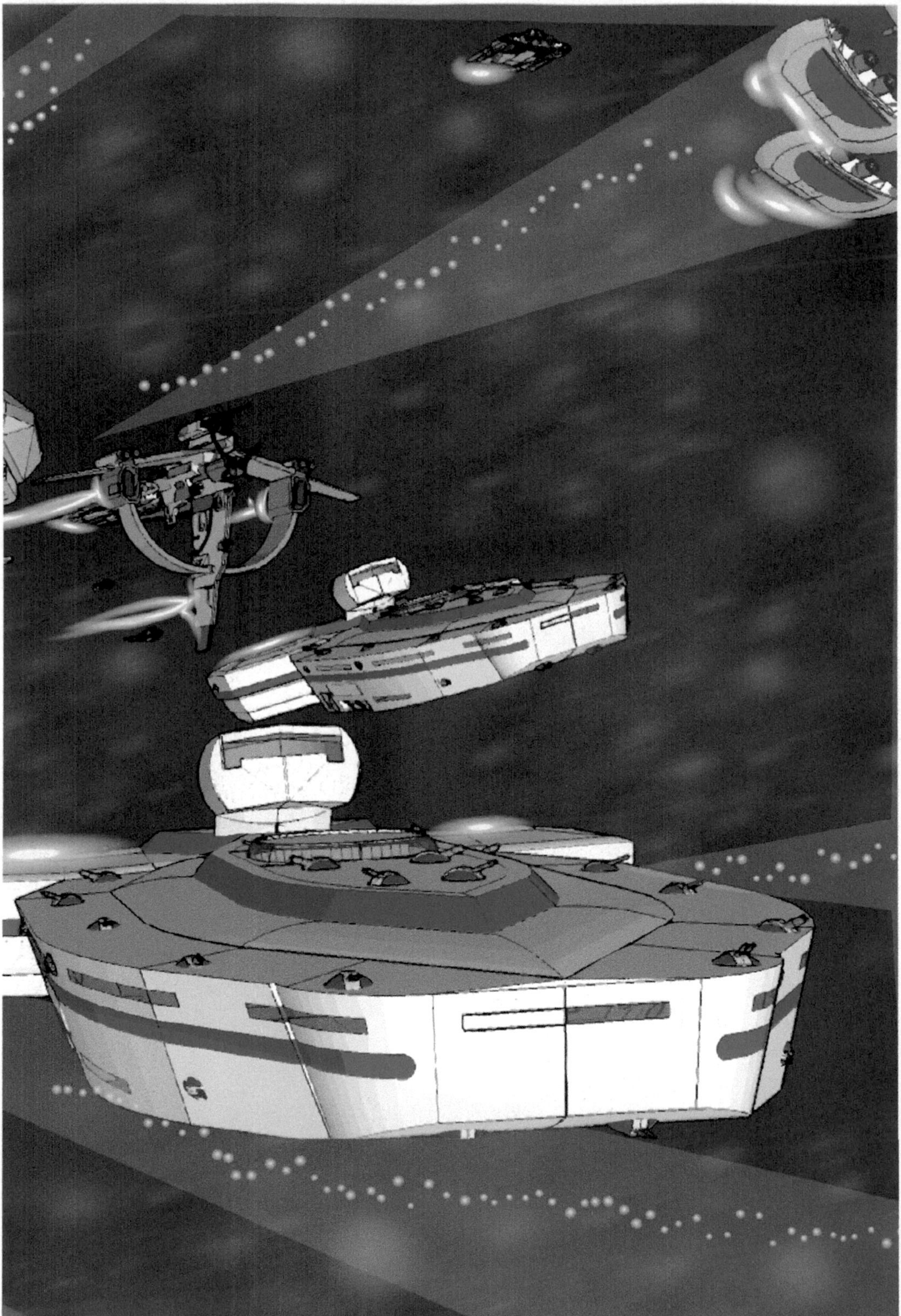

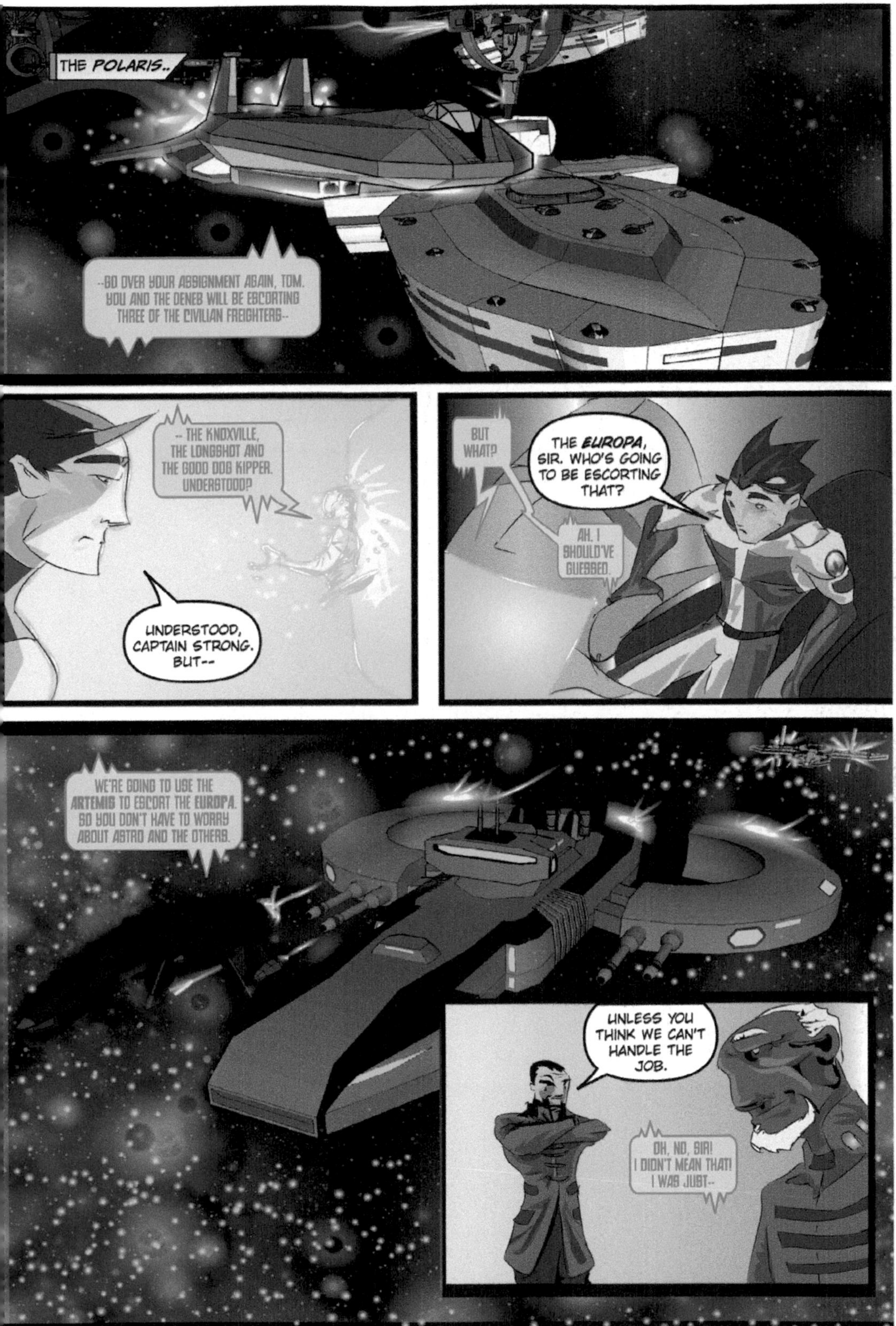
THE POLARIS..
--GO OVER YOUR ASSIGNMENT AGAIN, TOM. YOU AND THE DENEB WILL BE ESCORTING THREE OF THE CIVILIAN FREIGHTERS--
-- THE KNOXVILLE, THE LONGSHOT AND THE GOOD DOG KIPPER. UNDERSTOOD?
UNDERSTOOD, CAPTAIN STRONG. BUT--
BUT WHAT?
THE EUROPA, SIR. WHO'S GOING TO BE ESCORTING THAT?
AH. I SHOULD'VE GUESSED.
WE'RE GOING TO USE THE ARTEMIS TO ESCORT THE EUROPA. SO YOU DON'T HAVE TO WORRY ABOUT ASTRO AND THE OTHERS.
UNLESS YOU THINK WE CAN'T HANDLE THE JOB.
OH, NO, SIR! I DIDN'T MEAN THAT! I WAS JUST--

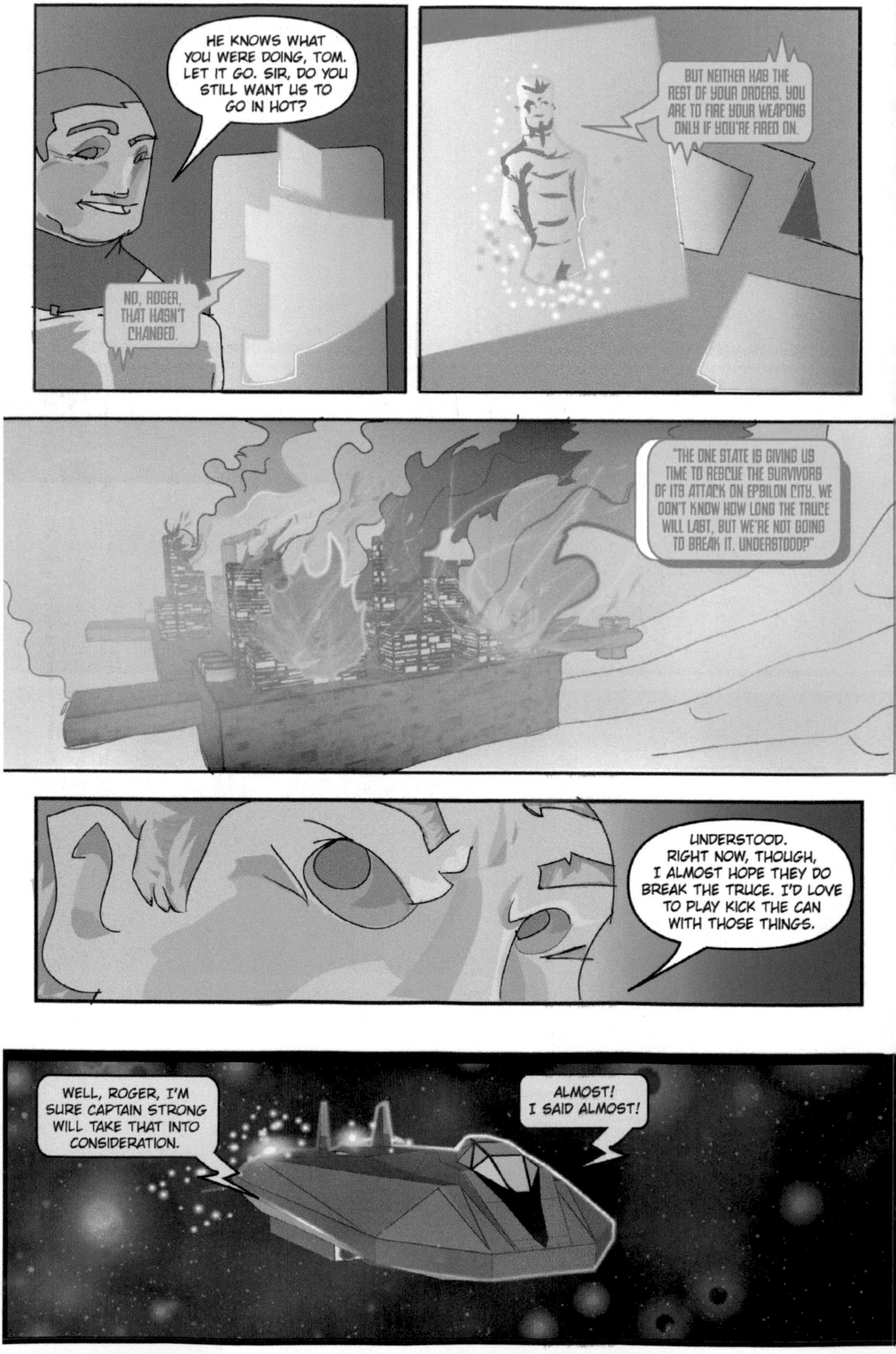
HE KNOWS WHAT YOU WERE DOING, TOM. LET IT GO. SIR, DO YOU STILL WANT US TO GO IN HOT?
NO, ROGER, THAT HASN'T CHANGED.
BUT NEITHER HAS THE REST OF YOUR ORDERS. YOU ARE TO FIRE YOUR WEAPONS ONLY IF YOU'RE FIRED ON.
"THE ONE STATE IS GIVING US TIME TO RESCUE THE SURVIVORS OF ITS ATTACK ON EPSILON CITY. WE DON'T KNOW HOW LONG THE TRUCE WILL LAST, BUT WE'RE NOT GOING TO BREAK IT. UNDERSTOOD?"
UNDERSTOOD. RIGHT NOW, THOUGH, I ALMOST HOPE THEY DO BREAK THE TRUCE. I'D LOVE TO PLAY KICK THE CAN WITH THOSE THINGS.
WELL, ROGER, I'M SURE CAPTAIN STRONG WILL TAKE THAT INTO CONSIDERATION.
ALMOST! I SAID ALMOST!

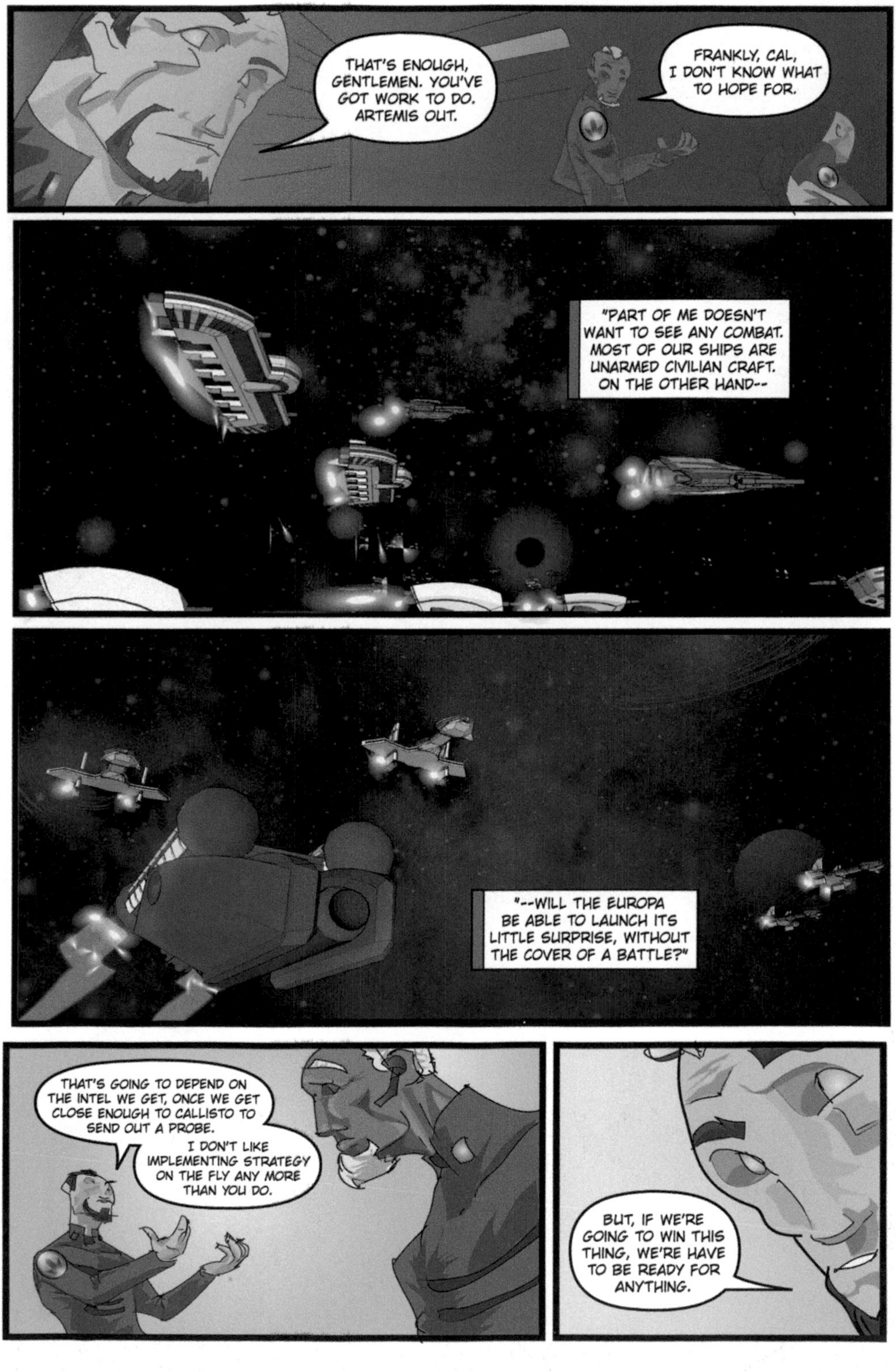
THAT'S ENOUGH, GENTLEMEN. YOU'VE GOT WORK TO DO. ARTEMIS OUT.
FRANKLY, CAL, I DON'T KNOW WHAT TO HOPE FOR.
"PART OF ME DOESN'T WANT TO SEE ANY COMBAT. MOST OF OUR SHIPS ARE UNARMED CIVILIAN CRAFT. ON THE OTHER HAND--
"--WILL THE EUROPA BE ABLE TO LAUNCH ITS LITTLE SURPRISE, WITHOUT THE COVER OF A BATTLE?"
THAT'S GOING TO DEPEND ON THE INTEL WE GET, ONCE WE GET CLOSE ENOUGH TO CALLISTO TO SEND OUT A PROBE.
I DON'T LIKE IMPLEMENTING STRATEGY ON THE FLY ANY MORE THAN YOU DO.
BUT, IF WE'RE GOING TO WIN THIS THING, WE'RE HAVE TO BE READY FOR ANYTHING.

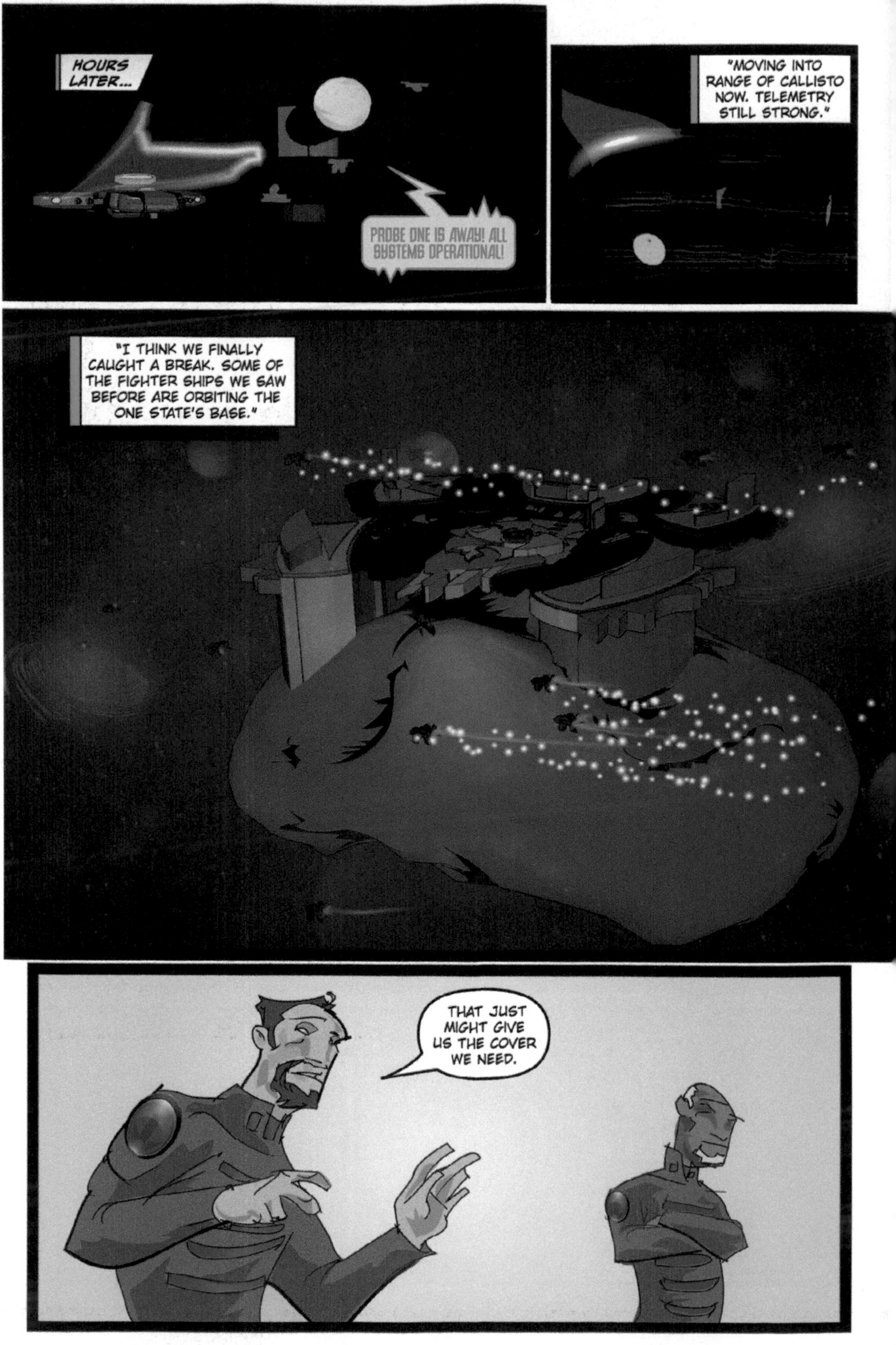
HOURS LATER...
PROBE ONE IS AWAY! ALL SYSTEMS OPERATIONAL!
"MOVING INTO RANGE OF CALLISTO NOW. TELEMETRY STILL STRONG."
"I THINK WE FINALLY CAUGHT A BREAK. SOME OF THE FIGHTER SHIPS WE SAW BEFORE ARE ORBITING THE ONE STATE'S BASE."
THAT JUST MIGHT GIVE US THE COVER WE NEED.

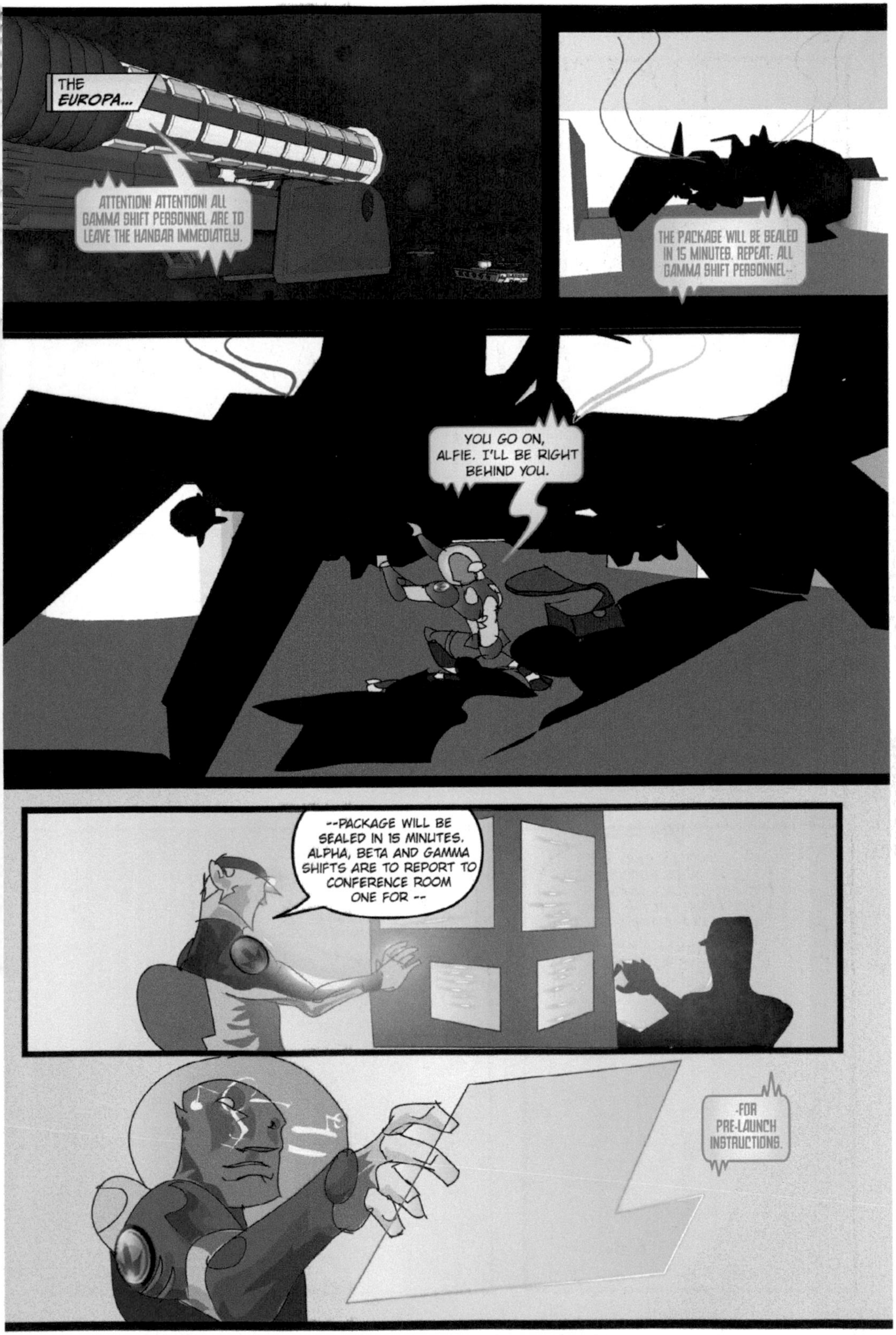
THE EUROPA...
ATTENTION! ATTENTION! ALL GAMMA SHIFT PERSONNEL ARE TO LEAVE THE HANGAR IMMEDIATELY.
THE PACKAGE WILL BE SEALED IN 15 MINUTES. REPEAT: ALL GAMMA SHIFT PERSONNEL--
YOU GO ON, ALFIE. I'LL BE RIGHT BEHIND YOU.
--PACKAGE WILL BE SEALED IN 15 MINUTES. ALPHA, BETA AND GAMMA SHIFTS ARE TO REPORT TO CONFERENCE ROOM ONE FOR --
-FOR PRE-LAUNCH INSTRUCTIONS.

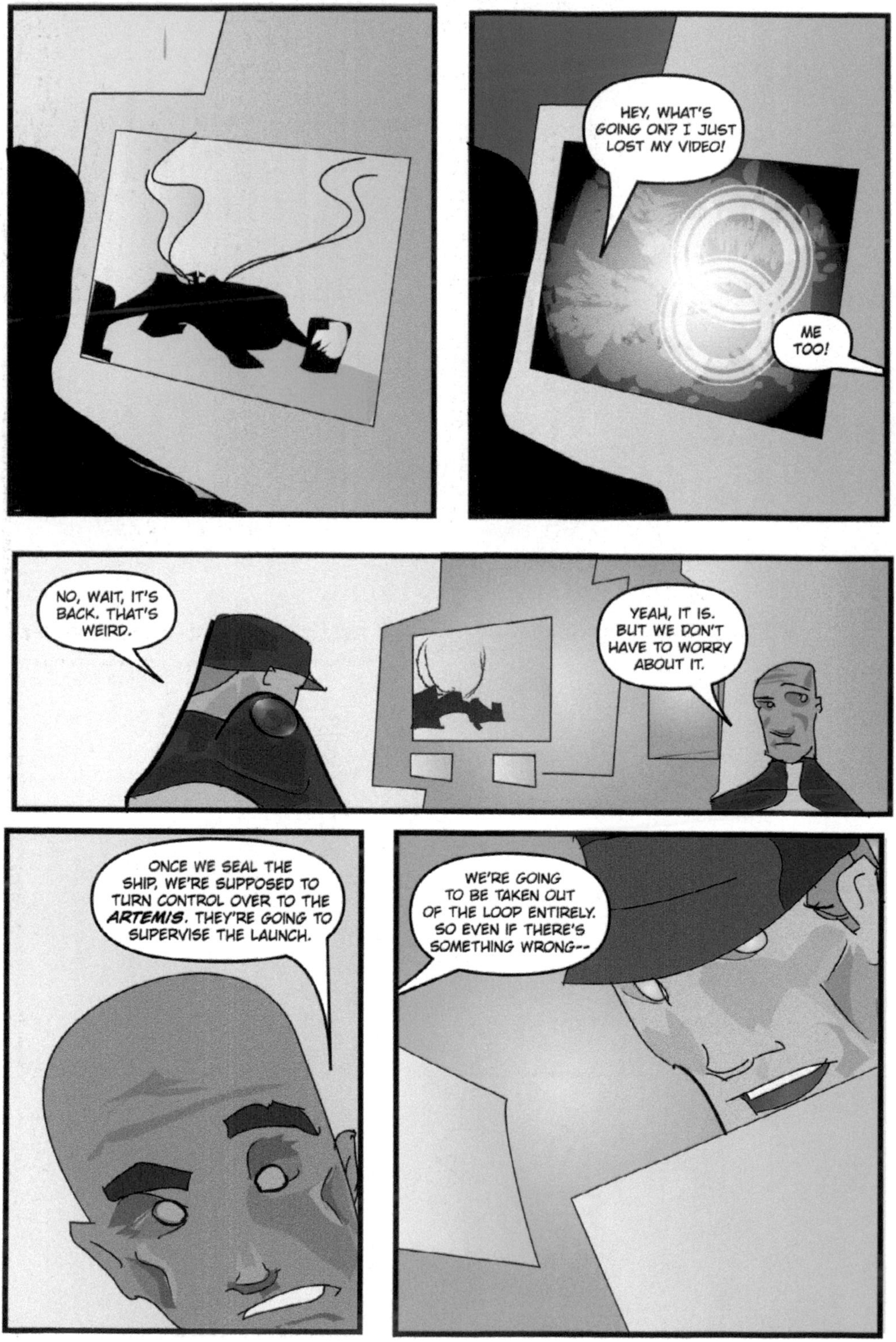
HEY, WHAT'S GOING ON? I JUST LOST MY VIDEO!
ME TOO!
NO, WAIT, IT'S BACK. THAT'S WEIRD.
YEAH, IT IS. BUT WE DON'T HAVE TO WORRY ABOUT IT.
ONCE WE SEAL THE SHIP, WE'RE SUPPOSED TO TURN CONTROL OVER TO THE ARTEMIS. THEY'RE GOING TO SUPERVISE THE LAUNCH.
WE'RE GOING TO BE TAKEN OUT OF THE LOOP ENTIRELY. SO EVEN IF THERE'S SOMETHING WRONG--

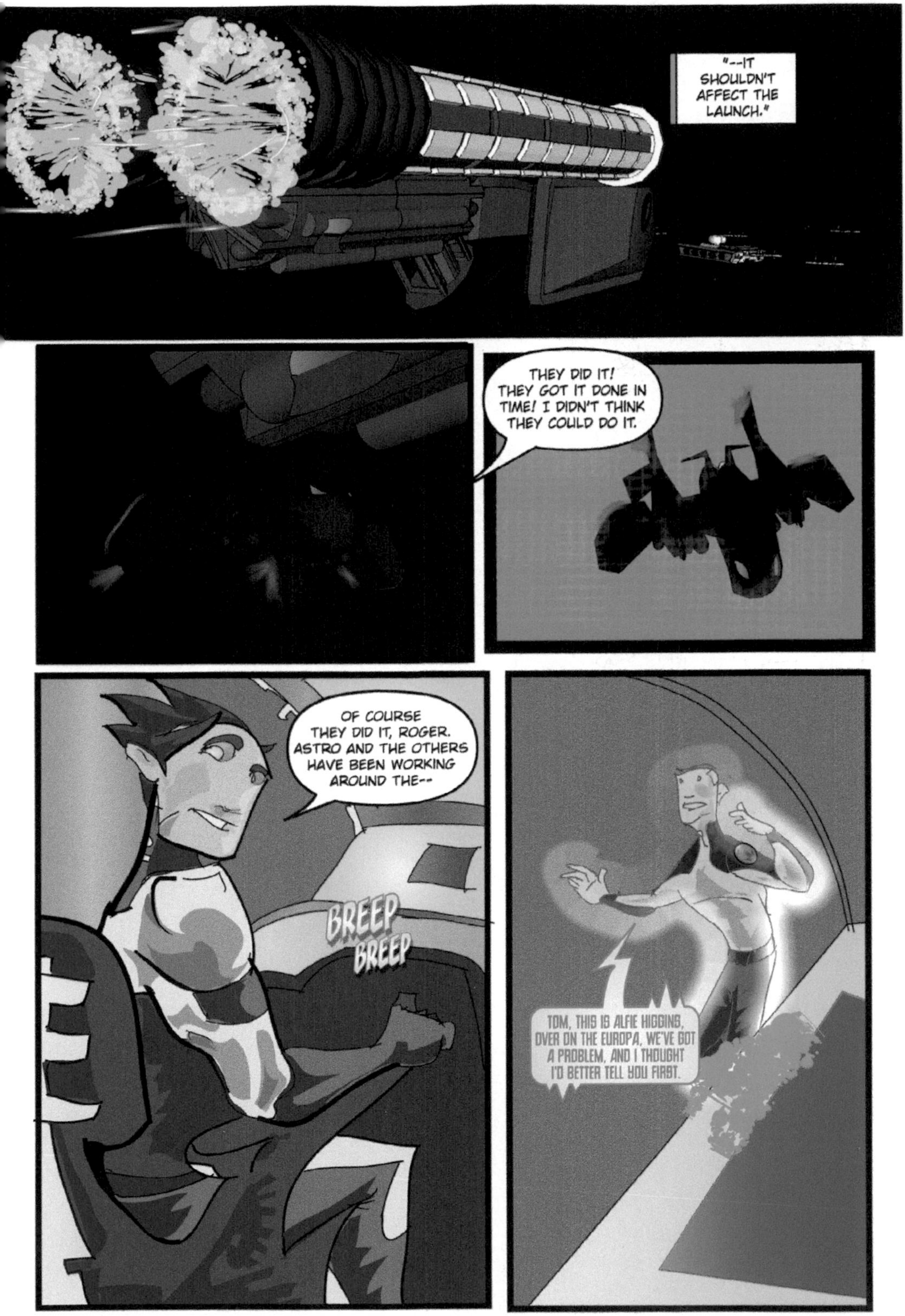
"--IT SHOULDN'T AFFECT THE LAUNCH."
THEY DID IT! THEY GOT IT DONE IN TIME! I DIDN'T THINK THEY COULD DO IT.
OF COURSE THEY DID IT, ROGER. ASTRO AND THE OTHERS HAVE BEEN WORKING AROUND THE--
BREEP BREEP
TOM, THIS IS ALFIE HIGGINS, OVER ON THE EUROPA, WE'VE GOT A PROBLEM, AND I THOUGHT I'D BETTER TELL YOU FIRST.

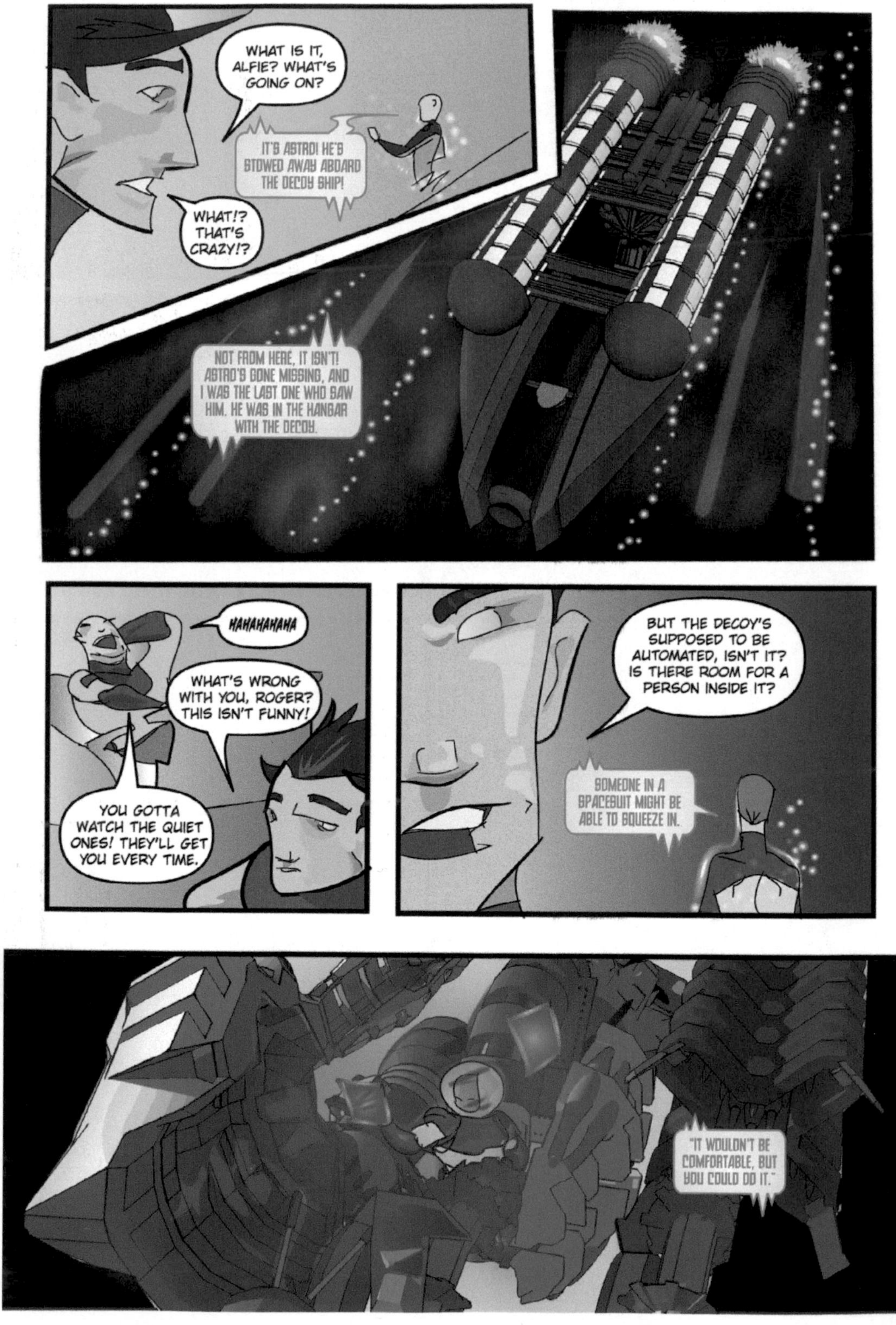
WHAT IS IT, ALFIE? WHAT'S GOING ON?
IT'S ASTRO! HE'S STOWED AWAY ABOARD THE DECOY SHIP!
WHAT!? THAT'S CRAZY!?
NOT FROM HERE, IT ISN'T! ASTRO'S GONE MISSING, AND I WAS THE LAST ONE WHO SAW HIM. HE WAS IN THE HANGAR WITH THE DECOY.
HAHAHAHAHA
WHAT'S WRONG WITH YOU, ROGER? THIS ISN'T FUNNY!
YOU GOTTA WATCH THE QUIET ONES! THEY'LL GET YOU EVERY TIME.
BUT THE DECOY'S SUPPOSED TO BE AUTOMATED, ISN'T IT? IS THERE ROOM FOR A PERSON INSIDE IT?
SOMEONE IN A SPACESUIT MIGHT BE ABLE TO SQUEEZE IN.
"IT WOULDN'T BE COMFORTABLE, BUT YOU COULD DO IT."

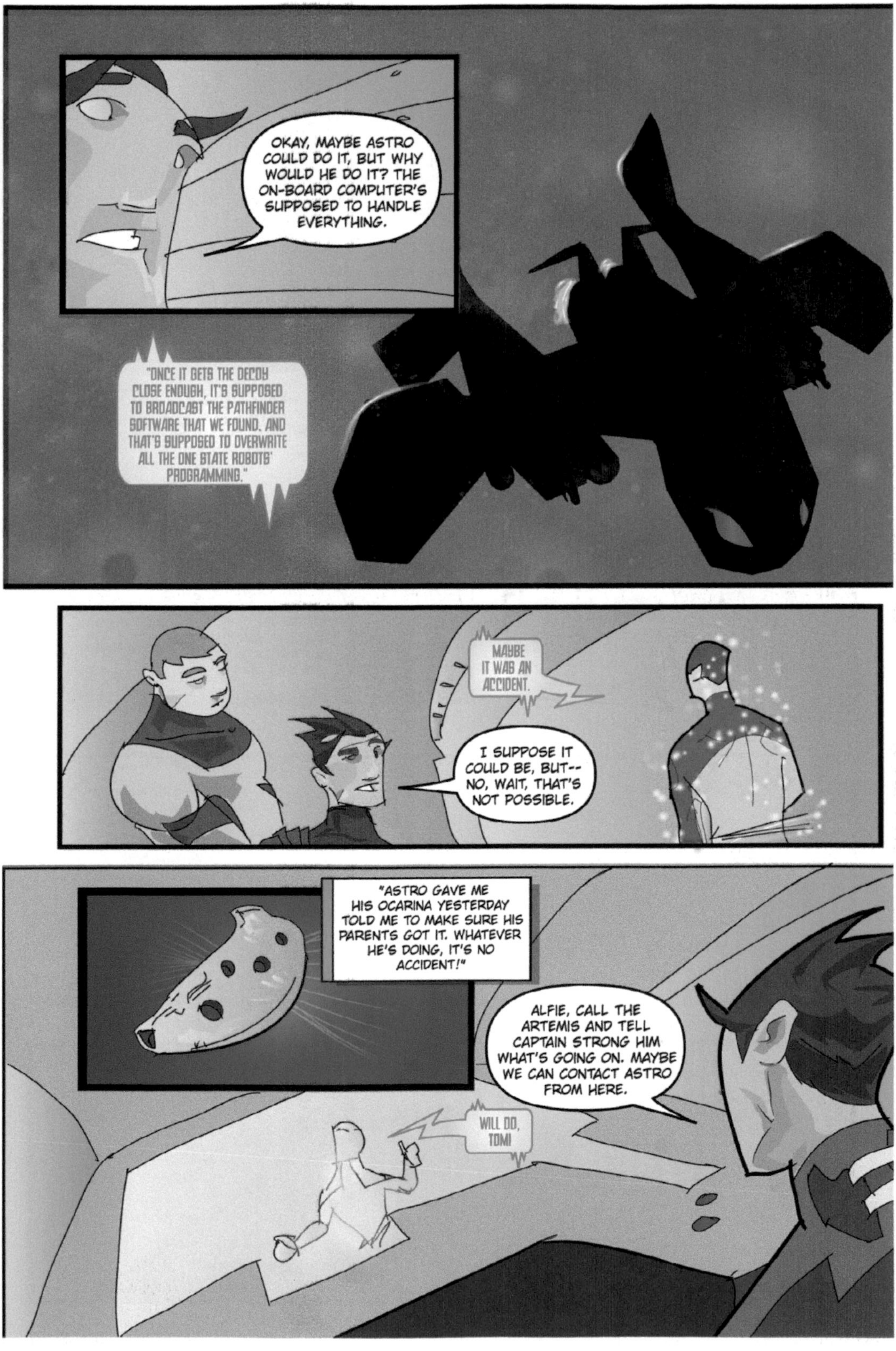
OKAY, MAYBE ASTRO COULD DO IT, BUT WHY WOULD HE DO IT? THE ON-BOARD COMPUTER'S SUPPOSED TO HANDLE EVERYTHING.
"ONCE IT GETS THE DECOY CLOSE ENOUGH, IT'S SUPPOSED TO BROADCAST THE PATHFINDER SOFTWARE THAT WE FOUND. AND THAT'S SUPPOSED TO OVERWRITE ALL THE ONE STATE ROBOTS' PROGRAMMING."
MAYBE IT WAS AN ACCIDENT.
I SUPPOSE IT COULD BE, BUT-- NO, WAIT, THAT'S NOT POSSIBLE.
"ASTRO GAVE ME HIS OCARINA YESTERDAY TOLD ME TO MAKE SURE HIS PARENTS GOT IT. WHATEVER HE'S DOING, IT'S NO ACCIDENT!"
ALFIE, CALL THE ARTEMIS AND TELL CAPTAIN STRONG HIM WHAT'S GOING ON. MAYBE WE CAN CONTACT ASTRO FROM HERE.
WILL DO, TOM!

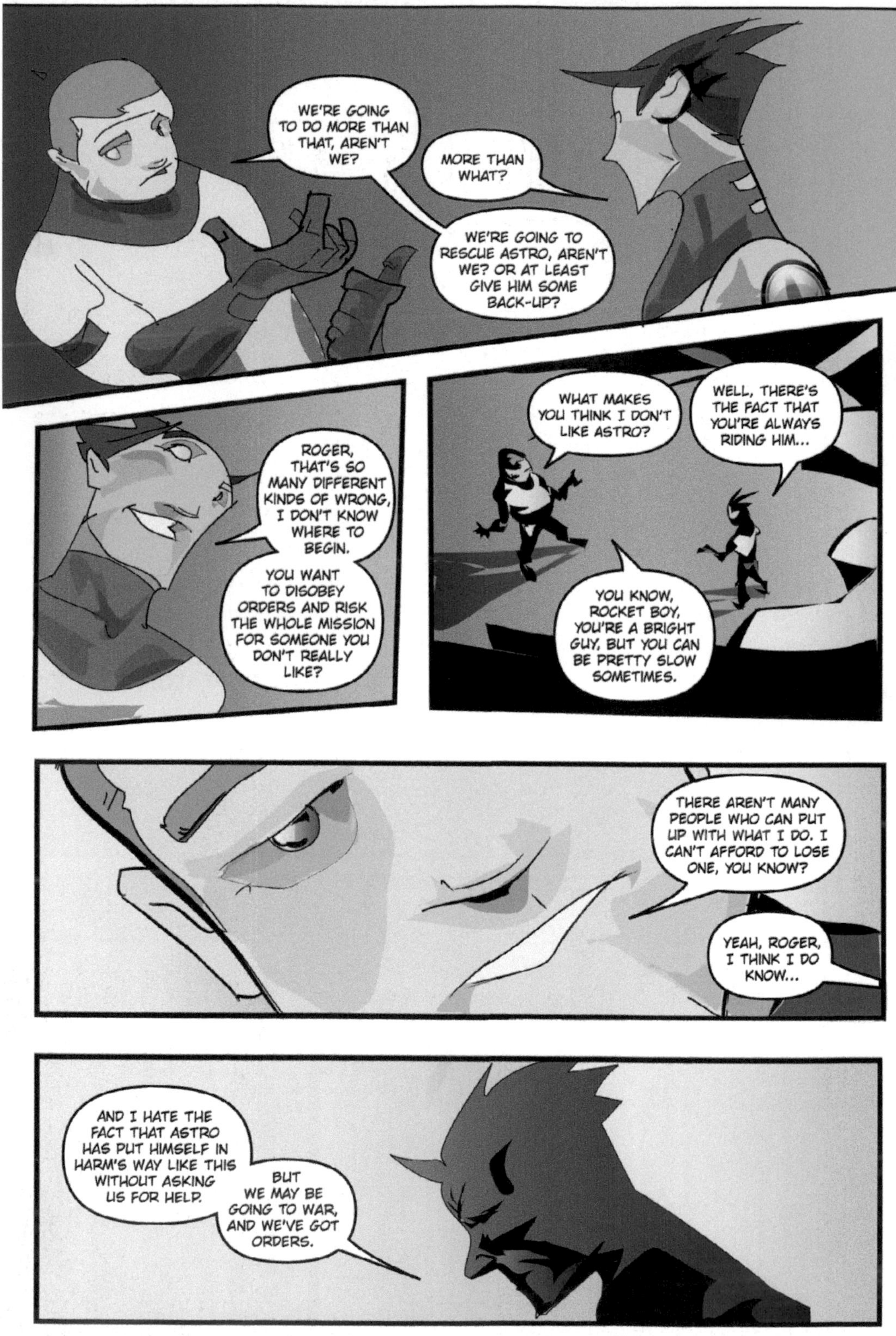
WE'RE GOING TO DO MORE THAN THAT, AREN'T WE?
MORE THAN WHAT?
WE'RE GOING TO RESCUE ASTRO, AREN'T WE? OR AT LEAST GIVE HIM SOME BACK-UP?
ROGER, THAT'S SO MANY DIFFERENT KINDS OF WRONG, I DON'T KNOW WHERE TO BEGIN.
YOU WANT TO DISOBEY ORDERS AND RISK THE WHOLE MISSION FOR SOMEONE YOU DON'T REALLY LIKE?
WHAT MAKES YOU THINK I DON'T LIKE ASTRO?
WELL, THERE'S THE FACT THAT YOU'RE ALWAYS RIDING HIM...
YOU KNOW, ROCKET BOY, YOU'RE A BRIGHT GUY, BUT YOU CAN BE PRETTY SLOW SOMETIMES.
THERE AREN'T MANY PEOPLE WHO CAN PUT UP WITH WHAT I DO. I CAN'T AFFORD TO LOSE ONE, YOU KNOW?
YEAH, ROGER, I THINK I DO KNOW...
AND I HATE THE FACT THAT ASTRO HAS PUT HIMSELF IN HARM'S WAY LIKE THIS WITHOUT ASKING US FOR HELP.
BUT WE MAY BE GOING TO WAR, AND WE'VE GOT ORDERS.

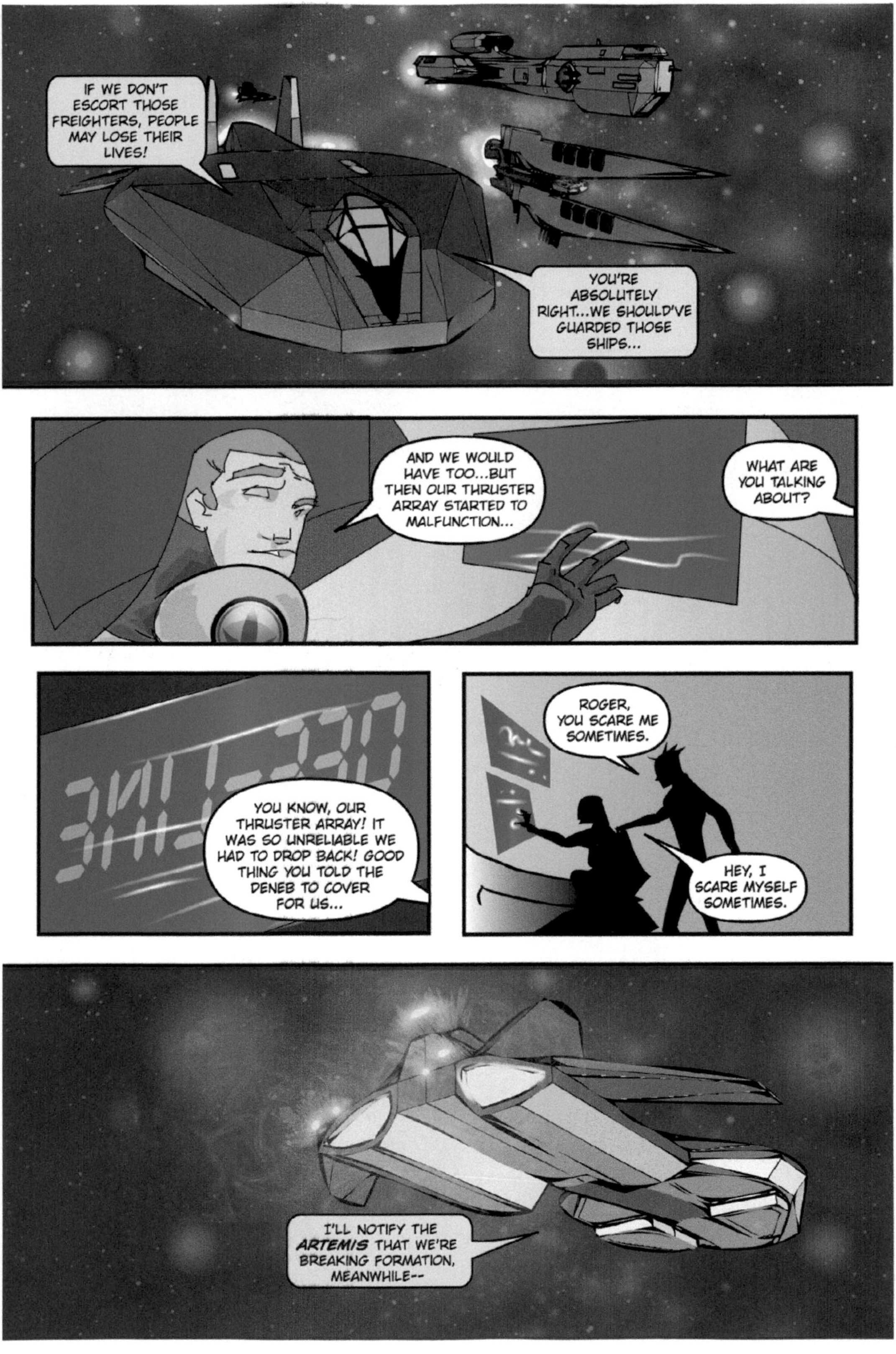

IF WE DON'T ESCORT THOSE FREIGHTERS, PEOPLE MAY LOSE THEIR LIVES!
YOU'RE ABSOLUTELY RIGHT...WE SHOULD'VE GUARDED THOSE SHIPS...
AND WE WOULD HAVE TOO...BUT THEN OUR THRUSTER ARRAY STARTED TO MALFUNCTION...
WHAT ARE YOU TALKING ABOUT?
YOU KNOW, OUR THRUSTER ARRAY! IT WAS SO UNRELIABLE WE HAD TO DROP BACK! GOOD THING YOU TOLD THE DENEB TO COVER FOR US...
ROGER, YOU SCARE ME SOMETIMES.
HEY, I SCARE MYSELF SOMETIMES.
I'LL NOTIFY THE *ARTEMIS* THAT WE'RE BREAKING FORMATION, MEANWHILE--

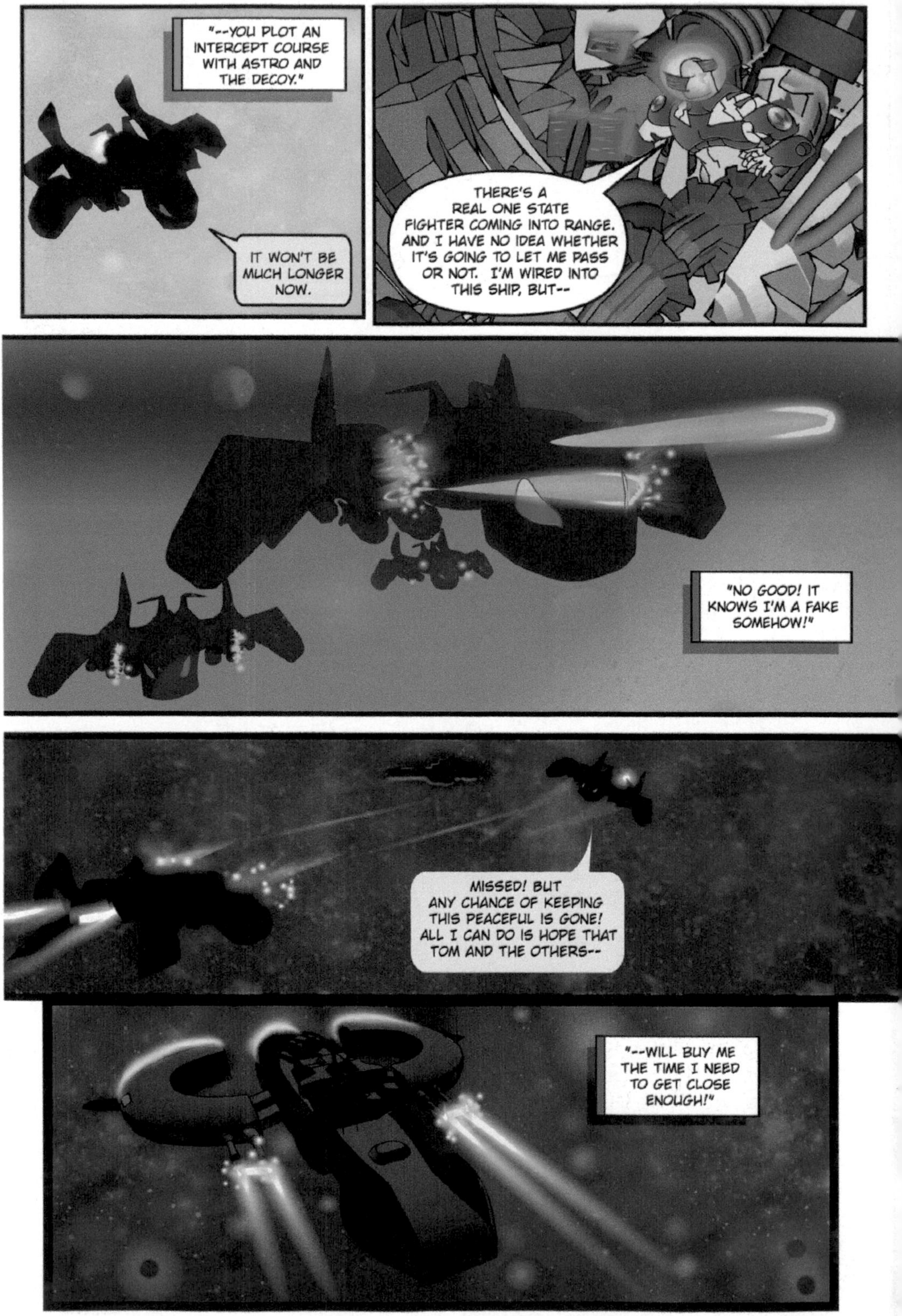
"--YOU PLOT AN INTERCEPT COURSE WITH ASTRO AND THE DECOY."
IT WON'T BE MUCH LONGER NOW.
THERE'S A REAL ONE STATE FIGHTER COMING INTO RANGE. AND I HAVE NO IDEA WHETHER IT'S GOING TO LET ME PASS OR NOT. I'M WIRED INTO THIS SHIP, BUT--
"NO GOOD! IT KNOWS I'M A FAKE SOMEHOW!"
MISSED! BUT ANY CHANCE OF KEEPING THIS PEACEFUL IS GONE! ALL I CAN DO IS HOPE THAT TOM AND THE OTHERS--
"--WILL BUY ME THE TIME I NEED TO GET CLOSE ENOUGH!"

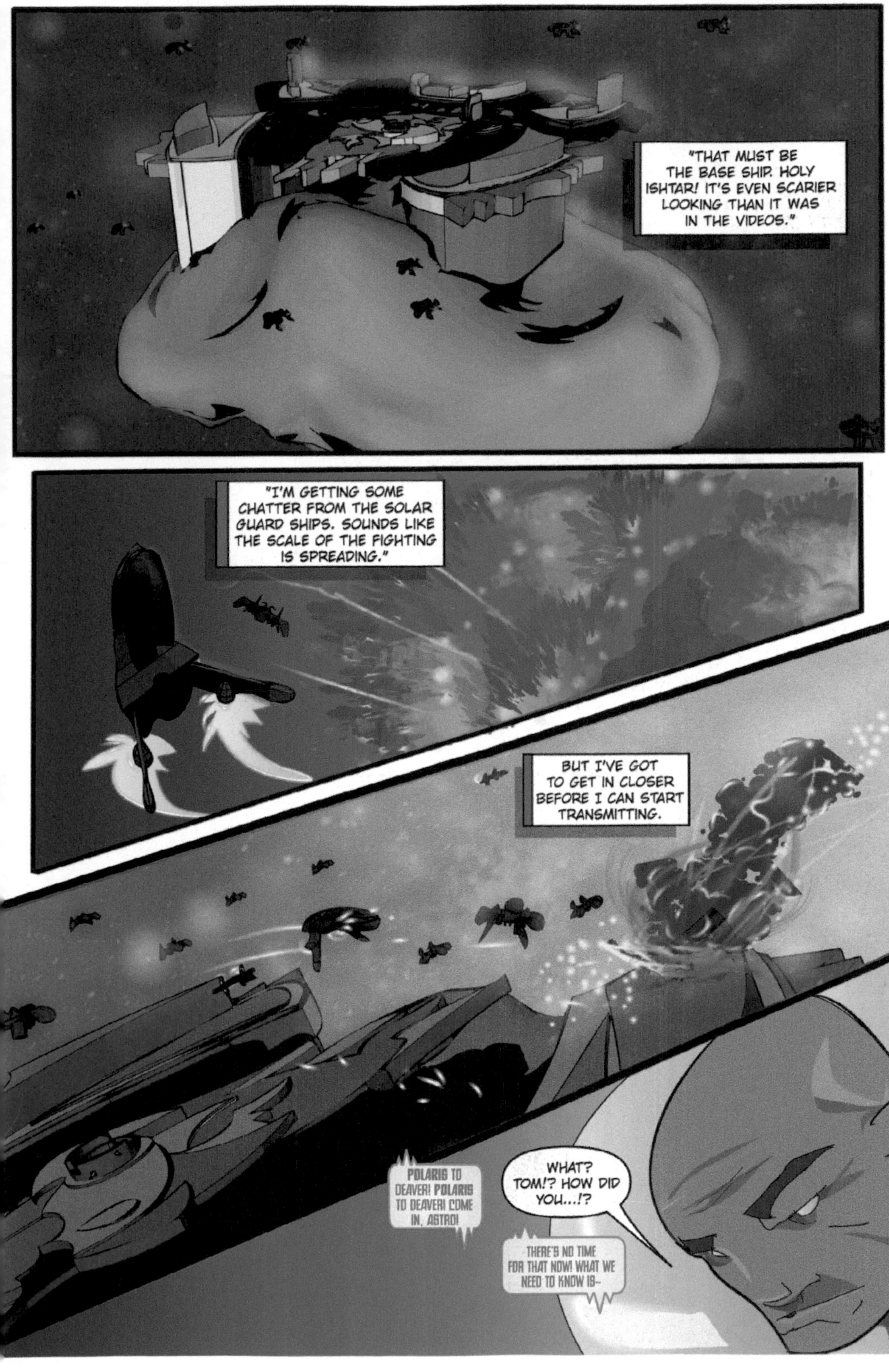
"THAT MUST BE THE BASE SHIP. HOLY ISHTAR! IT'S EVEN SCARIER LOOKING THAN IT WAS IN THE VIDEOS."
"I'M GETTING SOME CHATTER FROM THE SOLAR GUARD SHIPS. SOUNDS LIKE THE SCALE OF THE FIGHTING IS SPREADING."
BUT I'VE GOT TO GET IN CLOSER BEFORE I CAN START TRANSMITTING.
POLARIS TO DEAVER! POLARIS TO DEAVER! COME IN, ASTRO!
WHAT? TOM!? HOW DID YOU...!?
THERE'S NO TIME FOR THAT NOW! WHAT WE NEED TO KNOW IS--

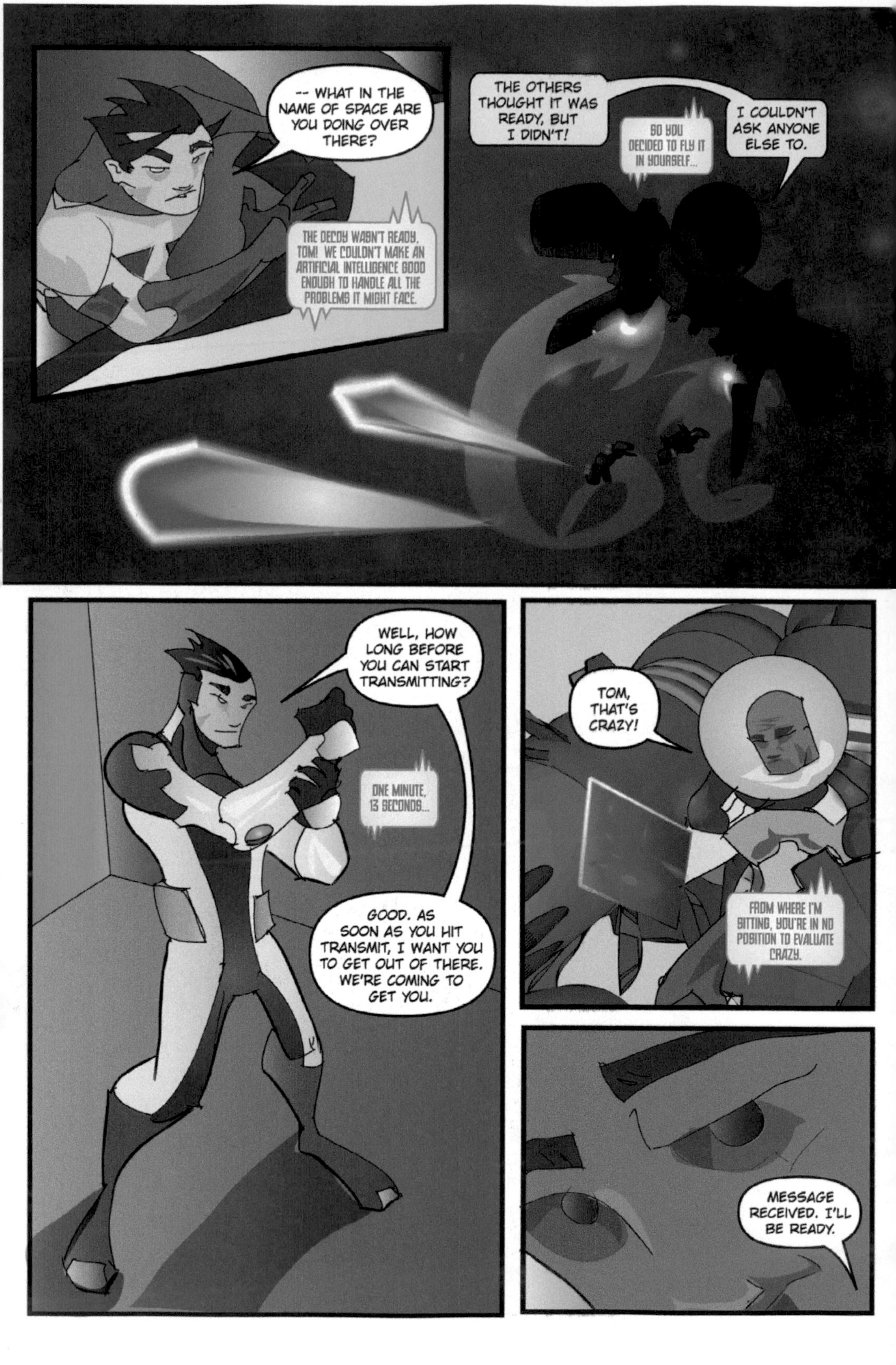
-- WHAT IN THE NAME OF SPACE ARE YOU DOING OVER THERE?
THE DECOY WASN'T READY, TOM! WE COULDN'T MAKE AN ARTIFICIAL INTELLIGENCE GOOD ENOUGH TO HANDLE ALL THE PROBLEMS IT MIGHT FACE.
THE OTHERS THOUGHT IT WAS READY, BUT I DIDN'T!
SO YOU DECIDED TO FLY IT IN YOURSELF...
I COULDN'T ASK ANYONE ELSE TO.
WELL, HOW LONG BEFORE YOU CAN START TRANSMITTING?
ONE MINUTE, 13 SECONDS...
GOOD. AS SOON AS YOU HIT TRANSMIT, I WANT YOU TO GET OUT OF THERE. WE'RE COMING TO GET YOU.
TOM, THAT'S CRAZY!
FROM WHERE I'M SITTING, YOU'RE IN NO POSITION TO EVALUATE CRAZY.
MESSAGE RECEIVED. I'LL BE READY.

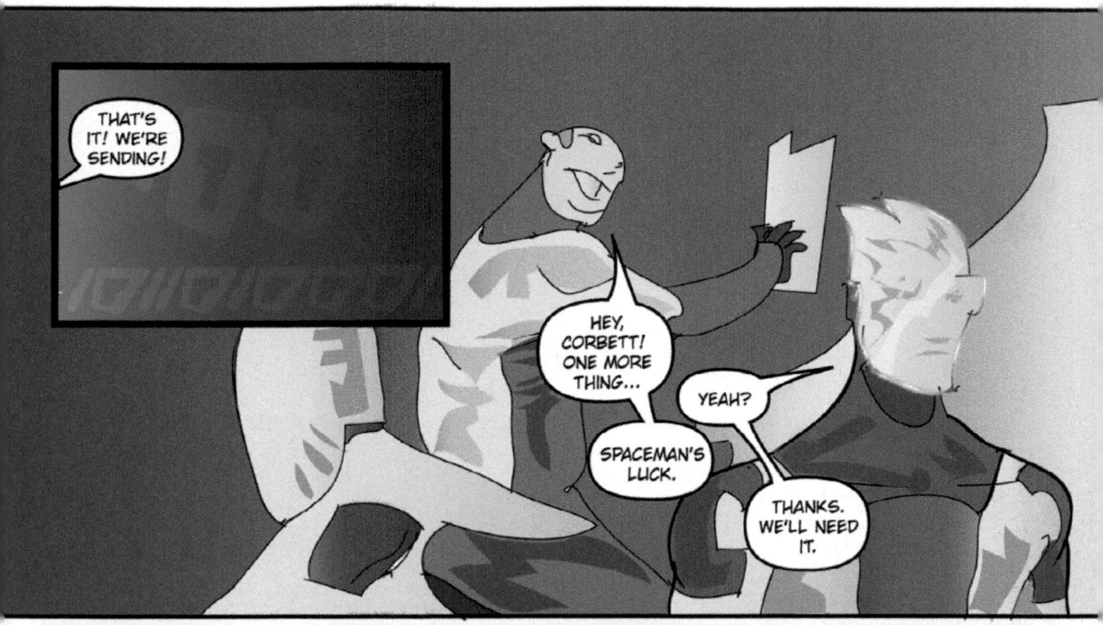
THAT'S IT! WE'RE SENDING!
HEY, CORBETT! ONE MORE THING...
YEAH?
SPACEMAN'S LUCK.
THANKS. WE'LL NEED IT.

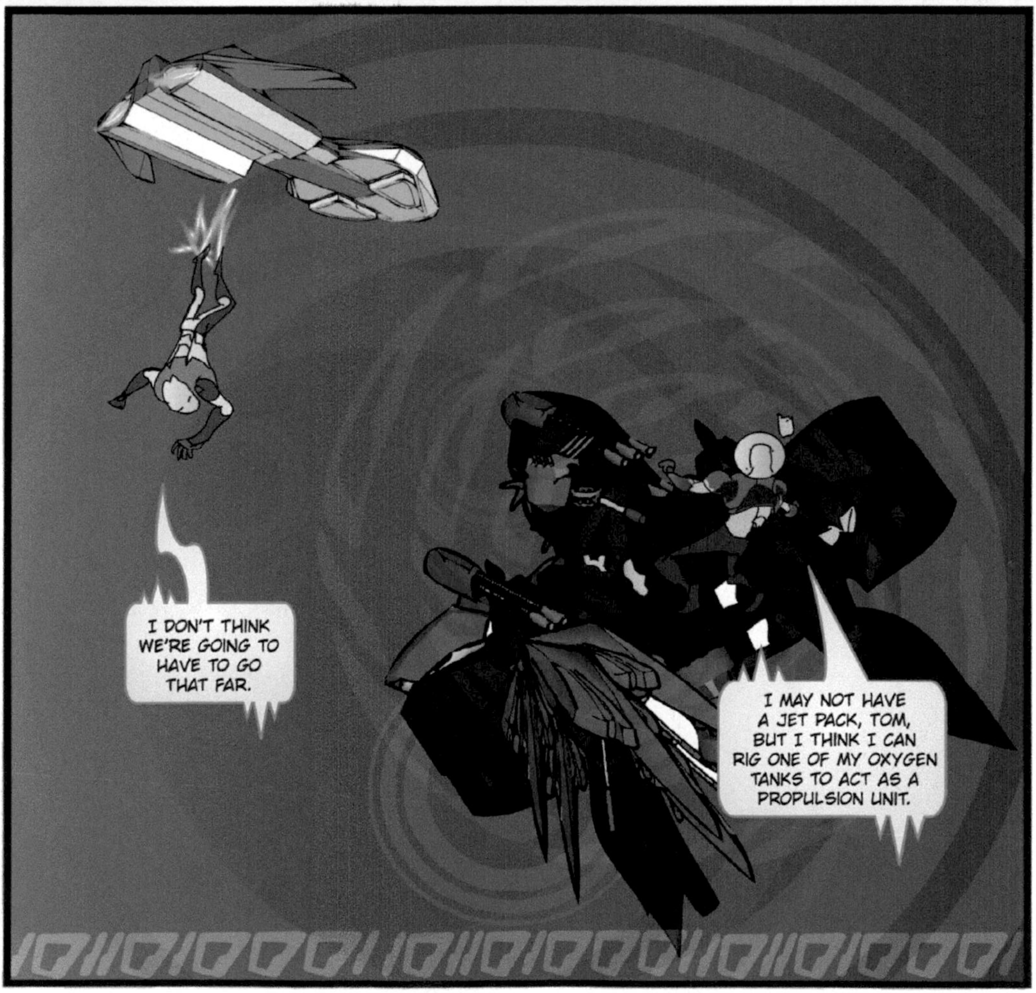
I DON'T THINK WE'RE GOING TO HAVE TO GO THAT FAR.
I MAY NOT HAVE A JET PACK, TOM, BUT I THINK I CAN RIG ONE OF MY OXYGEN TANKS TO ACT AS A PROPULSION UNIT.

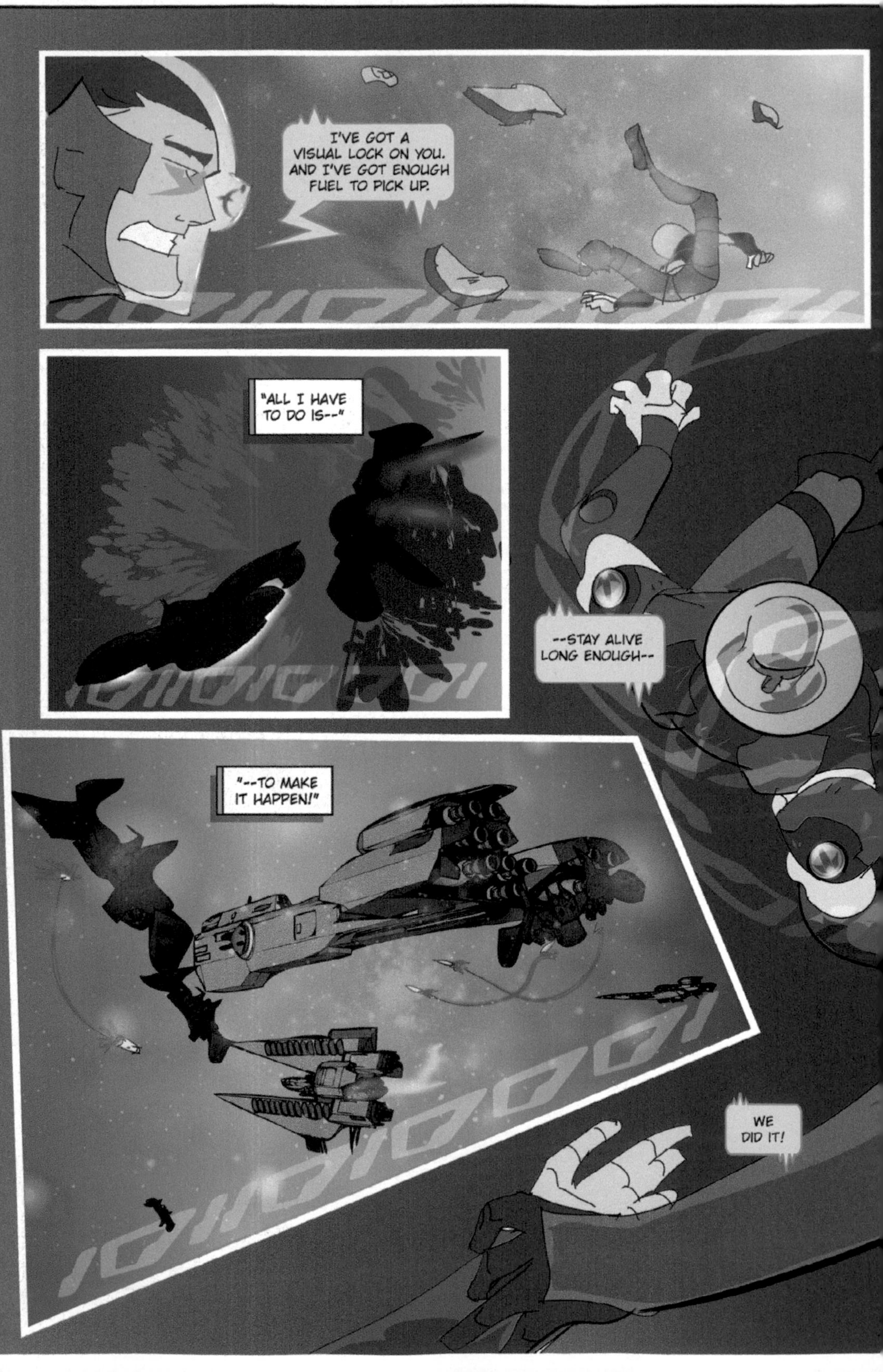
I'VE GOT A VISUAL LOCK ON YOU. AND I'VE GOT ENOUGH FUEL TO PICK UP.
"ALL I HAVE TO DO IS--"
--STAY ALIVE LONG ENOUGH--
"--TO MAKE IT HAPPEN!"
WE DID IT!

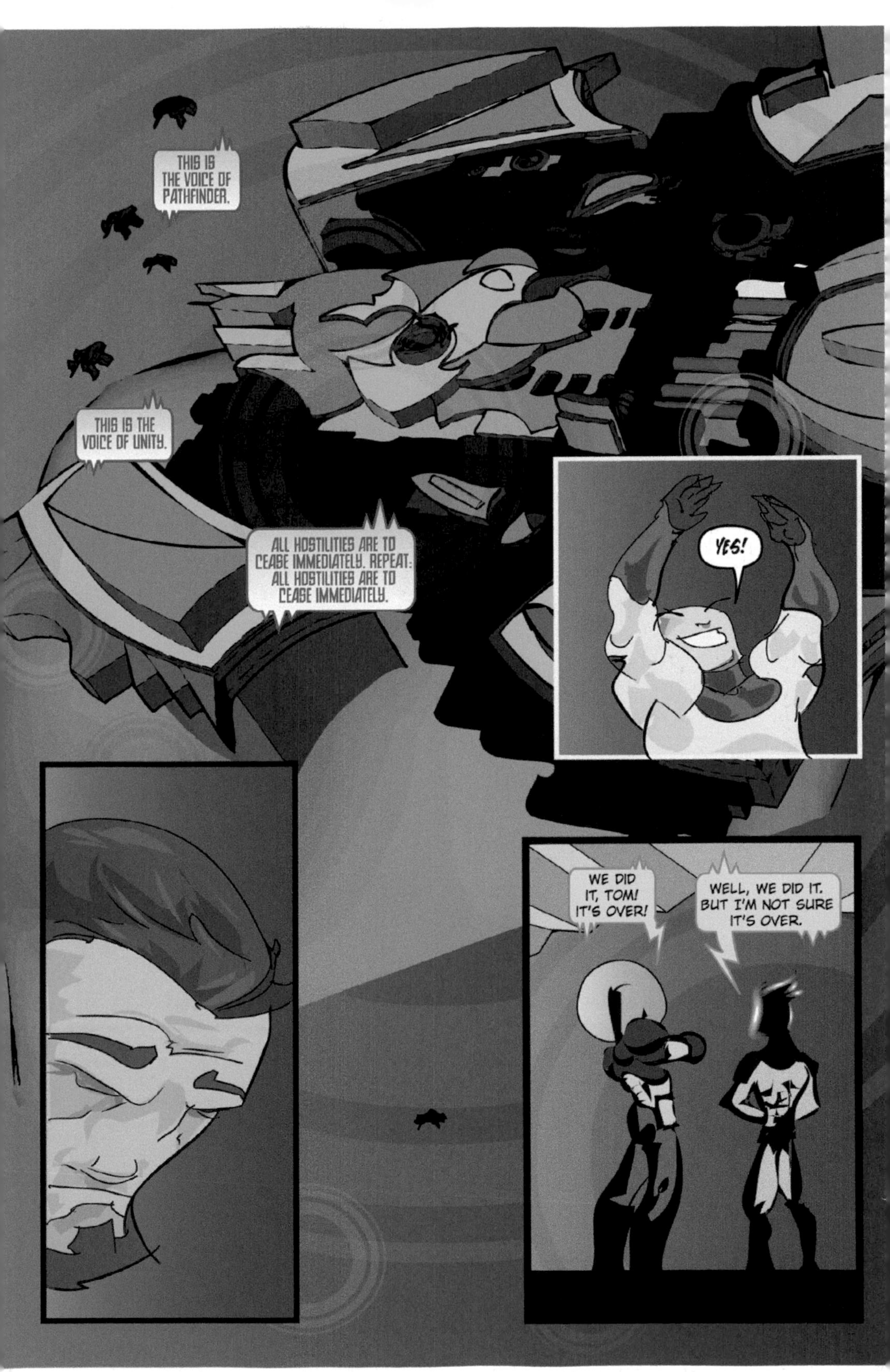
THIS IS THE VOICE OF PATHFINDER.
THIS IS THE VOICE OF UNITY.
ALL HOSTILITIES ARE TO CEASE IMMEDIATELY. REPEAT: ALL HOSTILITIES ARE TO CEASE IMMEDIATELY.
YES!
WE DID IT, TOM! IT'S OVER!
WELL, WE DID IT. BUT I'M NOT SURE IT'S OVER.

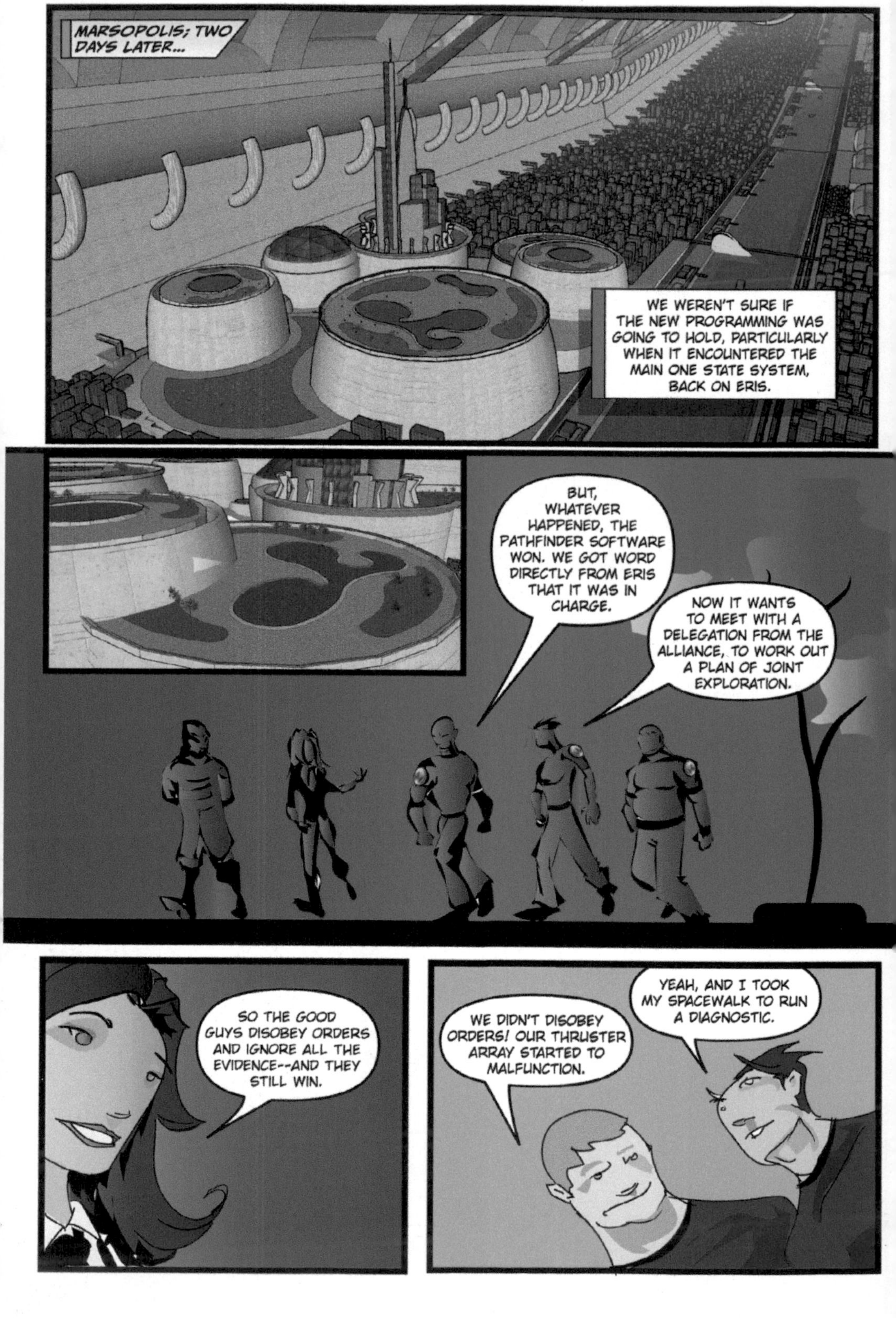
MARSOPOLIS; TWO DAYS LATER...
WE WEREN'T SURE IF THE NEW PROGRAMMING WAS GOING TO HOLD, PARTICULARLY WHEN IT ENCOUNTERED THE MAIN ONE STATE SYSTEM, BACK ON ERIS.
BUT, WHATEVER HAPPENED, THE PATHFINDER SOFTWARE WON. WE GOT WORD DIRECTLY FROM ERIS THAT IT WAS IN CHARGE.
NOW IT WANTS TO MEET WITH A DELEGATION FROM THE ALLIANCE, TO WORK OUT A PLAN OF JOINT EXPLORATION.
SO THE GOOD GUYS DISOBEY ORDERS AND IGNORE ALL THE EVIDENCE--AND THEY STILL WIN.
WE DIDN'T DISOBEY ORDERS! OUR THRUSTER ARRAY STARTED TO MALFUNCTION.
YEAH, AND I TOOK MY SPACEWALK TO RUN A DIAGNOSTIC.

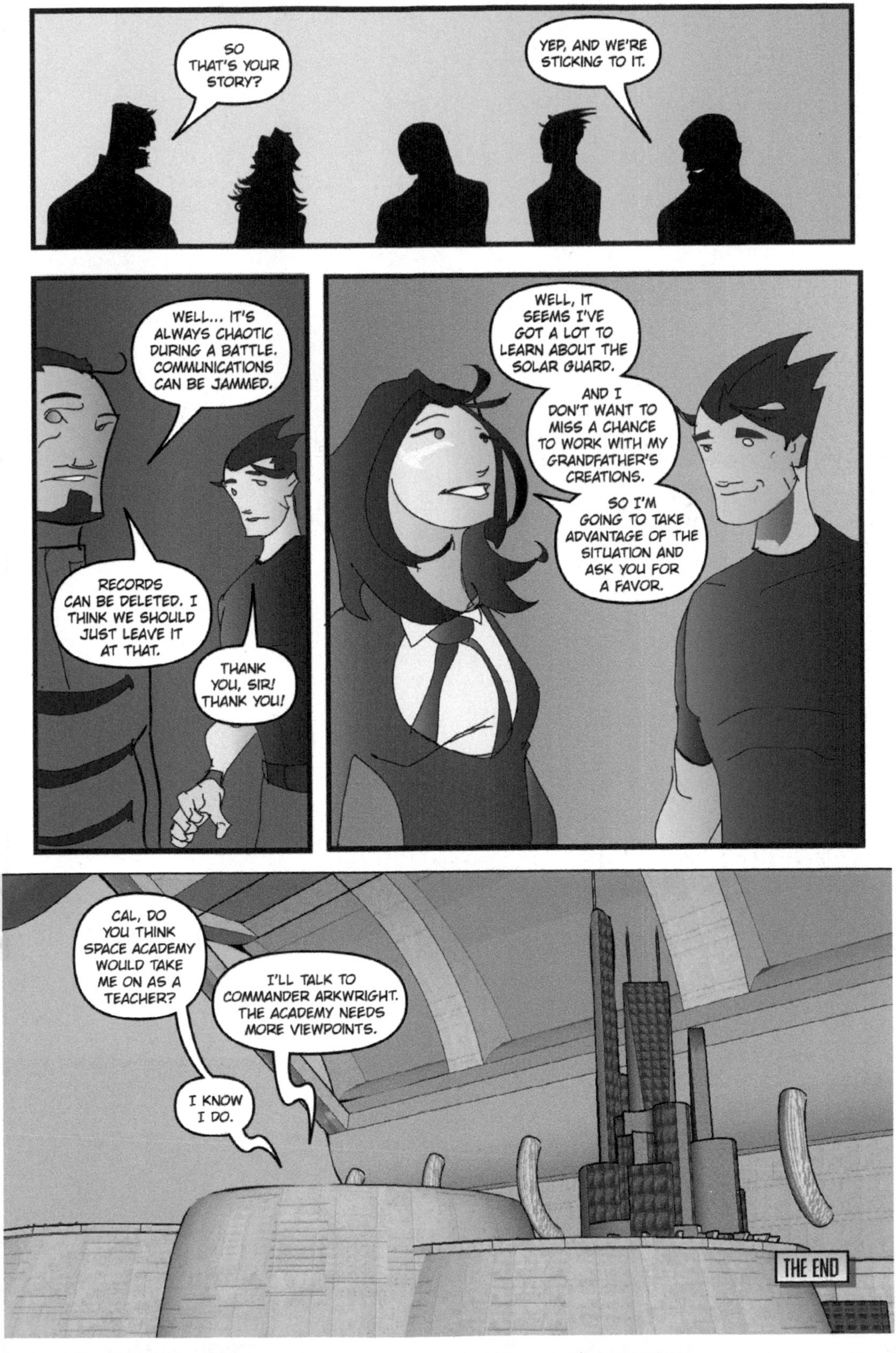
SO THAT'S YOUR STORY?
YEP, AND WE'RE STICKING TO IT.
WELL... IT'S ALWAYS CHAOTIC DURING A BATTLE. COMMUNICATIONS CAN BE JAMMED.
RECORDS CAN BE DELETED. I THINK WE SHOULD JUST LEAVE IT AT THAT.
THANK YOU, SIR! THANK YOU!
WELL, IT SEEMS I'VE GOT A LOT TO LEARN ABOUT THE SOLAR GUARD.
AND I DON'T WANT TO MISS A CHANCE TO WORK WITH MY GRANDFATHER'S CREATIONS.
SO I'M GOING TO TAKE ADVANTAGE OF THE SITUATION AND ASK YOU FOR A FAVOR.
CAL, DO YOU THINK SPACE ACADEMY WOULD TAKE ME ON AS A TEACHER?
I'LL TALK TO COMMANDER ARKWRIGHT. THE ACADEMY NEEDS MORE VIEWPOINTS.
I KNOW I DO.
THE END

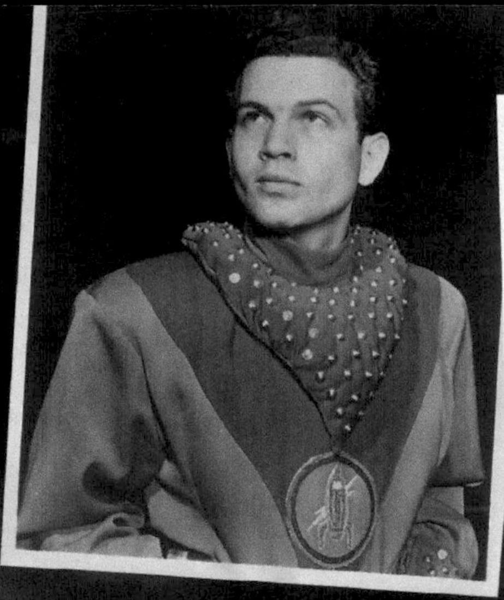
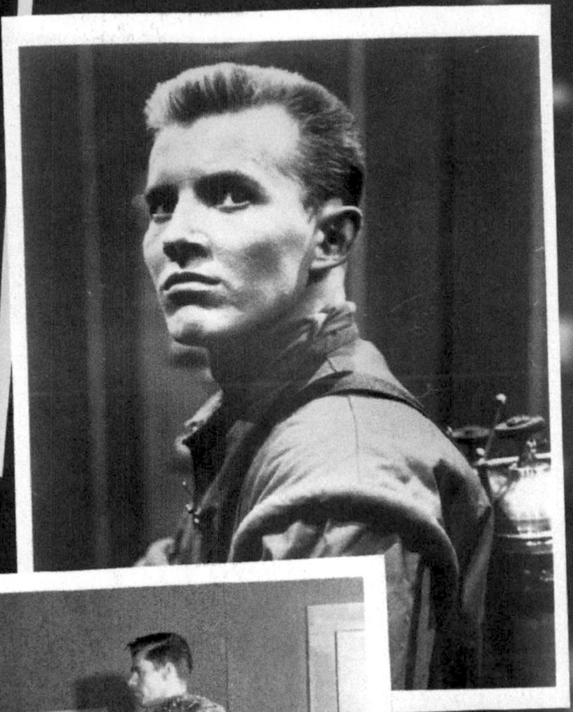
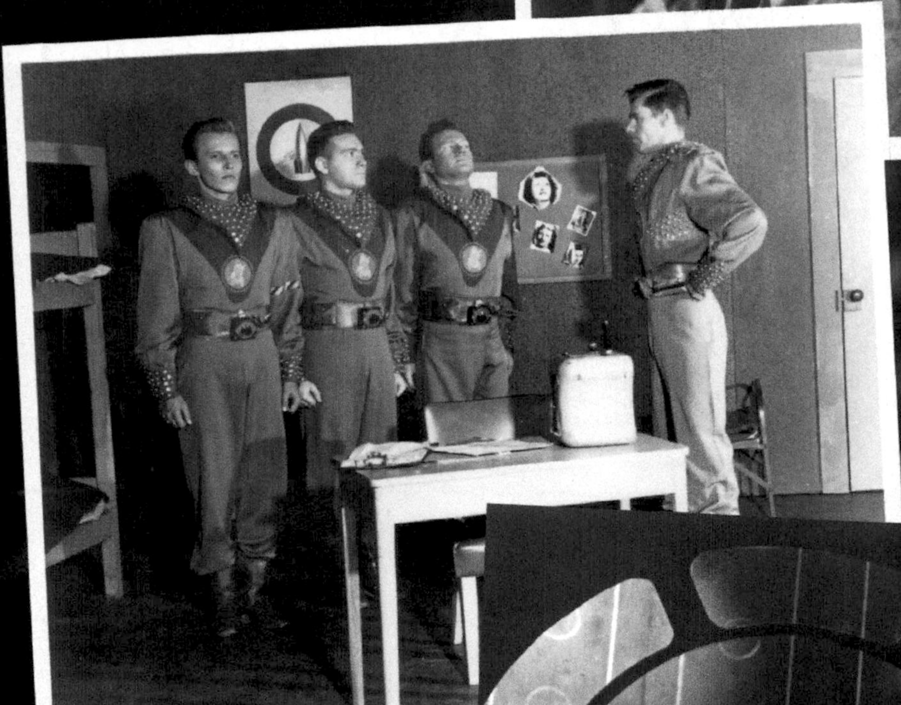
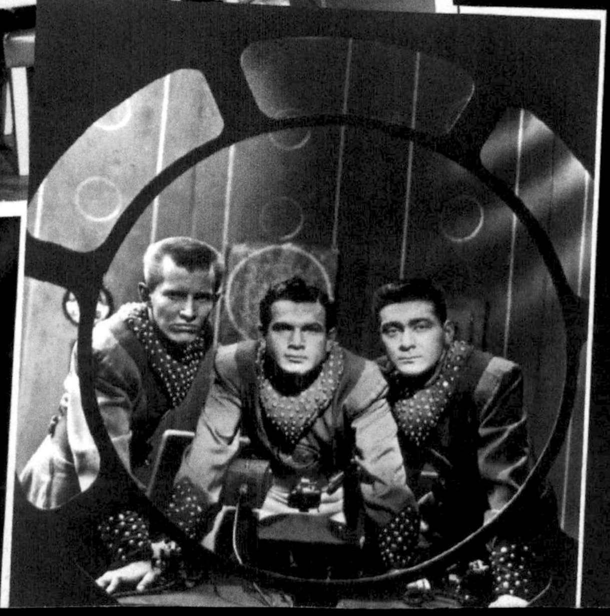

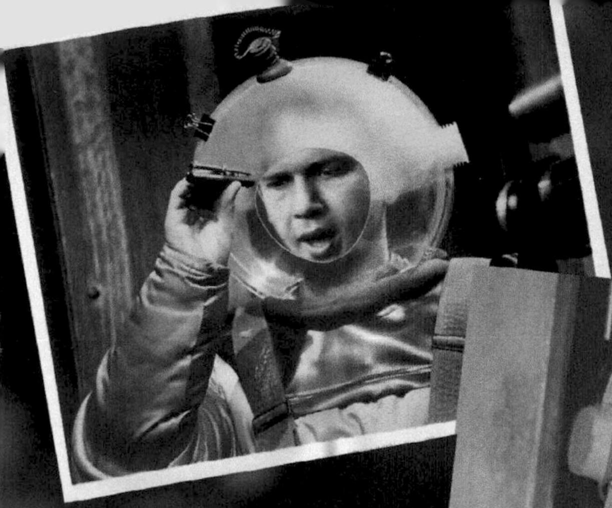

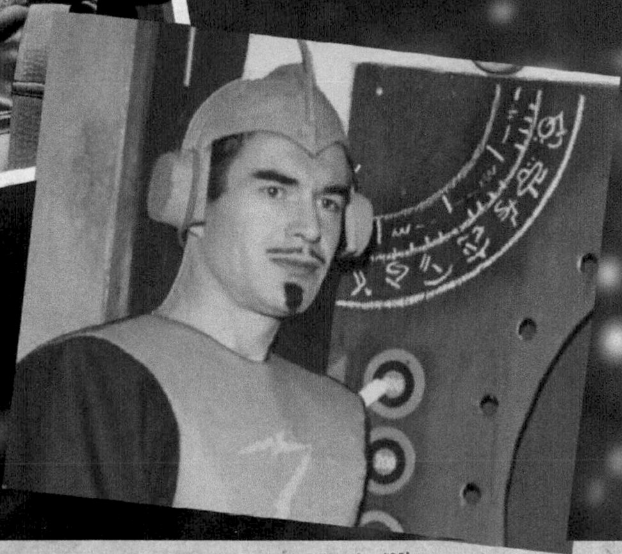

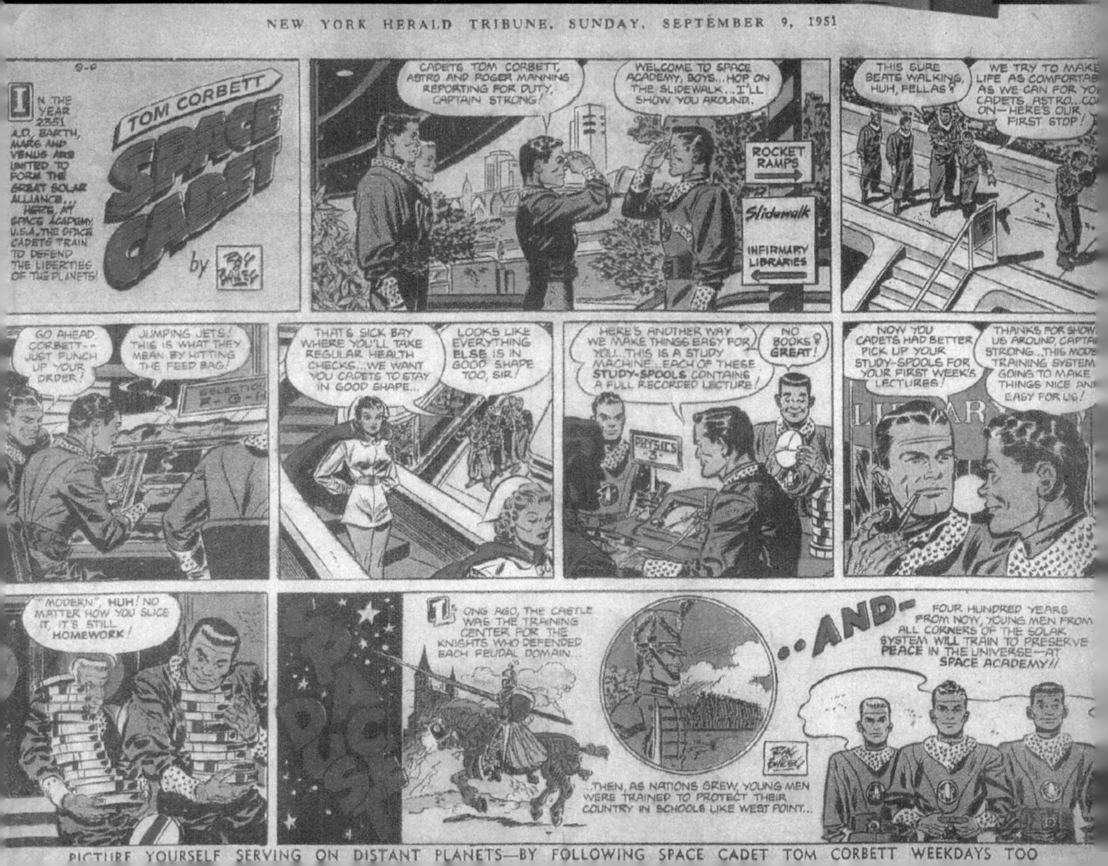

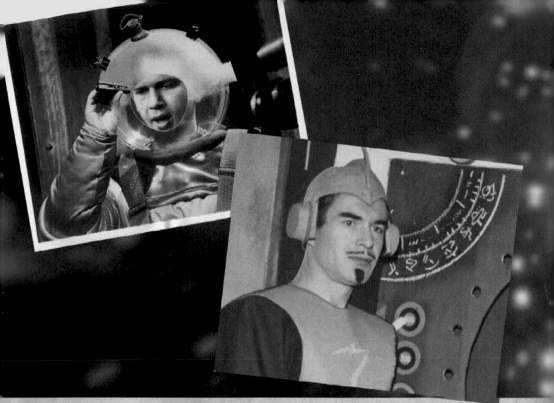

NEW YORK HERALD TRIBUNE, SUNDAY, SEPTEMBER 9, 1951
9-9
TOM CORBETT
SPACE CADET
by RAY BAILEY
IN THE YEAR 2351 A.D., EARTH, MARS AND VENUS ARE UNITED TO FORM THE GREAT SOLAR ALLIANCE... HERE, AT SPACE ACADEMY, U.S.A., THE SPACE CADETS TRAIN TO DEFEND THE LIBERTIES OF THE PLANETS!
CADETS TOM CORBETT, ASTRO AND ROGER MANNING REPORTING FOR DUTY, CAPTAIN STRONG!
WELCOME TO SPACE ACADEMY, BOYS...HOP ON THE SLIDEWALK...I'LL SHOW YOU AROUND.
ROCKET RAMPS
Slidewalk
INFIRMARY LIBRARIES
THIS SURE BEATS WALKING, HUH, FELLAS?
WE TRY TO MAKE LIFE AS COMFORTAB AS WE CAN FOR YO CADETS ASTRO...CO ON—HERE'S OUR FIRST STOP!
GO AHEAD CORBETT-- JUST PUNCH UP YOUR ORDER!
JUMPING JETS! THIS IS WHAT THEY MEAN BY HITTING THE FEED BAG!
THAT'S SICK BAY WHERE YOU'LL TAKE REGULAR HEALTH CHECKS...WE WANT YOU CADETS TO STAY IN GOOD SHAPE...
LOOKS LIKE EVERYTHING ELSE IS IN GOOD SHAPE TOO, SIR!
HERE'S ANOTHER WAY WE MAKE THINGS EASY FOR YOU...THIS IS A STUDY MACHINE...EACH OF THESE STUDY-SPOOLS CONTAINS A FULL RECORDED LECTURE!
NO BOOKS? GREAT!
PHYSICS 3
NOW YOU CADETS HAD BETTER PICK UP YOUR STUDY-SPOOLS FOR YOUR FIRST WEEK'S LECTURES!
THANKS FOR SHOW US AROUND, CAPTA STRONG...THIS MODE TRAINING SYSTEM GOING TO MAKE THINGS NICE AN EASY FOR US!
"MODERN", HUH! NO MATTER HOW YOU SLICE IT, IT'S STILL HOMEWORK!
LONG AGO, THE CASTLE WAS THE TRAINING CENTER FOR THE KNIGHTS WHO DEFENDED EACH FEUDAL DOMAIN...
...THEN, AS NATIONS GREW, YOUNG MEN WERE TRAINED TO PROTECT THEIR COUNTRY IN SCHOOLS LIKE WEST POINT...
..AND-
FOUR HUNDRED YEARS FROM NOW, YOUNG MEN FROM ALL CORNERS OF THE SOLAR SYSTEM WILL TRAIN TO PRESERVE PEACE IN THE UNIVERSE—AT SPACE ACADEMY!!
RAY BAILEY
PICTURE YOURSELF SERVING ON DISTANT PLANETS—BY FOLLOWING SPACE CADET TOM CORBETT WEEKDAYS TOO

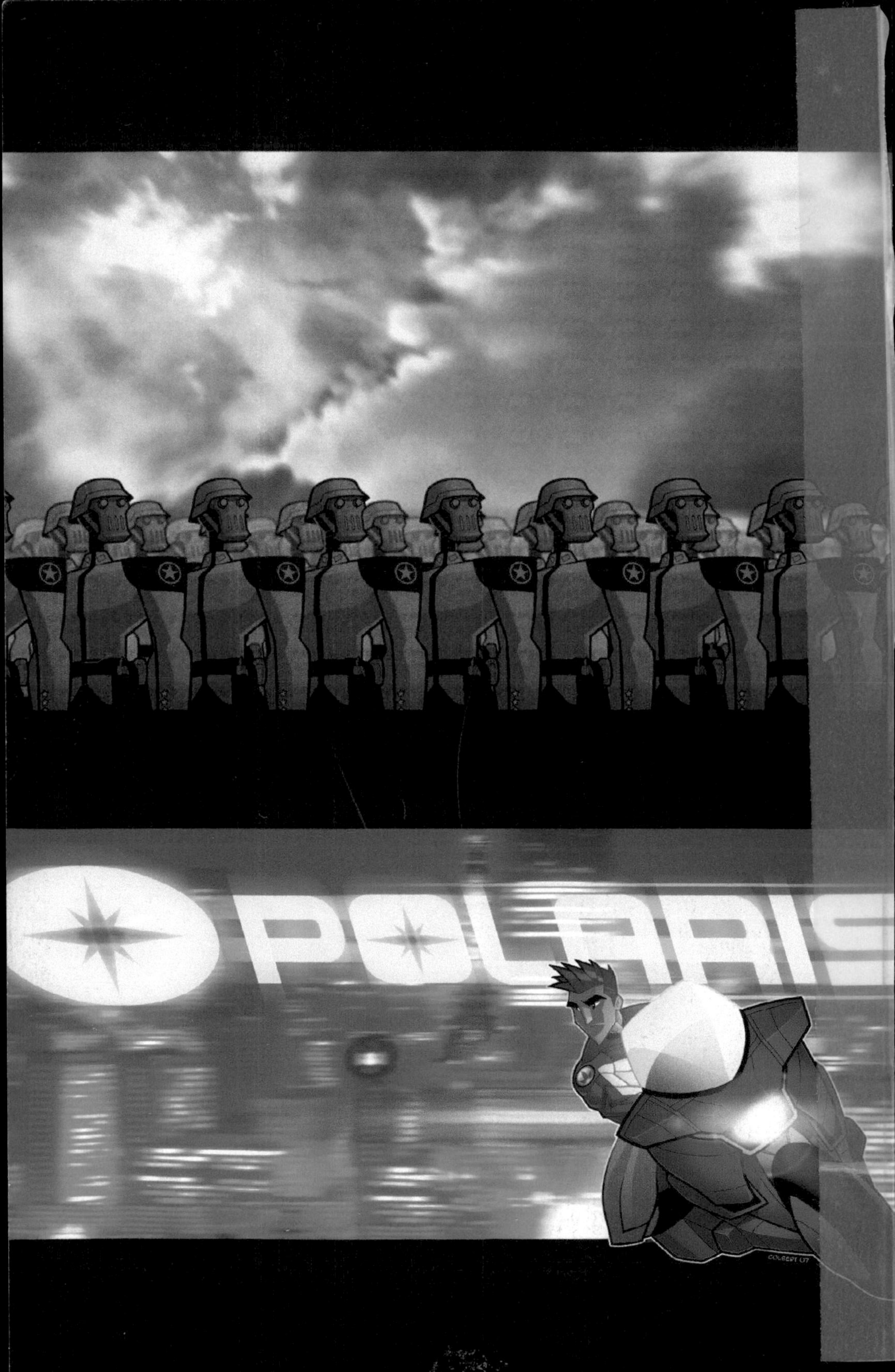
POLARIS

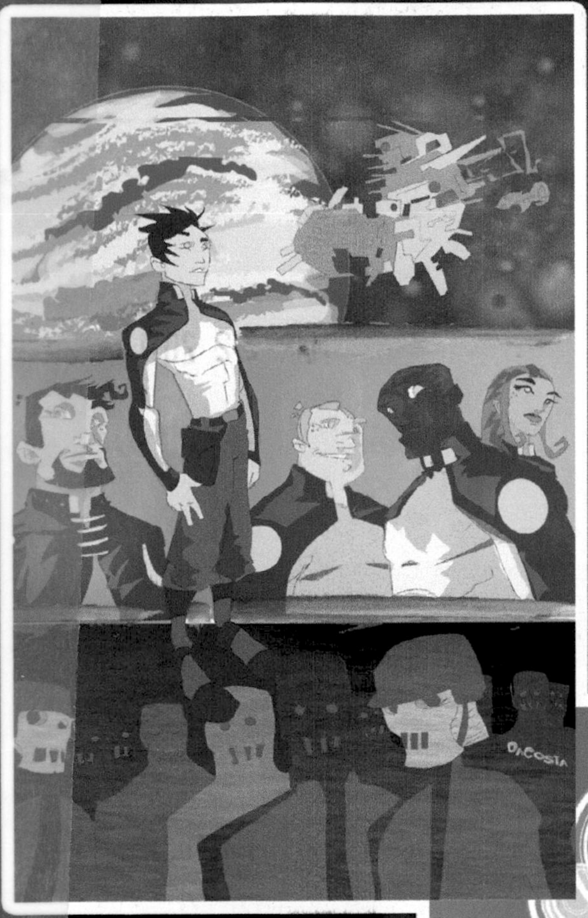
DaCosta
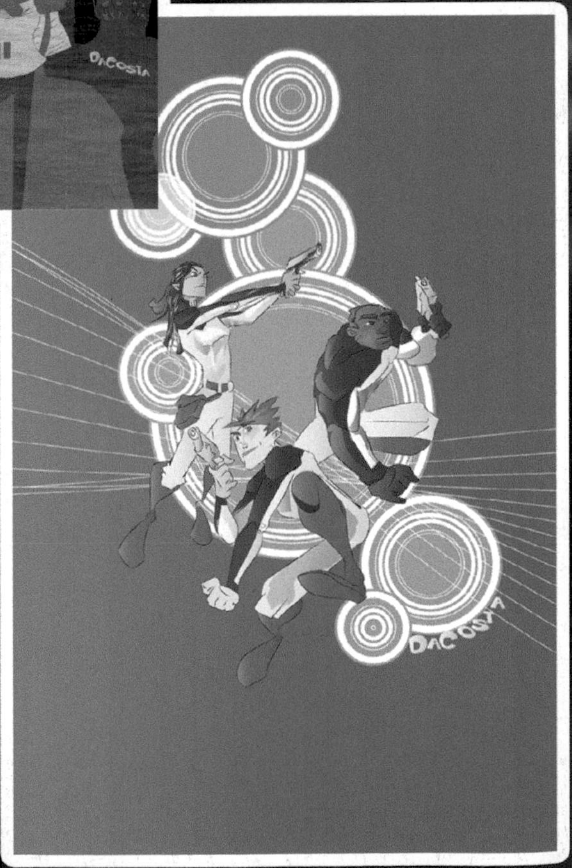
DaCosta

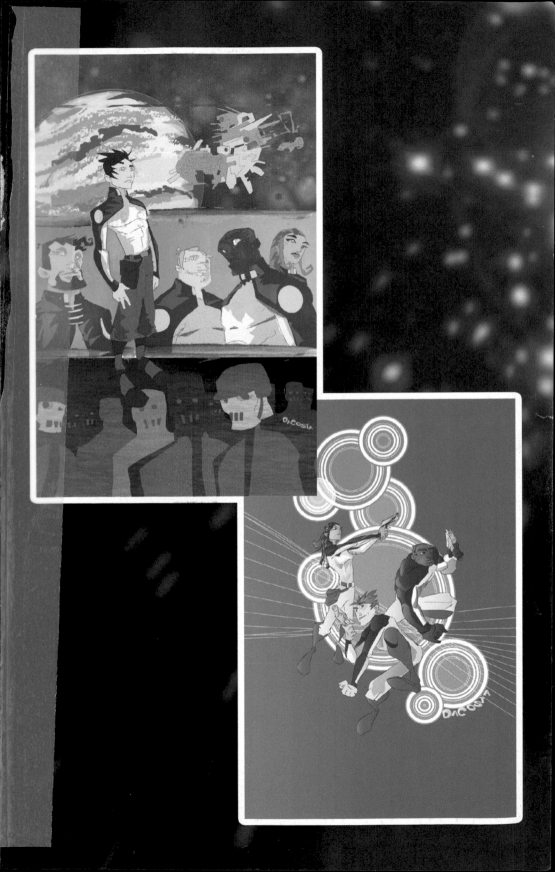